State of Grace

State of Grace is published in the United States in 2015
by Switch Press
A Capstone Imprint
1710 Roe Crest Drive
North Mankato, Minnesota 56003
www.switchpress.com

Originally published in 2014
by Hardie Grant Egmont
Ground Floor, Building 1, 658 Church Street
Richmond, Victoria 3121, Australia
www.hardiegrantegmont.com.au

Library of Congress Cataloging-in-Publication Data

Badger, H., author.

State of grace / by Hilary Badger.

pages cm

"Originally published in 2014 by Hardie Grant Egmont ... Australia"

Summary: Ever since she was created, Wren has lived with her friends
in an Eden created by Dot — but lately she has been troubled by
visions of a very different world, and when she meets Dennis who
comes from outside, she begins to confront the ugly truth at the heart
of paradise.

ISBN 978-1-63079-015-8 (paper over board) -- ISBN 978-1-63079-033-2
(ebook pdf) -- ISBN 978-1-63079-036-3 (reflowable epub)

1. Clinical trials--Juvenile fiction. 2. Drugs--Testing--Juvenile fiction.
3. Secrecy--Juvenile fiction. 4. Friendship--Juvenile fiction. [1. Clinical
trials--Fiction. 2. Drugs--Testing--Fiction. 3. Secrets--Fiction. 4.
Friendship--Fiction.] I. Title.

PZ7.B1378St 2015

823.92--dc23

[Fic]

2015003973

Cover photograph: Shutterstock: pio3

Book Design: K. Fraser

Printed in China.
042015   008865RRDF15

STATE
of
GRACE

by Hilary Badger

SWITCH
PRESS

THE BOOKS OF DOT

01

OH MY DOT, it's hot today. Majorly, seriously, *divinely* hot.

Fern and I are running across the lawn, and everywhere around us there's this haze that makes all creation shimmer. Literally nothing is still. The gazebo, the fountains, the lawn, every single flower, tree, and animal — all of them are rippling and wobbling and floating.

There's the smell of hot grass and frangipani flowers and ripe newfruit in the grove. And way, way off in the distance I can hear the waterfall gushing over the top of the escarpment into the lagoon below.

I grab Fern's hand and tow her along beside me.

Dot created Fern short with big deer eyes and a round, sweet face, exactly like a flower. She's a dawdler, not a runner. She's a wanderer and a daisy-chain maker, the type of girl who's always humming some dottrack or other. And smiling. Fern is always smiling.

As we run, my sungarb catches the wind and mushrooms out around me, sending a breeze gusting up between my legs. The grass under my feet is a bright saturated green, stretching on and on in every direction. The lawn is so huge, I could go on running forever.

From here, right in the middle of everything, I can't even see the fringe of trees that marks the edge of all creation.

But endless as Dot's creation seems, Fern and I eventually get to the lagoon. It's so packed, it looks like all one hundred of us are here at the same time. Splashing, shrieking, or just lazing around the way the big cats do, kind of sprawled out on the flat, warm rocks.

"Made it." Fern sighs, dipping her brown toes in the water. "Thank Dot."

She peels off her sungarb, which today is coral pink with a low V-neck and a fringe of periwinkle shells swishing around the hem. Fern lets her sungarb flutter to the rocks. The skin on her belly is the exact same shade as her arms and legs. The girl is tanned from her toes to the tips of her tatas.

Did I mention Fern has really nice tatas? Oh my Dot, she totally does. The whole of Fern is kind of round — her face and her eyes — but the roundest part is those tatas, for sure. They're like a pair of honeydew melons or ruby grapefruit, all *ripe* and everything.

No, I'm not planning to hook up with Fern or anything. Fern does hook up with girls. *Only* girls. But that doesn't mean the two of us are ever going to. It's so not like that between us. Never has been.

Right from the moment Dot created us, Fern and I have been the absolute bestest of best friends. Like, huts next door to one another, borrowing sungarb from each other, staying up all night together, *inseparable*. We know *everything* about each other. I know which girls

Fern most likes to hook up with. Number one would be Luna, number two, Sage.

And she knows which guys I like. (Right now, I'd probably say Jasper and maybe Drake, if I'm in the right mood.)

"Wren," says Fern. "Are you coming in or —"

That's when she disappears under the water, leaving this fan of blond hair on the surface. When she bobs up again, Fern's gasping and spluttering but also smiling.

Luna is clinging onto Fern's back, arms sort of slung around her neck. She looks like one of those little monkeys riding around on a bigger monkey's back. Luna is teeny-tiny, with glossy black hair and just a sliver of brown around the black circles in the center of her eyes.

Luna goes, "Sorry, Ferny," in a way that you know she doesn't really mean it.

Actually, it's pretty obvious Luna thinks the whole thing is super funny. There's this loud, smacky *mwah!* sound as Luna kisses Fern's neck then jumps off her back and into the water again.

"I was swimming right past your legs. What could I do? They're irresistible."

You can so tell Fern and Luna are going to hook up on completion night. That's if they don't do it before.

"Watch out, Fern! She's about to —"

But I'm too late, and anyway, Fern's too slow. Luna dives under the water and drags Fern down again. That gets the people beside them doing the same thing until there's just this bunch of legs and arms, tatas and willies flying all over the place. Just a typical afternoon in the lagoon.

I'm halfway through taking off my sungarb (parrot-wing green, mid-thigh length, with billowy sleeves to keep the sun off my dotmarks) when I hear this voice beside me.

Without even looking, I know it's Blaze. Dot gave Blaze a voice that's totally unlike anyone else's. It's slow and deep and kind of drawn out, and that's when you even get to hear it. Blaze isn't the type of guy who likes to say a whole lot.

"You swimming?"

I whip my sungarb over my head. The entire time, Blaze looks down at his feet like they're the most fascinating things Dot has ever created. It's like he's not sure where to look now that I have my sungarb off, which is sort of prenormal. I mean, bodies are Dot's creation and that makes them beautiful to look at — the same as a flower.

"Actually, no," I say. "As you can see, I'm about to go horseback riding."

I smile then, even though I haven't said anything particularly funny. Seriously, it doesn't take much to make me smile. That's how I am. Laughing, joking, having fun — it's how Dot created me. It's how she created *all* of us.

Except, of course, Blaze.

"It doesn't look like . . ." Then he glances away.

Let's just say Blaze is not the most light-hearted of Dot's creations. And if I had to explain what he *is* like — you know what? I probably couldn't. Blaze doesn't give a whole lot away.

That'd be intriguing if you happened to like that sort of thing. You know, quiet, mysterious, and oh-so deep.

"What about you?" I put my finger to my forehead like I'm thinking hard. "Oh, wait. I forgot. You never go in."

"Yeah, I do."

I just shake my head at him. No matter what he says, Blaze totally never swims or does anything the rest of us do, not really. "Swimming's fun. Jumping off the rocks is fun. And fun is possibly the most important of the —"

"Books of Dot," Blaze finishes for me, his mouth turning down and twisting sideways.

"You've heard of them?" I say. Another joke, obviously. "So I guess you are coming swimming, then?"

I reach out, snatch the hem of Blaze's purple sungarb, and start to lift it. But really quick, Blaze knocks my hands out of the way and tugs his sungarb down again.

"Later."

I make this huge deal of shrugging and folding my arms across my chest, where Dot's given me flat little tatas and a whole stack of gingery freckles besides my dotmarks.

"Sure, later. Uh-huh. Whatever you want."

Blaze lets go of his sungarb.

Dot didn't create us to hang around by the edge of the lagoon getting hot. She created us to have fun, so it's probably my duty to get Blaze into the water with me, right? Who knows? Maybe that's what Dot's looking for when she makes her choices on completion night. It kind of doesn't even need saying how indescribably awesome it'd be if I were one of the ones she chose.

So I make another grab for Blaze's sungarb.

All gruff and everything, he goes, "I said no!"

The way he's looking at me, it's hard to describe. Searching or scanning, if that makes any sense. So focused, I can't help but squirm.

"Fine. But you do realize you're supposed to be having fun?" And then I singsong, "And if you don't, Dot's not going to liiiike it!"

Blaze mutters something about fun being different for different people.

I think about that.

I do. I mean, Dot creates us all unique, and it says in the Book of Equality (Chapter 1, Verse 1, to be specific) that every creation is equally wonderful, so Blaze could have a point. It's just that, standing there, I don't know how holding back the way Blaze does, watching everyone else swim, could ever possibly be fun.

"Um, yeah. But I think *my* version's the one Dot's talking about in the Books."

"The Books . . ."

Blaze's voice sounds deep but tight and sort of tired, saying that. He even starts doing that mouth thing again.

While he's standing there, these two butterflies flutter out from behind a palm tree. There are palm trees all around the lagoon, along with mangos and avocados and some other type of tree that's always blooming with these waxy flowers in the brightest purple known to Dot. Anyway, the butterflies do this lazy loop around the top of Blaze's head before one of them finally lands right on top of his long, twisty-tangly ropes of hair.

He looks so funny, standing there all prehappy with a pink butterfly on his head, that I start laughing. I can't help it.

"What?" he says.

I shake my head and just keep on laughing. Blaze is trying his hardest to be stern, I can tell. But even he can't stay serious when the person next to him is losing it. He can't quite stop a little smile from spreading across his face.

"What's so funny?" he repeats, softer this time.

And he's looking right at me again, eyes stuck on my face like something pregood might happen if his gaze wandered anywhere else (say my tatas, for example).

"Nothing," I say, light and bubbly. "I'm getting in."

I bend at the knees and launch myself into the lagoon. I'm so hot and clammy that hitting the cold water feels like hooking up with someone for the very first time. As in, all tingly and fresh and surprising and stuff.

It's the feeling that makes you want to go straight to the gazebo and beg Dot to please, pretty please, make this last until the end of creation.

02

JASPER, FERN, LUNA, and I are swimming, the four of us just a bunch of bobbing heads on the surface of the lagoon. Underneath, Jasper keeps trying to hook his foot around the back of my right ankle and drag me under. Except every time I feel even the top of his big toe anywhere near me, I pull away and start splashing him.

Jasper says, "You know you want to. You know it's going to happen. It's just a matter of time till I get you."

I blink at him like I don't quite understand. "Pull me under, you mean?"

When Jasper smiles, his teeth look shiny white against his brown skin. "Maybe I do . . . and maybe I don't."

Since we were created, Jasper and I have hooked up a whole bunch of times. He's the kind of guy I like the absolute most.

I mean, I love everyone equally, like it says to in the Books. It's just, when it comes to hooking up, I obviously have my preferences. Jasper is definitely one of them, his skin all honey-dipped and his hair long and golden and dotly.

Plus, Jasper's *fun*. You know, the right-in-the-middle-of-everything type. Loud, energetic . . . out there, if that's the right expression. He is the first one awake in the morning and the last one to go back to his hut at night.

However it is she does it, Dot made Jasper and me from the exact same stuff. I guarantee it.

Jasper grabs me around the waist and pulls me over to him. And then (because, you know, I'm probably not even half his size), he lifts me right out of the water and drapes me over his shoulder so that my head's hanging down his back and my legs are churning the air.

"Not fair! Put me down!"

I twist around and kind of bite Jasper's neck, but he acts like he doesn't even feel it. I guess maybe Jasper and I will hook up again later tonight.

We could if we wanted, as long as one of us has hooked up with someone else since the last time we were together. We can't hook up twice in a row. No one can. It says so in the Books. It wouldn't be dotly to do that, since it wouldn't exactly be loving everyone equally.

I'll check. There's a chance Jasper and I might have to wait, maybe till completion night.

It's not long now, as I remind myself . . . oh . . . about every single time I breathe in or out. Three-hundred-and-fifty-eight days down, seven more to go.

Completion night is going to be huge. There's this whole big description of it in the Book of the Chosen, and I've read that section so many times, I swear my Books scroll there all by themselves.

You see, Dot wants us to have a big party on the lawn to celebrate the three-hundred-and-sixty-fifth night since we were created. That night, Dot is announcing her chosen ones. It says in the Books that Dot has a special purpose for them. We don't know what that's going to be, how many of us are going to be chosen, or why completion night is even called that.

But we do know that only the dotliest will be getting picked. At least, that's what we figure. It has to be, doesn't it?

Anyway, the one sure thing is every single one of us wants to be chosen. It'd literally be the best thing ever.

But anyway. Right now, I'm still upside-down, squealing and flipping around on Jasper's back when I see Gil wading toward us. Gil's all white, kind of like the underside of a lizard. He says something I don't hear, and Jasper lets go of me and I end up in the water. I'm so close to Gil that I'm practically standing on his feet.

"Say it again?" I ask him.

Dot created Gil to talk really softly, so quiet you have to lean in way close to hear him a lot of the time. But it's also what Gil says that makes him hard to understand. You know, he uses words I wouldn't think of ever using myself. Gil's one of Dot's creations just like the rest of us, but there's something different about him.

Sometimes I think Gil knows stuff the rest of us don't. That's how he acts, anyway.

"It's hardly worth repeating, Wren." Gil smiles. He has the kind of smile that doesn't show any teeth. It's more like his lips are a pair of snakes or centipedes or something, rearranging themselves into a curve. "I only asked if you two were having fun."

"Fun? Ha! Of course we are. That's what we're supposed to do, right? It says so in the Books! Having fun is a creation's duty. It's the dotly thing to do . . ." I'm babbling again, obviously.

Just lately, I've noticed Gil has this way of making me blank out. When he asks me a question in that soft voice of his, I can't think of how I should answer. What's been happening is I get totally precalm and start blurting out a whole bunch of stuff. I guess I'm hoping Gil will somehow pick an answer out of it all.

I don't think it's working, though, because Gil's totally eyeing me right now.

Which makes me feel even more precalm because Gil's eyes are different than any I've ever seen. The black parts in the middle are huge — the same as everyone else's. But the colored parts of Gil's eyes aren't a solid shade or anything. They're mostly brown, but the left one is kind of shot through with a bright blue color, which makes me think of a squid squirting its ink into the water. I guess you'd call that blue patch Gil's dotmark.

It looks nothing like mine. Dot created me with dotmarks all over my chest and arms and hands and everything. They're these thick, rough patches of skin edged with red, which get all itchy when the sun hits them directly. My dotmarks are the one part of me that never seems to sweat.

"Dot would be so pleased," Gil says.

I don't tell him I've already forgotten what we were supposed to be talking about.

Instead I say, "I'm going to jump. Who's coming?"

Jasper drops back into the water and floats on his back, completely relaxed. "I'm good right here."

And Gil smiles his snaky smile and says, "Why don't you show us how it's done, Wren?"

So I leave them there and wade toward the shallow end of the glimmering lagoon. That's where the rock pools are, and just next to them, three tall, jutting rocks. I'm pretty sure Dot created those rocks especially for me, because climbing to the top and jumping off them into the lagoon is literally my favorite thing to do. There's this joke that Dot made me part-monkey, since I like climbing and flipping and all of that. Obviously, that's pretty hilarious because, seriously, how could I have anything in common with a monkey? Talk about prenormal.

When I get out of the water, Blaze is sitting there, dangling his legs in one of the rock pools. It seems to me that Blaze has never really settled into the body Dot created for him. Tall, with wide shoulders and long legs, which are sort of thick and muscular and powerful-looking, like the rest of him. But I don't know how he stays that way, since Blaze isn't the most active person in creation. Dangling his legs in rock pools is about as far as it goes.

I guess the rock pools are super dotly, so that kind of explains why Blaze is so into them. They're shallow and warm and full of fish in every single color. Stripes and speckles and one fish that's completely clear with this bright blue head and an orange spot around its eyes.

Dot probably wanted to have a little fun creating the animals after she finished up with us.

My sungarb is spread out on the rocks, and I figure Blaze must have done that for me, since I'm pretty sure I just dropped it in a ball on the ground earlier. I scoop it up and put it on. Then I walk past Blaze, and he doesn't say a single thing.

It's only when I'm just about to start climbing the rocks that he goes, "It'd be even better off the escarpment."

I do the blinking thing at him, all slow and everything, but it doesn't work on Blaze the same as it does on Jasper. Actually, it makes Blaze look away.

"Um, are you completely prenormal or are you just acting like that right now?" I ask.

Blaze shrugs. I notice the way his coiled brown hair slides up and down his broad back as he nods up at the escarpment.

"Up there. That ledge is perfect for jumping."

The escarpment runs the entire length of one edge of creation, meeting up with the fringe of trees at either end. It's sheer, solid rock with these little specks of gold sparkling in the sun. Right here, where the lagoon is, the waterfall rushes down the rock face. The ledge Blaze is talking about, this little lip of rock, is maybe halfway up.

"Are you serious? I thought you said you read the Books!"

A soft little sigh escapes from between Blaze's teeth. "I've read them."

"The Book of the Beyond is kind of clear on this particular topic. We're not supposed to do anything presafe."

"Wouldn't be presafe for you." He pauses. "You can climb anything."

I don't know if I'm imagining it, but I think I hear the teensiest amount of admiration in what Blaze is saying. And I'll admit, that low voice of his makes me feel a little gooey.

Then the feeling passes, and I remember who I'm talking to here. Blaze. The guy who isn't quite like everyone else but doesn't seem to care. The one who comes up with the most prenormal stuff in creation.

"Trees maybe," I tell him. "Huts. But I can't climb halfway up the escarpment."

"Say you did climb. What do you think is going to happen?"

"I'm not even answering that because there's no way I *would* climb the escarpment."

"Really? Why not?"

"Um, okay. I could fall backward and smash my head open on the rocks. How's that for a reason?"

"Shouldn't matter, though," he says, half to himself.

"What in creation are you talking about? Smashing my head open on the rocks would matter a whole lot to *me*!"

There's the sound of rippling water as Blaze skims the surface with his toes. "If you fell, you'd go beyond. Beyond's even better than here."

There's this moment when everything goes quiet between us.

Until Blaze adds, "Supposedly."

When we fell from the sky, every one of us had a bag slung over our shoulders. Silver, drawstring, with everything we need inside it. By "everything we need," I mostly mean our capsules and the Books of Dot. The Books are thin and square, with a screen that lights up when you touch it. They're how we found out the way Dot wants us to be.

In the Book of the Everyday, there's all the practical stuff like which hut each of us should sleep in, who does which chores on what days, and what to eat and everything. (It's pretty easy to remember: we can eat everything in the orchard but never, ever the newfruit in the grove.)

In the Book of Contribution, there's a lot more about newfruit, how special and important they are to Dot and how we can show our thanks for creating us by picking them for her.

And the Book of the Beyond? That tells us the way life's going to be after we leave where we are right now. No one has actually gone beyond yet, obviously.

Creation began with a hundred of us, and we're still all here now. But it's not going to be that way forever. One day, every one of us will take a one-way trip beyond the fringe of trees. That's for certain. It's written right there in the Book of the Beyond (Chapter 64, Verse 3).

It's just, when it comes to the actual details of the beyond, Chapter 64's sort of hazy. Fern and I have spent ages talking about it, by which I mean Fern's dreamed up a whole lot of detail and I've just sort of listened.

According to Fern, going beyond is a whole big process. First, you'll lift off the ground and soar through the air until you reach the fringe. It'll be cool there, and the air will smell sweet and moist and mossy. You'll keep on soaring until you burst through the other side of the fringe and shoot up into the air. That's where Dot will be, in the beyond, waiting for you with her arms open. Behind her there will be a double rainbow and an entire field of daffodils, and you'll hear dottracks playing. Dot will smile, and this wave of total bliss will break over your head and wash down to your toes, and you'll know that you are home forever.

That's Fern's theory, anyway.

So now I tell Blaze, "Just because the beyond is super awesome doesn't mean we can act all presafe. Dot chooses when we go beyond, not us."

"Right."

There's this long, long silence, and I start thinking that the conversation's over.

Then Blaze goes, "You believe that?"

For some reason, the sound of everyone else splashing and laughing kind of fades away. It's only Blaze I can hear. In that moment, it's like there's only him and me in all of creation.

"Believe what?"

"Believe in going beyond."

I hear the jagged sound of my own laughter, even though nothing's even remotely funny. My voice seems to come out at half its normal speed, all stretched and everything. Around me, the colors and shapes of the lagoon begin to merge and blend. This blurring thing has happened to me before, but this time is definitely the worst.

Still, I manage to tell Blaze, "Obviously I believe it."

"Yeah?"

Pause.

"Because I've noticed stuff about you."

Inside my mouth, my tongue starts feeling giant and thick and furry. I get the prenormal sense that my entire head is expanding. It isn't, though. I have to keep on telling myself it totally, completely, utterly isn't.

It only feels that way because I'm completely precalm now. And that's because I've started wondering if there's any possible way Blaze knows about the stuff that's been happening to me recently. Stuff like the blurring, yes. But also the clammy skin and trembling hands. The things I keep asking Dot to stop.

"I *so* don't know what you're talking about."

He nods. Not a *yes* nod, though. A nod that's really saying, *I think you do.*

"Oh, so now you're Dot?" I joke, reminding myself he couldn't possibly know about the eyes and the trembling. It's not like I've shown anyone or told anyone, so how could he? "You know everything about me, just like she does?"

His only answer is a shrug. He stands up, shakes himself off, and gets ready to walk away.

Typical Blaze. He is so serious all the time, always way too busy thinking for jokes or fun.

"How about this? Did you know this was going to happen?"

And I do Jasper's thing to Blaze. I curl my foot around his ankle, then suddenly jerk it so that Blaze is thrown off-balance.

Blaze doesn't even smile. If you want to know, he pulls away like my foot is super hot or something.

If it wasn't for the Book of Acceptance, I'm guessing the two of us would be keeping our distance from now on. For sure *I* would be, especially now that Blaze has come out with all this prenormal stuff about jumping from the escarpment and noticing stuff and going beyond.

But Chapter 2, Verse 1, says Dot makes all creations different and that we should accept everyone for who they are.

So, nice and casual, I say, "Okay. If you're not coming in, I'll see you later, I guess."

I walk off, and even though I don't turn around, I can kind of tell Blaze is watching me the entire time.

03

THE THREE ROCKS next to the pools aren't even big or anything, definitely not presafe. Plus, I climb them practically every single day. So I'm not expecting anything different or special this time. I mean, why would I? My hands find the holds I always use, sun-warmed chunks of rock that are just as sturdy today as they were when Dot created them. I hoist myself off the ground, my toes curling into a crevice Dot put at the exact right spot for the length of my legs. Five or six more moves, and I'm practically at the top of the first rock, closest to the edge of the lagoon.

This huge *woo-hoo!* goes up from everyone down in the water. A jump from the very top of the rocks makes the best splash, and that's pretty much what everyone's expecting.

Fern is looking at me, shading her eyes. Gil's watching too, and Jasper's calling out my name, which is kind of funny. It's not like I need anyone to remind me who I am. I'm the same as I've always been. I'm Wren with the wavy hair that's sort of red and sort of brown. Wren who is good at climbing. Wren who loves Dot and every creation, the same way they love me.

So I can't figure out why I'm not just finishing the climb and jumping off the rocks right now. That's how I always do it. I have climbed these rocks tons of times since I was created, and never once have I stopped to think about what I'm doing.

Except for now. Today, there's a wild kind of feeling surging through me. A squeezing sensation in my stomach. My fingers are curled around two jutting pieces of rock, and my toes are all white from hanging on so hard. And suddenly, it's like all creation is a million shades brighter.

"Wre-en! Wre-eeeeen!"

Everyone in the lagoon seems to be calling out my name. Gil, Jasper, Luna, all of them. They just want me to jump and splash the way I always do.

Only I can't.

I'm literally stuck here on this rock. There's this picture inside my head, one that definitely wasn't there before I spoke to Blaze. It's me, sprawled on the rocks with my head caved in, blood pooling around my body.

I look down. Blaze has stopped walking away. In fact, he's completely still, staring up at me, as frozen as I am. And right in that moment, I think maybe Blaze saw on my face something I wasn't even aware I was thinking until now.

Dot only knows how, but he was right. I always thought going beyond was what creations did. Only now that I know *he's* questioning it, I realize I am too.

I could let go of the rock, I realize, and let myself tumble end over end down to the ground. Quicker than a butterfly flutters its wings, I'd be meeting Dot the exact way Fern and I had always talked about.

How super-thrilling would that be? Or should be, anyway. But now that it could be real, there's suddenly a whole lot of other stuff flashing into my head. All prenormal thoughts. Is it possible that I would soar off the ground and go beyond if my head was split open? Would I meet Dot? Could that actually happen? Really and truly?

I can still hear the others calling my name from the lagoon. Creations are begging me to jump. A whistle splits the air, but it's long and low and warped, just like before when Blaze and I were talking.

And over the top of all that, I think I hear Blaze and that voice of his, low and soft.

"You're okay," he says. Over and over again, just "You're okay," and "Hang on."

Blaze walks toward the three jutting rocks. He holds out a hand to help me down.

But I don't take it, because it's right then that I manage to unstick myself. I release one hand from the rockface, wipe it on my sungarb, and stretch my cramping fingers. Then I swing my way to the top of the rock easily. My bare feet slide into a crack, one on top of the other, and I know I'm going to jump and everything's going to be normal, the way it always has been.

The wind catches my hair and whips these long ropes over my face. I raise both arms up to Dot, out there beyond the fringe. I tip my head upward. I open my mouth, and out comes this huge whooping sound.

Everyone in the lagoon yells back because I guess they're as happy as I am right now. I'm Wren — Wren who believes in the Books exactly like she should.

That churning feeling before — it has completely disappeared. I mean, if I go beyond, I'm obviously going to meet Dot. How else could it possibly be?

At the base of the rocks, Blaze still has his arm out to me.

"I'm all good," I tell him, this huge smile on my face. "I'm jumping!"

In front of me, the lagoon's perfect and clear, fresh and crisp and dotly. I spread my arms wide. I bend my knees. Then I do it.

I jump. I swear, right then, my entire body is ringing with a love for Dot that's so powerful, I honestly feel like I'm flying.

04

OUR HUTS ARE right at the opposite end of the lagoon. Like I said, Dot's creation is huge. It's one gigantic rectangle that feels even bigger in the prelight, which is what it is now that the day's pretty much over. To get back to the huts from the lagoon, you have to pass the gazebo and the newfruit grove and everything else in creation too. The orchard is the one thing that lies beyond the huts, that and the fringe of trees.

So it kind of figures that Fern is practically collapsing after such a long walk.

"Come up," Gil says when Fern and I eventually make it back.

That's always how it is when Gil invites you somewhere. As in, he never puts it to you like a question. Gil is on the balcony of his hut with Brook. They're super-close friends, the two of them. You pretty much never see Gil without Brook by his side.

Anyway, I figure why not hang out with them? What else are Fern and I going to do except go to bed?

So I head up Gil's staircase to the balcony, with Fern following behind me.

Gil's hut is the same as everyone else's. Square, with stilts and a peaked wooden roof with a design of butterflies carved into it. The shutters have the same butterfly design, made out of these tiny little holes in the wood. There's a balcony all the way across the front of each one, which is where Gil and Brook are sitting, a whole pile of fruit from the orchard on the table between them. Pretty much every kind of fruit in creation, apart from newfruit, obviously. Blood oranges, apricots, cherries, lychees, these fat, fuzzy golden raspberries, and a pomegranate, torn open and spilling its seeds. There are even coconuts, which means Brook must have cut them down with the big knife nailed to one of the trees. Brook always likes to be in charge of the knife.

I grab a wedge of watermelon from the table and plop down on Gil's stairs. Fern settles into a hammock.

We don't get to sit there long before Gil tells us he has an idea. Before he'll say what it is, though, he waits, scooping hair out of his eyes and everything, until he is sure we're all totally and utterly listening to him and no one else.

Did I mention Gil's hair? It's shoulder-length, obviously, and blond. Not a yellow-blond like Fern's hair, or golden-colored like Jasper's. Gil's hair is practically white, and it's soft and flossy. Of course, every creation is good-looking, like it says in the Book of Beauty, Chapter 1, Verse 1. But on top of that, I guess you'd say Gil is striking. Or unusual, maybe. With his kinked nose and long fingers, he stands out from the rest of us, that's for sure.

"We're having a bonfire," he announces.

Fern yawns. "As long as I get to sleep next to it."

I spit out a watermelon seed, aiming for Jasper's balcony but hitting Blaze's instead. Blaze's hut is just across the path from Gil's.

In the orange light from the torches that line the path, I can see the shape of Blaze. He's out on his balcony in his own hammock, his Books lit up and resting on his chest. Asleep, I'm guessing.

"Brook?" Gil says.

And like Gil has directly asked him something, even though he completely hasn't, Brook gets up, brushing past me as he heads down the stairs. He disappears down the path, past my hut, and past Fern's. Past Luna's and Jasper's and Sage's as well, until he gets to the empty huts and I can't see him anymore.

There are more empty huts than there are full. Hundreds of them, wardrobes stocked with teeny-tiny sungarb and the beds already made. Dot only knows why. At first, we all looked in them a lot, but now no one really bothers. An empty hut just isn't that fun compared to everything else there is to do.

I ping a few more watermelon seeds in the direction of Jasper's hut. His door doesn't open so I guess he's inside hooking up. It's not like him to go to bed early for any other reason. But not every single seed hits Jasper's balcony. Some of them hit Blaze's again, and after a while he opens one eye, looks up at us, and switches off his Books. I guess he's coming over.

When Brook gets back, Gil meets him at the bottom of the stairs and takes the firewood he's collected. Without anyone saying so, it's just obvious Brook will be the one to get the fire going, and also that Gil's going to tell him exactly how to do it.

First off, Gil gets Brook building a pyramid of twigs right by the bottom of the stairs. Then he says to add the bigger branches and everything. When Brook has just a single twig left, he sticks it into one of the torches burning nearby and gives it to Gil. Gil uses the twig to light the pyramid and pretty soon the fire is really going, all toasty and warm and bright and everything.

Fern must be too tired to even walk, because once she's out of the hammock, she sits on the top step and bumps the whole way down on her butt. She sinks in front of the fire, not caring that the grass is kind of damp.

I'm about to follow her when Gil takes something out of his pocket. Of all the random things in creation, it turns out to be a bird. Gil stands there with the bird cupped in both hands, its mangled wing sticking out at an angle. The bird isn't exactly moving.

"Where did you get that?" I have to ask. It's totally obvious Gil wants me to.

"It flew into my shutters just a little while ago. Brook tried chasing it away, but it kept on slamming itself until . . ." He smiles, snake-lips curving all over again. Then he brings his hands together over the top of the bird, and there's this crunching sound. "Birds aren't like us, you know. They don't go beyond."

Gil moves the crumpled bird between his hands like he's testing its weight or something. There's hardly anything to it though, just a bundle of blue feathers and a pair of spindly legs.

"Why would it do that?" I ask, not looking at the little body. "Why would it fly into your shutters?"

"She could be sending a sign."

"*She* as in . . ."

Gil glances at Brook, who's looking from Gil to me and back again, then finally says, "Dot."

I tell Gil that I didn't know Dot sent signs. The Books don't say anything about it.

"If you think that, you haven't read your Books very well. Book of Communication, Chapter 6, Verse 6: 'Dot loves talking with her creations.'"

"That just means when we talk to Dot in the gazebo," Fern says sleepily.

Gil sort of chuckles then, like he can't believe Fern said that — let alone thought it to begin with. "Do you really think she'd ask us to talk to her and never say anything back?"

I totally see Gil's point.

Dot is kind. She loves us. It makes complete sense for her to talk to us, when you think about it that way. And if she decides to use signs to talk to us, well, that's her prerogative. She created us — she can do what she wants.

"Okay," I say. "It's a sign. So what does it mean?"

Gil stands up. He looks hard at me and says, "It's a wren." He tosses the little feathered body and it lands on the fire, making the flames flare and spit.

I give this small, sharp scream. I don't know if it's because Gil said the bird was a wren, or because he just threw it into the fire. Both, I guess.

For some prenormal reason, I kind of feel like Gil just hurt *me,* not the bird. Plus, I'm suddenly getting this picture in my head. Flames. Flames accompanied by a huge, roaring whoosh and a tight sort of feeling in my chest.

"Wren?" says Gil. He's sitting down again now, next to Fern, who already has her head in his lap.

Blaze is kind of hovering on the edge of things, still on the path, not quite a part of the group even though he's been standing there the whole time.

And me? I'm on the top step, as far away from the bonfire as I can get. Gil tells me to come down, but I don't want to — not with the flames hissing around the broken bird and that picture in my head.

Plus, that prenormal thing with my eyes is happening again. Everything is going from blurry to sharp, blurry to sharp, until I can't really see much at all. I wonder if this happens to the others too. I wonder if they can tell it's happening to me.

"Coming!" I go down the stairs, clinging to the rail. I sort of squat, still a ways back from the fire.

"Sit closer." Gil has his hands in Fern's hair, twirling it around one finger.

Brook is on his side, sprawled full-length on the grass. I wiggle over. I'm shivering. Not from the cold, though. It's because of watching that burning wren and, more than that, Gil's bonfire itself. The way the flames flicker and move around . . . it's like they are waiting for the first chance they get to swallow me up. How come I never noticed that about fire before?

"You don't look very comfortable," Gil says to me.

Fern has her head in his lap still. Her eyes are closed, and her hair is stuck to her cheeks.

I'm not sure what to tell Gil, so I do what I've been doing a lot lately. You know, blurt out a whole lot of stuff that sounds all fun and jokey and try to fill the silence. I want to at least *sound* like me, even if I don't exactly feel it right at this particular moment.

"I'm super good! Squatting is really . . . nice. You should try it. I can personally recommend it."

Blaze has been following my entire conversation with Gil, I can tell. Now he leaves the path and comes to squat down next to me. "Can I show you something dotly?"

I'm pretty surprised. Blaze is *so* not the type to initiate things. He never splashes you in the lagoon or throws his arms around you during a really powerful dottrack in the gazebo or anything like that. As far as I know, he's never hooked up.

"What, your willie?"

There it is again, the blurting thing. Anyway, Gil and Brook laugh. Fern would have too, if she wasn't asleep. Not Blaze, though.

"Yeah, no."

I think of how much easier it'd be to *get* Blaze if he were more like Jasper or someone. You know, a guy who never takes anything seriously. Someone fun. Someone who wasn't so *intense* all the time.

I sigh. "Okay, what then?"

"A pond."

"I have to say, a willie sounds waaaay dotlier. In my experience, anyway."

And right in the middle of Gil and Brook laughing all over again, something kind of occurs to me. If I go to see this pond Blaze is talking about, I could get away from the fire. It doesn't even matter what the pond looks like. I mean, who actually cares? I stand up from my squat, and right after me, Blaze does too.

"But maybe I just haven't seen the right ponds," I add.

Brook's watching me really closely now. "If you two want to hook up," he says, "why not just say so?"

"We don't," Blaze and I say at the exact same moment.

And if you asked me, I couldn't even tell you which one of us was louder. So I guess that sorts *that* out.

"Enjoy yourselves," Gil calls out as I follow Blaze down the path, back across the lawn, and away from the huts and the orchard.

I start talking, because it's super unlikely Blaze is ever going to. "So, where exactly is this amazing pond?"

Blaze kind of points with his head but stays pretty much silent until we reach this clump of magnolia trees, all thick with flowers. Blaze shoulders his way through them, and I follow him, only to stop in front of the plainest, globbiest-looking pond Dot ever created.

"You brought me that entire way for this?"

"Didn't think you wanted to stay."

Apparently my blurting strategy didn't work on Blaze. That thing with the wren and the bonfire? I'm pretty sure he noticed. Just like he'd somehow guessed what was going to happen when I climbed the rocks earlier. Dot only knows how, but he seemed to understand how I'd feel even before I did.

Blaze slides his bare feet into the pond, just like at the rock pools. But then, guess what happens? He swishes his legs in the water and, I swear to Dot, the pond lights up. Wherever Blaze's legs move, little specks of pale green light follow them. When he stops moving, the lights fade.

"How in creation . . ."

"Little animals."

Seriously, Blaze says the most prenormal things. I mean, there are obviously no animals in the pond. It's the rest of creation that's teeming with animals. Big cats dozing in the sun, deer grazing in the grass, butterflies flitting around, and monkeys chitter-chattering in the trees. Parrots, flamingos, eagles, macaws, snow owls, and even wrens, when they're not smashing into Gil's shutters. But nothing whatsoever in the pond.

I don't make a big deal about it, though. Mostly, I want to try the light thing out for myself.

When I slide my legs into the pond, the water does the exact same thing it did for Blaze. I try with my fingertips, and the lights follow them as well. I smile, and when I look over at Blaze — guess what? — he's already smiling at me.

"Cool, huh?"

I'm leaning forward. It would be so easy for Blaze to push me in, but I'm pretty sure he never even thinks about doing that. It would be totally different if Blaze were some other creation.

Jasper, for example. Jasper would have pushed me into the pond ten times by now. And I would have been so busy trying to get him back that I wouldn't have noticed the lights Dot put in the water.

For a long time, Blaze and I stay like that, trailing our fingers and kicking our legs. I keep on starting to talk, but Blaze never really allows any conversation to get going. One time he even tells me I don't have to talk if I don't want to.

"I do want to."

"If you're always talking, there's no time to think."

Exactly.

Think too hard, and you're going to end up stuck on the things you'd rather forget. Such as the eye blurring thing or that prenormal trembling in my hands. Feathered bodies in fires. Those things are way better ignored, in my opinion. I guess that's where Blaze and I are totally different.

At one point Blaze gets up.

"Where are you going?" I ask. I don't know why, but I want him to stay near me.

He disappears behind a magnolia tree, and I hear the sound of liquid hitting the dirt. For some Blaze-ish reason, I guess he feels like he can't just go in front of me like anyone else would.

When he's finished, I think he's going to say we should go back to our huts, but — surprise, surprise — he doesn't. He slides his legs back into the pond and goes on stirring up the lights. Over and over, so mesmerizing and peaceful and beautiful that I'm starting to wonder if Blaze has a point about being quiet sometimes.

In the end, I'm the first to suggest going to sleep.

I'm shaking off my wet arms and legs when Blaze goes, "How about here?"

I had been busy imagining the awesomely soft bed back in my hut. I definitely had not been planning on spending the entire night with Blaze. But now that he's said it, sleeping right here seems sort of okay. So I curl up in the grass and Blaze lies down beside me. Not touching or anything, but nearby, definitely.

"Comfy?" I ask. "I can shift over."

When I hook up with someone (which is basically the only time I'm ever sleeping beside someone else) I always have to be the last one to say something.

Beside me, Blaze's breathing has already gotten deep and slow.

"See you in the morning," I say.

"Yeah," he says. He lifts his hand and rests it on my lower back. *You're okay*, he seems to mean, without actually having to say it.

I tell him, "Good night."

In a soft, blurry mumble he adds, "Sleep tight."

And just then, this cold, precalm feeling starts creeping its way all over me. Even though I know *sleep tight* doesn't mean anything, it really feels like it does. There's something about that combination of words, but I can't say what. All I know is I suddenly don't want Blaze to keep talking.

Even though there's no way I can know what Blaze is going to say, I know what comes next even before he actually says it.

"Don't let the bedbugs bite."

Then Blaze makes this snuffling sound, which is how I know for sure that he's asleep.

Not me.

Goodnight, sleep tight, don't let the bedbugs bite keeps rolling around and around in my head. And suddenly I'm thinking a whole lot of things that make no sense at all.

05

IT'S LIKE LOOKING at pieces of a broken water jug or something. That's the best way I can describe it. All these fragments are tumbling through the air, and I can only glimpse each one before it's gone. Except the fragments aren't pieces of clay or anything like that. Instead, they're images. Pictures inside my head.

I'm sitting on a bed, but it's not my bed. At least, not the bed in my hut or anyone else's. I'm somewhere I've never seen before. Which, by the way, is impossible because I've been inside every hut in creation. I don't recognize the bed cover, blue with a pattern of clouds on it. Or the wooden X hanging from the roof with all the colored balls dangling off it.

A word swims into my head. *Mobile.*

Is that what it's called? How do I know that?

I see other things in the room. A fluffy purple animal with a little tongue showing in the corner of its mouth, not moving or anything. Apparently not real.

Rows and rows of what I somehow recognize as books. But they're not the Books of Dot. They don't even have screens.

Then it gets even more prenormal. Because the next thing I'm looking at is a whole entire person I don't know. He's much smaller than any of Dot's creations. Creations fell from the sky in all different sizes, sure, but there's not a single one as small as this. As in, this little person is maybe half my height. Perfectly formed, only in miniature. Stunted, I guess you could say. And he's just sitting all casually beside me in bed.

I reach out to smooth the little creature's hair but as soon as I flatten one curl, another springs up somewhere else. Seriously, it's major stomach-flop material because I realize that I feel something for him, whoever or whatever the creature is.

His hair isn't even down to his chin, let alone covering his neck, which is the minimum length according to the Books. And the thing about that is, my own hair is hardly any longer. It's the usual reddish-brownish color, but it doesn't spiral down my back the way it should.

That's not the only way I look different. I'm wearing some kind of sleeveless sungarb, and underneath it my skin is totally clear, not a single dotmark, as if I'd never had any to begin with.

Then the little creature cuddles up against me. The image in my head might be impossible, but right then it feels completely real too. So real, I can feel a little body all warm and soft against my leg in the fuzzy red sungarb the creature's wearing.

I see him hand me a book like he wants me to read it to him. There's a picture on the cover, a fat shape with whirring blades on top.

Hector the Littlest Helicopter. That's what the book is called.

Then comes a voice.

"Is Julius asleep yet?" it calls. It sounds all crisp and efficient, the kind of voice people listen to. When the creation and I hear it, we swap this *look*. We giggle. The two of us could not be closer.

"It's time he was asleep, Viva."

Even though that's not my name, I'm still one-hundred-percent certain it's me the voice is calling. Somehow the sound is as familiar to me as a dottrack. I even know who the voice belongs to.

Someone named *Mom*.

06

I JERK AWAKE, gasping. I say *awake* because I figure I must have been asleep. The things I saw, those prenormal images, were as dreamlike as it's possible to get. And just because I've never had a dream with my eyes open before doesn't mean it couldn't happen. It's the only way to explain all those impossible, nonexistent things. Miniature creatures and strange beds and someone called *Mom* calling me the wrong name . . .

That's where I stop myself. It's not even worth thinking about all that stuff because none of it is real. I must have imagined it. Somehow, for whatever reason, I made it all up.

Relief cools my flushed, sweating skin.

I'm still on the ground by the pond, next to Blaze. I feel like shaking him awake. A loose, wild kind of laugh is bubbling up inside me.

Guess what? I want to say. *Can you believe what I just dreamed? Isn't that ridiculous?*

But I don't. I let Blaze sleep, curled in on himself the way ferns do when the light fades. Dreams are never as interesting to other people as they are to the person who has them. Better to keep the whole thing to myself. Better, actually, to get away from here, right now.

So I creep past Blaze. All the way through the magnolias and back along the path, I remind myself, *It isn't real, it isn't real.* But all the same, I'm shaky and way overheated. Back at the huts, the open air is damp and the grass is wet with dew. Fern and Gil and Brook are sprawled out on top of each other near the cooling bonfire. I decide not to wake them up, either.

Sleeping would be a relief right now. But even when I'm back in my hut, I don't drop off the way I usually do. Nowhere near.

The Books are very clear on Dot's creation. Dot made everything and everything stops at the fringe of trees and there's nothing more past that except the beyond. *Definitely* nothing like all those things I saw. But what gets me is the pictures inside my head refuse to fade like dreams should. They keep hanging around, clear as they were the first second I saw them. I end up lying on my bed for a while, staring up at the carved butterflies and the fan on the ceiling, watching the light through my shutters turn from cool silver to the soft gray of early morning. When I can't stand that anymore, I pick up my Books from the table beside my bed. I touch the screen, and the text jumps straight to the part about chosen creations.

I scroll past that and go to Communications, Chapter 6, Verse 6. Dot loves talking with her creations. And like Gil said, what kind of creator would Dot be if she asked us to talk to her but never talked back?

Maybe she doesn't use words, but lying there, I'm suddenly pretty certain Gil was right. That wren, it must have been a sign. I guess Dot was trying to prepare me for the dream she was about to send me. That would explain why the two things happened on the same night. Not that I have any idea what it's all supposed to be about.

By the time I finish with the Books, the light on my ceiling has turned pink. It's morning, which makes it definitely late enough to go the gazebo and ask Dot if she'd mind giving me some answers.

In my personal opinion, the gazebo's the dotliest thing ever. Some creations feel closest to Dot in the newfruit grove. For others, it's when they're swinging in their hammocks in Dot's sunshine.

For me though, it's totally the gazebo. I've always loved it there. First off, it's super gorgeous. Completely white and everything, with lattice walls that let the breeze blow through. On the inside, attached to the lattice, are these big terracotta planters with flowers spilling over the sides. Hanging from the ceiling, billowing, are silky banners with Dot's picture on them. There's always a dottrack playing, piped from these little black boxes in all four corners of the ceiling.

The floor is just grass, but there are these huge, squishy cushions to lie on — green, purple, raspberry pink, and lemon yellow. And obviously, there are the bubbles. The whole gazebo's filled with them, which is how our conversations reach Dot all the way out there in the beyond. Whatever we think or say in the gazebo, the bubbles soak up. Then they drift out through the diamond-shaped holes in the lattice, into the fringe, and then into the sky. We only have to see the bubbles floating through the air to know Dot's listening to us.

When I get to the gazebo, it's empty, naturally. I'm pretty sure none of Dot's other creations have been awake half the night just thinking, the way I've been. It'll be a while before anyone else wakes up and comes here.

The Books say it doesn't matter when a person talks to Dot, as long as everyone makes sure to once a day. Most of us go to the gazebo after breakfast but before picking in the newfruit grove.

That's the best way to get maximum time in bed but also leaves the whole day after picking free for having fun. That's my thinking, anyway. Plus, I like to do stuff when everyone else does, obviously, because what's the point in doing anything if you're alone?

I'm not really the all-alone type. But right now, I'm sort of glad to find the gazebo empty. There's a squishy-squashy feeling inside me. Precalm, I guess you'd call it. I choose a purple cushion and drag it around until it's facing the extra-giant portrait of Dot that hangs on one lattice wall of the gazebo.

By this point I'm sweating all over again, even though the gazebo's one of the coolest places in creation. I'm guessing that's because I have no idea what to say to Dot or exactly where to start. So I sit down and just stare up at the portrait. It's the same one as on the banners, the same as in the Books. You know, just Dot's head and shoulders, her sheet of long, pale hair, her dark skin, and her eyes shaped like two almonds, rounded at one end and tapering to these little points on either side. Even now, in the state I'm in, I notice how the portrait always looks like it's smiling.

The only choice I have is to jump into it.

Hello, Dot?

I don't need to talk out loud or anything, because Dot knows everything I'm thinking. I mean, the gazebo is full of bubbles. She's going to hear me, right?

It's Wren.

That's a kind of pointless thing to think too, obviously, since Dot knows who I am already. Apparently now I'm a blurter inside my head as well as when I'm talking out loud.

I had this dream.

Pause.

But I guess you know that.

More pausing.

I was in the dream. Well, a different version of me was. But I wasn't here. I was . . . I don't even know where. Can you tell me? It has something to do with the wren Gil found, doesn't it? Or something to do with Blaze?

Parked there on the cushion looking up at Dot's face, I tell her the whole prenormal story in this waterfall gush. How Blaze said the rhyme that I somehow knew without knowing. The miniature creature with his curly hair. The person called Mom. I even remind Dot about the blurry eyes and stuff, although I've already mentioned that a million times before.

Bubbles go floating past, all silent and serene. I'm sitting there, watching them soak up everything I'm thinking and feeling, carrying it all off to the beyond, when it hits me.

It doesn't matter that I don't understand what all this is about. I'm not *supposed* to.

Dot has her reasons for prenormal wrens and blurred vision and making me see the things I did. That's all I need to know. My only job is to follow the Books. The rest of it, well, Dot has it covered. So what am I even doing thinking so hard? When she decides I'm ready, Dot will explain.

If she wants to, that is.

If not, I can handle it. I mean, I only need to look around at her perfect creation to realize that Dot completely knows what she's doing.

I let myself sink back into my big, soft cushion. I stretch my arms and legs across the silk, yawning as Dot smiles down at me and the sun makes yellow-gold pools on my skin.

I'm light again, relaxed and smiling. Right here is where I leave all those precalm feelings behind.

Dot will work it out. And that means I'm free to make today the best day in creation. You know, just another installment in Dot's never-ending series of minor miracles.

07

On the edge of the newfruit grove there's a stack of empty picking bags, the way there always is. That's how it works (Book of Contribution, Chapter 5, Verse 2). Every day, everyone fills a picking bag in the grove. Then we empty all the newfruit into a chute built into the ground that leads . . . well, I guess it leads directly to Dot. The Books aren't specific about how that part works. All I know is that when the bags are empty, we leave them stacked up beside the chute, ready to fill the next day.

That's it. That's all Dot asks from each of us. Just one single, perfect bag of newfruit, which is nothing when you think about all the stuff Dot has given us.

"Throw me a bag, will you?" I say to Fern.

She has a glazed look on her face, with her nose way up in the air and her nostrils practically quivering. That sounds prenormal, but it isn't, not when you understand how totally dotly the smell of the newfruit grove actually is.

Imagine warm grass and dripping honey, fresh sungarb, vanilla beans and bark, sunshine on a warm rock, and a creation's neck as you nuzzle into it, all rolled into one. That's close to what the smell is like, except the real thing is a bazillion times better.

It's the blossoms that make the newfruit grove smell so incredible. Obviously Dot created tons of other flowers as well as the newfruit blossoms. There are flowers all over the place — in the orchard, by the gazebo, near the lagoon.

But newfruit blossoms are a whole other thing altogether. Newfruit trees only grow in the grove. Their blossoms fall off their branches, and there are so many different colors. There are purple flowers with gold speckles. Bright yellow ones with fuzzy pink centers. Blue bell-shaped things that leave dust on your fingertips when you touch them. And, I swear to Dot, the smell of newfruit is the most incredible thing in all creation.

"Hello, Fern?" I wave my hand in front of her face. "Anyone home?"

Fern stoops and takes a picking bag from the pile at our feet. But with her short arms and everything, she ends up flubbing the throw.

"Careful," Gil says, arriving at the exact right moment to see the bag hook itself over one of the newfruit trees.

Gil is walking with Brook and Drake, the three of them in sungarb as bright as the blossoms all around us. Drake has his sungarb unbuttoned lower than the others, which gives me a perfect view of the creamy-yellow skin underneath. Arms, legs, chest, willie. Drake's pretty much hairless apart from the black hair on his head, which brushes his shoulders as he walks. He smiles, and I think about hooking up with him again, about feeling that smooth skin. Maybe at the completion night party, if I don't end up with Jasper. Or maybe I could hook up with Drake as well as Jasper. Dot would probably like that. Hooking up as much as possible would be a dotly thing to do, I'm pretty sure. I notice Drake's kind of looking at me with that hooking-up expression, so I figure he's thinking about it too.

"Wren?" says Gil. "Are you listening to me?"

All around us, people are drifting up from the gazebo in pairs and threes. Except for Blaze who (gigantic surprise) is walking by himself. When I see him, of course I end up thinking about the pond and what he said there, that prenormal rhyme.

Goodnight, sleep tight, don't let the bedbugs bite.

But I shove it away pretty fast. I don't know how I know it and I don't know how Blaze knows it, but I do know that I don't want to think about any of it.

It's not like it matters or anything. Going to the gazebo reminded me that all that stuff is for Dot to handle, not me. End of story. I guess Blaze didn't get the message that I feel this way, though, because he keeps trying to get my attention, to catch my eye or something super awkward like that. So what I do is turn around to Drake, Gil, and Brook and start chatting the way I always do, as bright, bubbly, and fun as is possible.

"I'm totally listening," I say. "I was just thinking about the completion night party at the same time. Who's looking forward to it? Drake?" I flick my spiraling hair and let it fall so it covers one eye. Now Drake definitely knows I'm interested. As a bonus, I can't see Blaze's face and he probably can't see mine.

As Blaze goes past, Gil untangles my bag from the tree. Before he hands it to me, he makes this big point of checking to make sure the fruit underneath is okay. Newfruit are Dot's fruit, so it's common sense that no one would ever want to damage one. The fruit is fine, thank Dot. Round with thin, silver speckled skin, exactly the way Dot created it. Perfect.

Gil hands me the bag and walks deeper into the grove, leaving me and Fern to find two trees side by side. We need trees with enough ripe newfruit to fill our picking bags, but that isn't exactly hard. Like everywhere else in creation, the trees in the newfruit grove are covered with fruit pretty much constantly.

When I find a tree, I climb into the lower branches. Beside me, Fern's in her own tree humming "We Belong 2 Dot."

I reach for the nearest branch and pull it closer to me. Then I scan the newfruit dangling down. It says in the Book of Contribution that newfruit has to be picked at the exact right time.

Too firm, and Dot might find it sour. Too ripe, and it could drop from the branch overnight and split, and that would mean one less newfruit for Dot to enjoy.

So I look hard till I find the ripest, most perfect fruit. Really gently, I press around the stem with the pad of my pinky finger. Newfruit skin is so thin that it bruises if it isn't handled the proper way. I mean, if you even *breathe* on a newfruit wrong it could bruise.

I turn to Fern. "What do you think about this one? Does this look ripe to you?"

Fern is holding a branch herself, but instead of picking anything, she's just cupping a newfruit in both hands. Then she strokes it against her cheek and holds the newfruit under her nose to take this great big sniff.

"Um, Fern?" I say, all chirpy. "Pretty sure Dot wants us to pick the newfruit, not smell it."

"Oh, I know." Fern sighs. She starts stroking the newfruit against her cheek again. "I just love thinking about it. This newfruit, the one I'm touching right now . . . Dot's going to eat it. Isn't that incredible?"

An actual tear spills out between Fern's lashes and rolls down her cheek. I guess you could say Dot created Fern sentimental. Everyone loves Dot, obviously, but Fern really shows it on her face. As in, the whole time.

Everyone agrees she's probably going to be one of the ones chosen on completion night. On top of following the Books, Fern is always doing extra stuff to please Dot. Like right now, she's making every single person in the garden a garland of flowers to wear at the completion party. You know, just because there's a picture of someone wearing a garland in the Books and Fern has decided that means Dot really wants all of us to wear them.

According to Fern, weaving those garlands makes her feel closer to Dot. Which is *so* Fern. Everything about her is adorable.

I reach over and poke Fern's arm. "Can you hurry up and fill your bag? I want to go riding after this."

Dot created horses for us to ride, which me and Fern like to do before we go swimming so that we're nice and hot by the time we jump in.

I'm thinking about spending the whole afternoon having fun, smiling to myself, when this voice goes, "Riding?"

I look down, and Blaze is there standing by the bottom of my tree.

"If Fern ever finishes," I say.

Blaze has a full picking bag slung over his shoulder. By the looks of it, he's ready to empty his newfruit down the chute and go back to his hut or whatever exactly it is he does for fun. But he doesn't. Instead he says, "Can I talk to you?"

I give him this really big smile. The glowing pond is no big deal to me, not anymore, and I want him to know that. Just in case he's thinking something big happened, or that the little rhyme he said in any way affected me. Or that I was obsessing over it or something.

"Not if I'm riding," I say. "That would be kind of difficult, don't you think?"

Blaze doesn't smile or anything, which is fair enough because I guess it wasn't that entertaining a thing to say. It was just the quickest way I could think of to tell him that I don't want to talk to him about what he said. Not now. Not ever.

I've already spoken to Dot, which is all I need to do. She is the only one who will ever know about the pictures in my head. The best thing right now would be for Blaze to walk away.

He picks that moment to put his bag down. "Move over," he tells Fern. "I'll help you."

"She's fine," I say as Fern starts making room for Blaze on her branch.

He scales the trunk in that stiff way of his and starts picking newfruit twice as quickly as Fern could. Not even once do I see him touch a stem to check if the fruit is ripe. He hardly even looks at the newfruit before he slides it into Fern's bag.

I have to ask, "Wait. How did you even know that one was ready to pick?"

Blaze looks at his bare feet, huge against the branch of the newfruit tree. "Seemed dotly to me."

Am I imagining he sounds different from everyone else when he says *dotly*?

I feel like there's a sourness to it, exactly like biting into a preripe plum. He reaches for a branch and *ping-ping-ping*, he twists the newfruit from their stems and rolls them into his picking bag. He's so quick, he sends blossoms and leaves showering through the air.

The blossoms make this beautiful flickering shadow on the grass underneath us, which catches Fern's attention right away. In her head, Fern's probably already thanking Dot for putting on the display.

Blaze grabs his chance. "I really want to talk to you."

"I'm kind of busy right now."

"After picking."

"I'm busy then too."

"Skip riding?"

The way Blaze asks questions is the opposite of Gil. When Gil asks a question, you can tell he already knows the answer. With Blaze, it's like he's never sure about one single thing. Anyway, for once he's looking at me. Not at my eyes or anything, but at my cheek, which kind of dilutes the impact of my favorite long, slow blink technique.

"I'm not going riding. I changed my mind. I think I'll go to the gazebo instead. There's nothing in the Books that says I can't go twice a day, right?"

Blaze shakes his head.

"Because I really want to tell Dot something."

Like I knew he would, Blaze asks, "What?"

I pick a newfruit, this gleaming silver orb, and for a while I just let it roll around in the palm of my hand. "I want to tell her how perfect things are. How much I love all creation, and how I never want anything to change."

I put the newfruit into my bag and turn my back on Blaze. "Not that anything ever will."

* * *

Then it happens again. It's the afternoon, not long after Fern and I get back from riding and swimming and everything. I'm in my hammock, out on my balcony. I'm not even doing anything, just feeling the breeze on my skin and waiting for the sun to dry my thick hair.

Fern and Drake and Jasper are down on the grass outside their huts, close enough that I can talk to them whenever I want.

I see Luna coming out of her own hut, sneaking down the stairs with a jug of water in her hands. When she walks up behind Fern she doesn't make a sound. She smirks at me, then tips the entire jug of water down the back of Fern's sungarb. Fern squeals, and suddenly I'm somewhere else altogether.

08

IT'S GREEN LIKE Dot's creation, but there's no lagoon or gazebo in this other place. Not a single deer or monkey or any of the normal stuff you'd expect. There are pieces of bark on the ground, as well as grass. And instead of a fringe of trees there's just black wire mesh with a door cut into it, which creaks whenever someone goes in or out. I find myself reaching for words without even wanting to. Words like *park* and *gate*.

There's no one I recognize. Instead, the *park* is full of miniature people. They're running around all over the place while bigger, normal-sized people stand around watching. The little ones swarm all over this hut-type thing, which is bright yellow. It's hard and shiny, with stairs and bridges and ropes dangling from it. Across the other side of the park, there's a tall wooden crossbar with pairs of chains hanging down and this sort of seat attached. On each seat, there's a small creature swinging back and forward, all gleeful smiles like it's the best thing Dot ever created. I feel like I've seen that kind of seat before. If I thought hard, I could probably think of the name for it.

Then I'm looking at the creature I saw last time.

Julius?

Right away, I recognize the curly hair, which in the light I can see is the exact same reddish-brown shade as mine. I'm lifting him up onto my shoulders, laughing as I hoist him high into the air. There's a bar across two vertical wooden poles, and he grabs it. He swings there, arms above his head. He's wearing prenormal sungarb again, this time it's a blue-and-yellow thing with the outline of a rearing horse on the front. On the back, the number sixteen. As he swings, the top part of his sungarb rides up and shows off his soft white tummy.

I'm looking the other way when he falls. I hear him calling out, and when I turn he has already landed in a crumpled heap on the ground. I rush over and scoop him up.

"Are you okay?" I croon. "Poor dear. Poor little guy."

The zigzagged crown of a tooth has pierced the wet, pink skin of his bottom lip. Blood is trickling down. His mouth is now wide open, and he's really howling. This isn't a noise like anyone else in the park is making. Everyone's looking at us. Big creations and small ones, all of them staring at us as Julius screams, the trail of blood mixing with tears.

Outside the park, beyond the gate, a group of people about my size are watching too. I see them in a series of quick, bright images. Long, glossy hair. Heavy lashes sweeping pink cheeks. Otpen mouths, giggling at me. Familiar unfamiliar names appear in my head. Allie. Kristin. Gianna. Maya. *Oh my God*, they shrill. *So embarrassing.*

And in the middle of them, another face. A guy — maybe the most gorgeous I have ever seen. Hair all swept to one side, golden brown. Shirt with the collar twisted up. He's not whispering to the others, at least, but he's watching Julius and he's watching me.

"C'mon," I beg Julius. "It doesn't hurt that much. Everyone's looking. Can't you just be quiet?"

Next thing, another figure appears. She's slight and pinched, with the same red-brown curls as mine. I recognize her even though I've never seen her before.

Mom.

She hugs Julius to her.

"What were you thinking?" she says to me in this prenice way.

"I'm sorry. I just . . ."

I flick a glance at Julius, then another at the guy. Back and forth, like I can't quite decide who is more important.

Mom makes this clicking sound and pulls Julius out of my arms. And it takes a while — like, a long while, because I'm telling you, these sobs are *powerful* — but slowly the crying stops as she closes her arms tight around his little body.

09

My eyes are open, so I snap them shut. Open, shut, open, shut. I want to be sure that the dream, or whatever it was, is totally finished. Not that I can stop thinking about it, even once I'm sure it's over. I mean, it's hardly been half a day since the last time.

It takes me a moment to realize where I am. I'm inside my hut, stretched out on my bed. Right there beside me, of all people in creation, is Blaze. You know, with his solid chest and muscled thighs and knotty hair and everything.

On top of that, though (and excuse me if this sounds prenormal), it's like there's all this extra detail to Blaze I never noticed before. His eyes, for one. The circles in the middle are smaller than they're supposed to be, and the colored brown parts are way bigger. Everything about Blaze is sharper too. As in, I can see every one of the little hairs bristling on his jawbone. I can see the actual texture of his skin.

It's the same thing all over my hut. Even from the bed I can make out every little hole in the butterfly design punched into my open shutters. I can see the wood grain on each one of the slats. Outside, the individual leaves on the trees stand out from each other. Since the blurry eye thing started, I guess I'd gotten used to trees looking like green smudges against the sky. But now that seems to have stopped. Everything is sharp and clear and glittering like broken glass.

The whole time I'm looking around my hut, Blaze is looking at me. All intense and everything, the way he does.

"Sore?" he asks.

I don't feel sore. Sort of the opposite. I'm awake, but somehow I'm even more awake than usual, if that makes any kind of sense.

But I tell Blaze, "Um, I guess." He seems to be expecting I will be sore.

"Big bruise coming up." Blaze rubs his own forehead. "Right there."

There are a couple of butterflies circling the fan on the ceiling. The wind comes in through the shutters and turns the blades. I keep thinking the butterflies are going to get all tangled up or mashed or something, but you know what? They never, ever do. It's like they know how to keep out of the way. They go on swooping down, flapping around my head and everything. For whatever reason, the butterflies won't leave me alone.

"Wait . . ." I say. I'm remembering the dream. I saw all that prenormal stuff, the *park*. Before, though . . . what was I doing before? "Did I fall or something?"

"Rolled out of your hammock."

A fall. A bump on the head. That's what caused me to see all that

56

stuff — this time, anyway. It makes sense. As much sense as anything else.

"Has that ever happened to you?" I ask. I notice my hands are skittering across the top of my sheet. I take one hand in the other and lace my fingers together. On and on and on. My fingers are moving all by themselves, and I can't seem to stop them. But I've spoken to Dot about the dreams. I need to remember I have complete and total faith and that she has everything under control.

Blaze answers, "Once or twice."

"What was it like?"

Now he looks at me with those prenormally brown eyes of his.

"What's it like for you?"

I'm getting the feeling Blaze means more than falling. And now I'm wondering if he's talking about the things I saw. *Stop*, I tell myself. Blaze can't see the contents of my head. Anyway, none of it is real. There are no screaming mini-people. Parks with gorgeous guys in them do not exist.

Blaze is waiting for me to answer. So I do what I'd normally do, which is laugh. "How would I know? I was out of it, remember?"

"Your eyes were moving. You were looking at something."

"Oh my Dot. You were *watching* me?"

"You fell. I came to help."

I can't stop myself. "Even if you were watching me, it still doesn't mean you have one single clue —"

"Yeah, I do."

Then, I swear, I snort. The sound is like something an animal would make. It's so un-Wren. As in, it's a totally prehappy sound.

"Yeah, um, that's impossible. There's no way you could ever know what I see when my eyes are closed."

Blaze's eyebrows go up.

I blurt, "Not that I ever see anything prenormal or anything. I mean . . ."

That's when Blaze starts to smile. An actual grin, maybe the first one I've ever seen from him. "So there is another you," he says. "A real you."

He runs his hand over his chin, and I can hear the little hairs there crackling under his calloused fingers. Mostly the hairs on his chin are brown, but there are some glimmery gold ones too.

I try another laugh. "There's only one me."

"Happy, fun, bubbly Wren." He goes on stroking his chin.

"Can you not do that?"

"You don't like stubble?"

I smile like Blaze has made some hilarious joke. Snorting, prehappy Wren is gone. I force her to disappear. "Dot created it, so why wouldn't I?" I ask.

The ceiling fan turns lazy circles above our heads. The butterflies dip and hover in front of my eyes.

Then, out of nowhere, Blaze goes, "We're the same, you know."

Underneath me, the bed is kind of tipping and lurching, but I manage to act like it isn't. "Last time I looked, I don't have stubble. No willie. So no, we're *nothing* alike."

Blaze's shoulders draw together. Then he sighs and says, "It happens to me."

"Seriously, I don't know —"

"You've seen outside. Places. People. Words you shouldn't know," Blaze says.

Right away, I hear those screams in the park again. The feel of that little body in its fuzzy red sungarb. Completely imagined, wispy little nothings. They're things Dot chose to put in my head for reasons only she understands. Not worth talking about, which is why I'm not even going to admit to Blaze that they exist.

"Um, try *no*? I do *not* see anything outside, because there's no such thing."

Blaze's chin-stroking goes from thoughtful to totally determined and focused, like his entire existence hinges on it. "I don't know what it is or why it happens. I don't know why it's only you and me."

That's when a wild, pure, raw prehappiness surges up inside me.

Somehow, we're talking about stuff that isn't real as though it is. We're thinking about things that should be left to Dot.

Then Blaze veers off again. "Did you like climbing the rocks by the lagoon?"

I prop myself up on my elbow. "I loved it."

"You looked prehappy."

"When?"

"When you froze."

How does Blaze know what I felt when that happened — the squeezing of my insides, my hands all wet and clammy? And how much does he know about the other part, the part where I wondered whether or not I would really meet Dot?

"Are you kidding me? I was absolutely *fine*."

"Not precalm about falling?" He slams his hands together and makes this huge crashing noise. "*Wham!* That's it. Gone."

Blaze's hands drops to his knees. He's kind of rubbing them or kneading them or something. I don't even think he knows he's doing it, same as the thing I've been doing with my fingers.

"I have no idea what you're talking about," I say. I'm so ready to stop this conversation.

"You knew you'd meet Dot if you went beyond? You were sure?"

"Definitely," I say. Blaze leaves another gap, and I end up plunging on with this conversation, even though another part of me is begging myself not to say what comes out next. "What else is there to think?"

"I want to find out." Blaze watches the butterflies up by the ceiling fan, flitting around the blades, never once getting caught. Very softly he says, "What if the places we see are real?"

That's it, right there. That's why Blaze and I are nothing alike and never will be.

It sounds like he sees stuff too — prenormal dreams or visions he thinks are real. Even worse, he's really desperate to talk about them and find out more. Whereas I know there's no way in creation any of it can exist.

I mean, if it did, then there'd have to be something outside the fringe of trees, in the beyond, where there's only Dot. *That* would mean the Books are wrong, and not just a little wrong. I'm talking majorly, completely, totally wrong. And if they can be so far off about that, then it could be that none of the other stuff in there is right. Everything would be upside-down, and that's just not possible.

"I don't know how many ways I can tell you this. I have no idea what you're talking about. Forget it, will you?"

Then I do the only thing I can think of, which is to pull my sheet up over my face. Hidden there in my own private pearly bubble, it's easier to act like I don't know what Blaze means.

I groan. "This conversation is messing with my head. Seriously. There are parts of me that weren't prehealthy before you got here, and now they are."

"If you don't want to talk about it . . ."

"I really don't. In so many different ways."

Blaze peels back the corner of the sheet and peers in so that I can just see a little bit of hazel eye and a square of bristly skin. "When you do, come to my hut. Any time."

Okay, so now we're back to a place I'm familiar with. A way out, it seems. "You want to hook up," I say. "Is that what you've been trying to tell me this entire time?"

Oh my Dot, you should see Blaze's face then. His cheeks are like dragon fruit red. Raspberry red. Raspberries and dragon fruit all mushed together. Totally, totally red.

"You do!" I say. "Why didn't you just say so, instead of all that prenormal stuff you were going on about? My head is fine. I'm fine. I could hook up now, if that's what you want."

I reach my arm out toward him. His hand is right there, grabbing the edge of my sheet still. It's the easiest thing in creation to put my hand on top of his and mesh our fingers together. It would be, if Blaze hadn't whipped his hand away instantly. The sheet drops over my face again and from underneath it, I see his shadow rippling across my bed as he stands up to leave.

"So that would be a 'no,' then?" I say. I'm pretty glad to be under the sheet. I have no urge to look at Blaze right now, none whatsoever.

He stops and stands still. "I just . . ." Then he gets all fumbly. "Not everything's about . . . *you know*. Hooking up."

"Hooking up is no big deal. It's what people do. It's *dotly*."

Even as I'm saying this, I can't believe I'm bothering. It's not even like Blaze is my type of guy. In no way is he entertaining like Jasper or Drake. He isn't fun to be around — at least not my version of fun. And I know he's beautiful according to the Books, but in my opinion, his hair is too twisted and his skin is too weathered to be the kind you want to brush up against. Maybe there was a moment back at the rocks . . . but it's over now. Very, *very* over. I swear to Dot, I'm not even sure that moment happened at all.

"If that's what you believe."

From underneath my sheet I say, "I don't believe it. I know it." Then I pull it back just a little to look at Blaze. He's sort of staring at nothing, or maybe it's the dust mites.

"See you later," he says.

"Right. Whatever."

Does that sound enough like I don't care? Because I *don't* care. Really.

Not even when he backs away, opens the door, and leaves.

I pull the sheet off my face completely and just lie there. Outside my hut I can hear people talking. Who's coming to the lagoon for an afternoon swim, who's down at the orchard, who was slowest to finish filling their newfruit bag.

Only the thin wooden walls of my hut separate me from them. But you know what? That's really not the way it feels. From where I'm lying, those people and their light, delicious conversations suddenly seem impossibly far away. Or it feels like I'm impossibly far away from them. Like I'm somewhere else, somewhere that shouldn't exist.

I think of that small creature with the curls. I think of his soft, round tummy.

"Julius."

It comes out suddenly. I realize I've only thought the word before. This is the first time I've ever said it out loud. For a simple collection of letters, it has a powerful effect. I am shaking.

I don't want to say the word again. But at the same time, I can't stop myself.

"Julius."

There is this loose thread on my sheet, and I start flicking it back and forth with my fingertip as I lie there. Gradually, the thread works itself looser and looser, until a whole row of the weave starts to come undone.

I know what I should do. Get up and stop being so prenormal. Stop talking to myself. Go hang out with Fern, maybe hook up with Drake or Jasper or whoever.

Whatever would help me erase this whole little scene with Blaze — that's what I should do. That would be dotly.

But guess what?

I just go on fiddling with that loose thread in my sheet, thinking things I don't even want to put into words because once I do, they'll be out there in the air and I won't ever be able to take them back. And the whole time I keep tugging at the thread even though I know that if I don't stop right now, pretty soon the entire thing will unravel.

10

It's the perfect late afternoon, the kind only Dot could create. Everyone's either swimming or lazing in the huts or maybe, like Fern, picking flowers. Everyone except for me. The only place I want to be right now is in the gazebo, talking to Dot. You know, just watching my thoughts float away in a bubble the way they always have before.

When I arrive at the gazebo, it's not empty like I expected. Gil's already there.

"I didn't know you came here twice a day," I say. I'm working really hard to keep my voice all frothy light. There's no way I want Gil asking me why *I'm* here for the second time (which, incidentally, would be a totally Gil-like thing to do).

If he did, I wouldn't know how to answer. I mean, I'm here because I want to forget about the prenormal conversation I had with Blaze. I want to stop thinking about the way it made me feel to say the word *Julius*. I'm here because I have to keep reminding myself Julius isn't real and that Dot has her reasons for making me see him, which aren't for me to know. There's no way in creation I'm explaining all of *that* to Gil. Even if I wanted to, I don't know if I could.

But it ends up being beside the point, because Gil never even turns around. There's a whole lot of silver hair flopping over his eye, the one with the dotmark. He's kneeling on a cushion staring up at the portrait of Dot on one lattice wall of the gazebo. And even though I kneel down right beside him, it doesn't seem like he notices me.

"So you're pretty much going to ignore me. Am I right?"

Gil's eyelids flutter. His lips close, and he starts to hum. Not in time with the dottrack that's playing in the gazebo or anything like that. No, Gil's hum is one long, low, continuous stream.

"Ha! Okay. I'm going to take that as a yes."

Underneath my knees, the cushion shivers. That would be because Gil's entire body has started shaking. His silver hair falls across his face again, but he doesn't scoop it out of the way. All he does is kneel there while his shaking turns into rocking. Back and forth, side-to-side, Gil lurches all over the place. His arms are circling now, his mouth drawn back in a sort of snarl.

Next Gil starts making this high-pitched moaning sound. His arms stop circling. Instead they rise up and reach out for Dot's portrait like he's not even controlling them, like Dot's literally pulling him to her. In the middle of his moaning he starts to talk but not in words I've ever heard before. It's just a whole lot of garbled letters.

I want to ask him what's happening, but when I say Gil's name it just gets lost in all the noise. Then his eyelids open. It's like Gil can't see me even though I'm right there next to him. His eyes are blank white. As in, no colored parts whatsoever. His head tips back. He's really shrieking now, jerking and rolling and sweating and everything else. It's like Dot's portrait is watching him and only him, like Dot and Gil are joined by some invisible, unbreakable thread.

Then he says, "Yes, Dot. I understand."

And suddenly, without any kind of warning, the whole thing is over. Gil flops sideways, all limp and splayed out. His head's on the cushion, his hair brushes my leg, and he's breathing hard. I touch his forehead and brush away the damp silver ropes of his hair until he opens his eyes and gazes up at me.

"Okay. Oh my Dot. Are you all right?"

Gil's eyes are back in the proper place, pale as a wolf's with huge black circles in the center. "No one has ever seen me like that, except Brook."

"Are you, like, *prehealthy* or something?"

"No." Gil smiles. "The opposite. That's just what happens when Dot is inside me." He lets this sink in before he adds, "I can hear her, you know."

Gil says this like it's so ordinary there's no reason for me to act surprised. But obviously I can't help it. I've never seen anyone do anything like whatever it was that Gil just did. Not in a dream, and definitely not in real life.

"At first I couldn't understand her. I only felt her. But now I see her too. Now she talks through me."

I feel this sharp stab of prehappiness.

Gil sees Dot. She *talks* to him. It's obvious he's been chosen, that he'll be singled out on completion night. Whereas Dot shows *me* stuff that isn't real and definitely isn't dotly. I don't know what it means, but I don't think it's anything good.

"What does she say to you? I mean, is this how you knew about the signs?"

"I see our lawn, washed in pale golden light. Dot steps out of the fringe and takes me in her arms. She always says the same thing. 'Defend the dotly.'"

"'Defend the dotly?' I don't get it." A bubble drifts between Gil and me. He waits for me to fill in the gaps, to figure it out. "'Defend the dotly,'" I repeat. "Um . . ."

"Come on, Wren. Dot created you to be intelligent."

"But everyone's dotly. It says so in the Books."

"We're *created* dotly. Dot's saying we don't all stay that way."

Images whirl into my head and out again. Gil's hands crushing that wren. Flames licking at the feathered body. Then those prenormal images inside my head. People who shouldn't exist. Places that aren't here. Can Gil tell just by looking at me? Does he know? Dot's inside him, so maybe . . .

I have to act like Gil's conversation is having no effect on me. Gil has to think I'm normal.

So I say, "What other way is there to be?"

Gil gives me this smile like I couldn't possibly understand. "There's happiness and prehappiness. Calm and precalm. Why not dotly and predotly?"

"*Pre*dotly? Is that a thing?" It pops out of me in this little squeak before I have time to think or moderate in any way. So much for looking normal.

"Dot wants us to defend the dotly," Gil says coolly. "It's simple logic that there has to be something to defend it against."

"Totally," I say in a rush, trying to recover as fast as I can. "It makes sense. Wow, though. *Wow.* That's major. Who's predotly? I mean, is Dot going to give you names and everything?"

By now, I'm kind of babbling.

"There are the signs," Gil says. "There's a lot you can tell from behavior too. Who does the dotly thing and who doesn't."

He crooks his finger in a come-here kind of way. Still on my knees, I shuffle across the cushion toward him. When I get close enough, he reaches out the same finger and touches my cheekbone.

"We should all read our Books." Gil's hand moves from my face to the top of my head. He strokes it like I'm a deer or something, with my head bent down, eating grass. "We should follow her instructions. Be kind. Have fun. Hook up."

"I do. I do those things."

"Of course, Wren. No one said you didn't."

Gil's hand goes on smoothing my hair, and his fingertips start to circle their way downward until they're edging under the neck of my sungarb. Is it dotly to do this in the gazebo? *If it were predotly, Gil would know,* I tell myself. He's the one who found out about predotliness in the first place. If he wants this, then Dot wants it too. That'd be right, wouldn't it? I don't want to do anything predotly.

Then somewhere behind us, a voice says, "Gil? You ready to go?"

I do more than just jump. I swear to Dot, my entire body leaves the cushion and hovers in midair before crashing back down again. Gil does the same.

I whip around, and there's Brook over by the door of the gazebo, half-hidden by the late afternoon shadows streaking the ground. "Have you been there this whole time?"

Brook rolls his shoulders and gives me this single nod.

Gil laughs. "He's never far away."

Brook is as tall as Blaze but twice as lean. It's like, when Dot created Brook she didn't waste a single speck of her materials. There's almost not enough skin on him. What's there is stretched so tight that you can see the bones underneath.

Not that Brook isn't strong. He is. He's powerful, especially with the coconut knife in his hand. On his ankle, there's a prenormal dotmark. A little colored circle, right there on his skin. I've often thought of asking him what it is, but Brook has this way of discouraging questions.

Gil's hand clamps around one of my shoulders like a claw or something.

"I hang around when Gil's talking to Dot," Brook says. He's looking at Gil's hand on my shoulder.

"It's quite a draining process," says Gil. "Emotionally and physically."

Brook says, "I'll take you back to your hut."

But Gil's voice gets crisp as he says, "I'm fine for now."

"Yeah? Because I can . . ."

"Now that Wren has seen this, I want to share it with her."

Brook turns to me. "What are you doing here anyway? Didn't you come earlier?"

I flick my eyes from the bubbles to the billowing banners to Dot's portrait on the lattice wall. I swallow. I force out a laugh. "What, are you following me or something?"

Brook's face is blank as a hut wall.

"Anyway, who said you can't come twice a day?" I say. "The gazebo is sort of awesome, you know."

Then Gil goes, "Let's walk."

"Is that a good idea?" There's a prehappy edge to Brook's voice. He looks at me. "Do you want to?"

"Thank you, Brook." Gil's voice is sharper than ever. "I think Wren knows what Dot wants her to do." He gets to his feet and holds his hand out to me.

Brook folds his arms across his chest, and there's a loud huff as he breathes out.

Gil kind of steers me past him and out through the doorway. Before we go, Gil turns back around to Brook and says, "You know what would be useful? Collecting some fruit for me." He turns to me and adds, "I'm ravenous. I always am when she's been inside me."

For a moment, Brook blocks the doorway, not saying yes and not saying no.

"Meet me back at my hut in a little while?" Gil says. "We'll spend some time together, and I'll tell you what Dot shared with me."

"You want cherries?"

"And apricots." Gil smiles. "Please."

Brook shoots me one more look before wheeling around and disappearing in the direction of the orchard.

* * *

Obviously Gil and I aren't just walking. He has something particular in mind, so he takes me somewhere special, to a bunch of magnolia trees with glossy green leaves and a pond in the middle. Blaze's pond, which in the late afternoon isn't glowing yet.

"How did you know about this place?" I ask.

"I looked for it, after Blaze mentioned it." Gil smiles. "At least, Brook looked for it. We like to know everything that goes on." We bash through the trees, and Gil says over his shoulder, "Dot's definitely created more spectacular things."

From which I figure out Gil hasn't seen the pond glowing. As in, he's missed the point of it completely.

"You took one today, I assume."

A capsule, Gil means. And by asking that, Gil is telling me that what I thought was going to happen really *is* going to happen.

"As if I wouldn't!"

The capsules are what make it safe for us to hook up all the time. I keep my bottle beside my bed. The bottle's green but the capsules inside are see-through, filled with multicolored balls that rattle around when you shake them. I take mine as soon as I wake up, the same way I've done ever since I was created. The bottle is the first thing I see when I open my eyes — if I spend the night in my own hut, that is.

Capsules are just one thing that the Books say about hooking up.

There's also stuff about all creations having natural desires and how it's fine in Dot's eyes to hook up with whomever you want, as often as you want. It's not like we *have* to hook up once a day or anything like that, though. It's just about having fun and being happy.

"I'm surprised Dot's never wanted you and me to do this before." Gil has his hand on my shoulders, and I know he wants me to sit down. So I do. The green grass at our feet is long and soft and littered with glossy leaves that the trees all around us have dropped. Gil pulls me onto his lap so our faces are close enough to touch. I creep my hands across his back, the way I know he wants me to. The way *Dot* wants me to. My fingers find bumpy things underneath his skin and across his shoulders. Gil closes his eyes. I feel his lips against my cheek. He wants to hook up, that's obvious. It's just, I'm not sure I do.

For one, there's the way Gil feels, all cold to the touch. His snake-lips are thin and papery as a page of one of Julius's prenormal books. Dry too, which explains why he's always licking them.

I notice all these things about Gil because our first kiss isn't one you lose yourself in or anything. What I mean is, I don't start kissing Gil, then suddenly look up and see the sun has gone down and nighttime's here. Every rotation of his head, every time our teeth clank, I notice it all.

"This is nice," Gil says. "Very dotly."

That's when I get it. I finally figure out what's going on with those dreams. Those people and places aren't real, just like I always thought. I'm seeing them because Dot wants to test me. That's why she made them up and planted them in my head. Some creations are dotly and some are predotly, and Dot wants me to prove to her which one I am.

If I were a less dotly person, the wide-awake dreams might make me doubt my faith in Dot. Maybe that's what's going on with Blaze. It could be that he's predotly.

Not me, though. I'm absolutely, definitely, one-hundred-percent dotly. I'm going to show Dot that my faith is unshakable. I'm going to show her I *believe*.

The best time to start, obviously, is right now. Gil has always been super dotly. So even if I'm not totally convinced I want to get close to Gil, I'm going to do it because it's what Dot wants.

I close my eyes. So far I've been kind of holding myself apart from Gil just a little, but now I make myself relax against him. Gil drops his head to my neck and starts kissing it, eating it practically. He moves his mouth from my neck back to my lips. We kiss fully, his dry lips to mine again.

The whole time, I'm thinking, *See, Dot? See how dotly I am? I'm doing just what you want.*

At the same time, I start wondering about completion night, whether if I show Dot I'm a good believer, I might be one of her chosen ones. And obviously I'm desperate to be chosen. I want it more than anyone has ever wanted anything. Those prenormal images of life outside Dot's creation have given me a little taste of what it's like to feel your faith slipping. I know for sure I don't want that to happen anymore.

Gil pulls away. "You're somewhere else." Even though he says it quietly, it comes out as shocking as a slap.

I laugh a high little laugh, as though Gil has got it completely wrong. "Oh yeah? Like where exactly? The lagoon? No, I know. I'm climbing the rocks!"

"Are you prehealthy?" Gil says this slowly.

"What? No. Are you serious? I feel great. Why would you say I'm prehealthy?"

"You're acting distracted, Wren." He sort of considers me then. "It's your eyes as well."

My hands fly up to my face, like feeling my eyes is going to tell me something. But of course, everything up there feels the same as always. Lashes, lids. You know, the standard stuff, all still in place.

"My eyes?" I squeeze out another laugh. Can Gil see I'm being tested just by looking at my face? "My eyes are fine."

Everything is fine. I'm going to repeat that to myself, over and over, until I make it true. Until I pass Dot's test.

Gil lifts his face and says, "Are you enjoying yourself?" If Gil wasn't holding me up, I'd probably collapse right there on the ground.

"Obviously! This is completely dotly. *I'm* completely dotly so of course I'm —"

"Good."

Gil tugs at the hem of my sungarb. "You should take this off."

"Okay."

If this is what is takes to prove myself to Dot, then I'll do it. I'll do it a million billion times over if I have to.

11

THE LAGOON IS TOTALLY different at night. For a start, it's empty. The sun went down ages ago and now, in the thick, still prelight, I'm the only one here. And the water, which is normally bright blue, now looks deep and mysterious. The only light comes from the bottom, which is dotted with silvery pinpoints that start to sparkle when the sun fades.

I pull my sungarb over my head and drop it so it puddles in a damp pile at my feet. Since Gil and the gazebo and the magnolia trees, I've been sweating like that's all I was created to do. I spent ages — too long — examining my eyes in the mirror in my hut. At first, the black circles looked normal to me. At least, that's what I told myself.

But the longer I looked the more I had to admit they were pretty small, just like Blaze's. So to forget about that, I tried sleeping in my hammock. Except every time I closed my prenormal eyes I saw things I didn't want to see.

You know, places called parks and creations called Julius and Mom.

I guess I thought hooking up with Gil might erase all that, or dilute it somehow. I hoped it would show Dot she didn't need to test me anymore. But the images inside my head are as clear as ever. Apparently in Dot's eyes, I'm no better after the thing with Gil than I was before. Now, basically all I feel like doing is getting clean.

I slip into the water. Under the surface, my legs look bleached, nothing like a creation's skin normally does. It's sort of like I'm someone else altogether, someone I don't even know. In the shallows, I drop to my knees and slide under the water completely. About a million fish slip past me, and I stay down there as long as I can, hidden, until everything inside of me is at the point of bursting. It's only then that I shoot up again, flip onto my back, and lie in a starfish pose, arms and legs pointing outward.

I open my eyes, and I can see the ledge Blaze wanted me to climb to jutting out from the rocky wall of the escarpment. Above the ledge, the escarpment goes higher and higher, and that gets me wondering. If Blaze thought I could climb to the ledge, then maybe I could climb to the very top. From up there, I could see the whole of creation.

Floating under the great big velvety dome of the sky, the idea of seeing Dot's brilliance laid out in front of me makes me feel so happy. I can't help wondering why Dot doesn't want us to climb the escarpment so we could see all of creation for ourselves.

Then I remember. I *know* why. It'd be presafe to climb so high, and Dot only wants to protect us. She knows what's best for us. That's what I'm busy telling myself when I first hear the noise.

I plant my feet on the bottom of the lagoon and stand waist-deep in the water, listening. The sound has stopped, but I know I heard something. I definitely did, and I'm pretty sure it was coming from the trees around the lagoon. I look up, figuring I'll see a monkey springing from branch to branch or an owl with those big glossy round eyes or whatever. But there's nothing apart from a bunch of leaves shivering in the night air.

Diving under the water, I start convincing myself I imagined the noise. It could happen. I mean, I have to admit my head's not in the clearest state in all creation right at this moment. But when I pop up and look back to the trees, I see a flash of movement. I swear it. An arm pokes through the leaves of an avocado tree, then quickly disappears.

"Gil?"

I have no clue why I think it's going to be him. I can't even work out if I hope it is or if I wish it isn't.

Whatever, because there's no reply anyway. Nothing. If this is a joke, it's kind of prefunny. Whoever is playing it should really be owning up by now. That's pretty much the whole definition of a joke. When it's not funny, it's not a joke anymore, right?

"Brook? *Blaze?* Hello? I saw you, you know." I haul myself over the edge of the lagoon and onto the cool, flat rocks. It's kind of difficult, and I realize that it's because my arms have started shaking. "I'm getting out," I say. Completely pointless really, since whoever is in the trees can obviously see every single thing I'm doing. "I'm coming over."

Water rolls down my skin, leaving a trail of droplets behind me as I walk toward the trees. Right away I see something. Well, some*one* really. A person.

Suddenly I remember the word. A *boy.*

The *boy* is crouched behind the avocado tree. His face is round and open and shiny with sweat. His hair is short and cloudy soft. And he's way smaller than anyone else in creation. *Not much bigger than Julius*, I think. Except Julius is only an image in my head, whereas this boy is right here in front of me.

The boy stands up, staring, looking away, staring again, and the whole time he's got this tiny little smile on his face. Smiling to himself — not to me, if you get what I mean.

I think my mouth is hanging open, I don't know. I'm absolutely sure that my cheeks and tongue are all numb.

"Nathan is never going to believe this," he says. "You really don't wear any clothes."

The boy is pretty happy, I can tell.

"Come here," I say.

If I touch him, I'll see my hand pass through him. Then I'll know he isn't real. I mean, of course he isn't. This must be part of Dot's test. Another phase or something. She has realized the images in my head are never going to shake my faith. So now I guess she's wondering what I'd do if someone new, someone who shouldn't exist, appeared right in front of me.

Then something forces its way out of the boy's mouth. A bubble, melon-sized. It's like the gazebo bubbles except it's purple and smells of . . . of . . . I know the smell. I know the name.

Bubblegum.

The boy's feet are encased in fat, white things. And his sungarb isn't like mine, either. He has on some grubby thing that reaches as far as his knees. It doesn't even ripple free. Instead it's split in two so each leg can move independently. On his top half, he has something with yellow-and-blue stripes and the outline of a horse.

"You're the one they were talking about on Nathe's computer."

I have no idea what the boy means, but I can guess from the way he's talking that something prenice is involved. And I'm not prenice. I'm good. I'm kind. I'm dotly. This is a test, so I need to be clear about that. But if there's ever been a time when I don't know what to say, this is it.

So naturally, I'm blurting. "I'm not a computer. I'm one of Dot's creations, just like everyone else. Not you, though. You're just here to test me. You're not even real."

The boy's mouth drops open. He looks a little less certain, a little less pleased. "Is this . . . is this Club Naturelle?"

My eyes sweep up to the sky. I wish I were in the gazebo right now. That way, I'd be sure my words would find a bubble and make it to Dot. Right now, I don't have that option. I'm just going to have to hope she can hear me anyway.

I say, "Hello, Dot? I know you need to be sure everyone loves you and everything. But you can rely on me. You don't need to test me. No matter what happens, I'm never going to change my mind about you. I love you, Dot. I really do."

The boy says, "Who's Dot?"

Apparently Dot didn't hear me. Or maybe she didn't want to stop the test for whatever reason. Which makes a whole other feeling sweep through me. It's prehappiness, I guess you could say, only not the ordinary kind. This prehappiness is like the most intense ever. It's bitter and hard and tastes sour. I picture Gil's face moving above me as I lie by the pond. I'm doing everything I can to be dotly. But it still isn't enough.

The boy blows another purple bubble and pops it. He opens his mouth to talk, and I notice something prenormal about his mouth. Where there should be teeth, the boy has a gap.

He says, "You're weird."

I sigh. I want to pass Dot's test, and that means I can't ignore the boy. I'm going to have to engage with him, to play along.

That must be what Dot wants.

So I ask, "Where did you come from?"

"Woodend."

"Oh, *Woodend*. Sure. That's a place, is it?"

I figure Dot wants to see if there's any way I'd believe something exists beyond the trees. And, I guess, whether or not this boy can tempt me to go there.

The boy wrinkles his nose. "You haven't heard of Woodend? It's the biggest town for miles. Woodend. Where Shepherd is?"

"Town," I echo. The word is familiar, but I'm not totally sure what it means.

The boy shakes his head at my blank expression.

Inside, I'm thinking how amazing it is that Dot would dream up this whole story about a *town* called Woodend just to test me.

"Okay. So how do you get there?"

"Easy. You fly."

"You mean, like a butterfly?" There must be ten of them circling around us right now. "You can do that?"

Now I'm confused. In the awake dreams, the smaller creations don't fly. Not that I've seen, at least. I figured this boy would be the same as them, only right here with me.

"You're not pretending, are you? You really think I can fly?" The boy laughs. "Woodend's over there. You can walk there in ten minutes." The boy jerks his head toward the fringe, like a place called Woodend located right there is the most obvious thing in all creation.

"That's enough, Dot. Please?"

The boy doesn't get that I'm not talking to him. He turns a finger in one ear. "I don't know Dot. I already said that."

Not knowing Dot is like not knowing your own hands exist. Or like saying you've never taken a breath or gone to sleep or had a sip of water. I know that. Somehow I have to let Dot know I know.

So I tell the boy, "Obviously you don't. You're not real. You're a test. If you were real, you'd live here with us in Dot's creation."

"Don't believe me." The boy shrugs. "It's not like I'm hanging around here or anything. I only came to show Nathe I could." And he smiles a gappy smile.

For a moment, the boy and I are totally still. I can hear the soft hum the butterflies make, the one that comes from those single, unblinking green eyes of theirs.

It can't be long now, I think. *Pretty soon, the test is going to end. Okay, Dot. I'm ready now. I've had enough. Please?*

The boy twists an avocado off of a tree branch. Just a small one, the size of his hand. He squashes it so the skin splits open.

"Yuck," he says, as the creamy green contents ooze out. There are bright green smears all over his hands. Avocado streaks his fingers the way it would if he had actual, solid hands. If it happened to turn out that the boy was real, not part of a test at all . . .

Suddenly, I'm lunging toward the boy, but he turns and runs away, crashing through the avocado trees, the palms, and the mangos, away from the lagoon as fast as he can go. I hear his footsteps through the trees, heavy for someone so little. On his back, there are two blocky numbers. One and six. Sixteen.

I snatch up my sungarb. And now I'm moving, dodging around the trees, following the test boy, catching up to him. His little legs make him a slow runner, just like Fern. Plus, he doesn't know his way around. He runs across the lawn, not realizing he's doubling back in a huge loop until he finds himself at the lagoon again.

I call out to him, "Stop! I only want to touch you."

But the boy doesn't listen, and he definitely doesn't stop. He blunders on, in a sideways direction now, all along the length of the escarpment. I want to catch him, pass my hands right through him just to prove that one little avocado doesn't mean anything. That way I'd know he's as insubstantial as air after all. I'd be sure my theory was right. The boy is nothing more than a test.

"Get away!" The boy is close now. He's trying to shout, but it comes out more like a whimper.

The boy from before, the boy who smiled and laughed, is gone. Now he's small and precalm and not at all sure what to do.

"Don't . . . you can't touch me. I'm going to tell Nathan," he says, and he brings his wrist up to his face. Around it is a sort of strip, see-through as water, with words and little lights blinking on it. I notice his arms are shaking.

The escarpment looms up in front of us, a solid black wall in the prelight. I throw my arms out toward the boy, but he veers away. He's looking over his shoulder at me when his foot finds a loose rock on the ground. He pitches forward. There's a crack, which sounds a whole lot like real forehead against real rock (trust me, it's something you never want to hear).

He lands on his side and lays there sprawled out like an animal basking on the rocks in the sun. Apart from the fact that it's night and no animal in creation basks then. I want to ignore the puddle of blood under his head, creeping slowly outward across the rocks. But I can't exactly do that, not when I dab my finger in and find it's all warm and sticky and red.

"Hello?"

The boy has his eyes shut, but surely he can hear me. Surely he's going to start crying or something.

"I'm sorry. I didn't mean for this to happen, I swear."

The boy doesn't answer. Right now, the boy isn't doing anything at all.

12

I SLIDE MY BACK down the rocky escarpment wall and squat next to the little body. I reach out a finger. It hovers there, right above the boy's shoulder, the whole time looking like someone else's finger on someone else's hand. I pull my finger away.

Try again.

I tell myself that my finger's going to pass right through the boy anyway. There's no reason to feel precalm about the rocks and the cracking sound his head made.

He isn't real. Not even a little. He's a test because, really, there's no other explanation. So it shouldn't be that hard, giving him one little touch.

I force myself. All over again, I reach out and this time the crescent of my fingernail connects with the boy's sungarb. The fabric's all thick and damp. Now I touch him with the pad of my finger, tracing the stripes on his sungarb and the rearing horse too. I even touch his skin.

The entire time, the boy stays completely still.

And guess what?

He's solid. As in, absolutely and definitely real.

"Hey. Can you hear me?" I start prodding the boy, and it isn't long before an explanation presents itself. When I think about it, it's obvious. Dot wanted to make a really convincing test for me, so she created a real, live boy.

But even the thought of a real boy stabs at me, hard. For one, if the boy is real, then he must really be feeling prehealthy right now, all because of me. But two, a real boy makes the whole test thing way harder to handle. I mean, when it was only images appearing in my head, the test was confusing. But at least it was hidden.

No one had to know I was being tested apart from me. But now, lying right in front of me, there's proof that Dot thinks she needs to test me. Apparently, the creator of everything thinks I'm a pregood person.

I must be, or else why test me in the first place? Fern and Jasper and Drake, Gil and Brook and anyone who's ever mattered to me would think the same thing if they found out.

Then the boy blinks. He makes this low, soft moan followed by a choking sort of cough. He moves his head a little bit, from side to side. Just enough to streak his face with the actual, real blood that's oozing out of his actual, real hair. The boy seems to be trying to fix his eyes on me, but they just keep sliding around all over the place. He goes, "That really hurt, Nathan."

I start to tell him about how he tripped, but all he says is, "I'm telling Mom."

Then he rolls onto his side and tries sitting up. He struggles up as far as his knees, then stops, saying, "Whoa. Hang on. Whoa."

He opens his mouth, and this stream of yellow comes out, in pumping kind of waves. In between the waves he makes a prenormal groaning sound before finally he says, looking up at me, "You're not Nathan." He touches his head and moans. "I feel sick."

It's pretty obvious what I have to do. I have to show Dot that I won't be tempted by anything he says. He's trying to make me think there's a place outside the trees, a place that's different from and better than here. So what I need to do is make sure Dot knows I'm not swayed, so that she'll make this boy go away.

And I need to do it before anyone else finds out Dot ever sent him.

But I know I can't leave him lying here by the escarpment. For one thing, the first person who comes along will find him, and the boy will tell them how Dot created him to test me. Then everyone will know I'm predotly.

I need a strategy, and thank Dot, I come up with one pretty fast. I decide I'll take the boy back to the huts. I'll hide him in one of the empty ones until I can work out how to make him disappear. If no one sees him, it'll almost be like he was never here in the first place. And Dot will know I love her, the same as I always have.

* * *

Nice plan, Wren. I think. *This whole "hide him in an empty hut" thing is working out really well.*

It really isn't working out at all. Because, you know, when I pull myself out of the prenormal whirl inside my head and start actually trying to move the boy, I figure out that it's not going to be the easiest thing in all creation to do.

I put his arm around my shoulder and try hauling him onto his feet, but it doesn't happen. Not even close. The boy is smaller than me, but he's floppy and super heavy and he really, really doesn't want me touching him. It would be a whole lot easier with someone else to help, but I can't exactly ask. That would mean explaining everything, and avoiding *that* is the point of this whole plan in the first place.

And anyway, there's only one person who might understand. But knowing Blaze, he probably wouldn't believe the boy's a test. I bet Blaze would insist the boy is real or something. He'd want to find out all about him. Chances are he wouldn't worry about anyone else discovering him, either. So basically, I'm going to have to sort this out by myself.

"Get up," I tell the boy. No, I *beg* him. "Please? Here, hold on. Put your arm around me."

"My head hurts. I want to go home."

I get a prenormal twinge inside when he says that. All because of Dot and the test, I figure. I mean, that would have to be it. So I say, "I want you to go home too. That's possibly the best idea anyone's ever had. It's just, I can't leave you lying here while we figure out how to make that happen."

About then, I guess the boy decides he needs my help. As far as I can tell, he doesn't know he's a test. From his point of view, he's a real boy, and he's all alone. I'm his only choice if he wants to get back home. So he puts his arm around me and tries to stand. He even takes a staggering, wobbling step. Then he sees the pool of red on the rocks, the tuft of hair, and skin stuck there. He must connect the whole mess with his own head, because he releases another hot yellow wave all over both of us.

Vomit, spew, upchuck.

A lot of unfamiliar words pop into my head, and I'm not sure which one is the right one or even what they mean, exactly. Whatever you call it, the force of it seems to wring the last of the energy out of the boy. He loses his balance, tipping sideways so I have to shoulder all his weight just to keep him standing up.

And that's just one step. Only about another million to go before we reach the huts.

Even when it was just Fern and me, running to the lagoon the day I froze on the rocks (*forever* ago, it feels like), the lawn seemed ridiculously massive. But I can personally guarantee the distance is even more ginormous when you're dripping in gooey yellow stuff and trying to prop up one prehealthy and generally prehappy test boy.

Plus, even though it's prelight, it's still really steamy in the garden, so pretty soon I'm panting. I have to keep stopping, and every time I do the boy starts talking softly to me. Sometimes he reminds me he wants to go home. That his mom will be *freaking out*. Other times, he says Nathan's going to get me if I do anything funny. And then there's stuff that just doesn't make the remotest sense whatsoever.

It takes us so long to get anywhere that all I want to do is beg Dot for help. Just go to the gazebo, send my thoughts up in a bubble, and ask Dot to make everything right for me. But then I realize there's no point in doing that. I mean, Dot can't fix things when she's the one testing me in the first place. Solving this on my own is the only way to pass the test and show Dot how much I love her. It's just, right now, the sky above my head feels so big and empty. Beneath it, I've never felt so wobbly and tiny and weak.

But still, I finally get the boy to the huts. I half-carry, half-haul him across the lawn, up the stairs, and into the first hut I come to. An empty hut, obviously, its back directly to the orchard, with this giant coconut palm bending right over the roof.

The boy wants to know where we are, and I tell him somewhere he can rest until he's ready to leave. I think maybe he's going to object or something, but he doesn't. When I plunk him down on the bed, he closes his eyes right away. Almost immediately, he's asleep.

There's a chair near the bed, so I sit down and watch the boy for a while. He's perfect, as real-looking as you could ever hope for. Curled up there on the bed, a purple mound on his forehead, the boy looks paler and weaker than he did over by the lagoon. His mouth hangs open just a little as he sleeps, and his breath comes out all snuffly.

And suddenly, I have this prenormal urge to hug him. I almost do it too. My arms reach out toward him, but at the last moment I pull them away. A hug doesn't seem that dotly a thing to do. So I pull the sheet over his chest and get up, which is when I have this idea. I've dragged the boy a long way. I've spent all this time with him, and not once has he said anything that's made me doubt Dot. Maybe that will be enough?

I could leave the hut now, and when I close the door behind me he might just disappear the same sudden way he arrived. Out of nowhere, into nowhere.

I mean, why not? It wouldn't be the most prenormal thing to happen tonight.

* * *

I make myself wait. I don't know how long I lurk around outside the hut, but it feels like forever. And when I do go back inside, guess what? The boy is still there, all sort of floppy on the bed, with those big clompy things still on his feet.

Sighing, I go over and take them off for him because it occurs to me he'd probably be a whole lot more comfortable that way (that is, if test boys can even get uncomfortable). It's when I'm up close that I start to notice stuff about him. There's a graze on his knee with a kind of white strip stuck over it. On his hand, the words "math homework" are scrawled in blue. And inside the collar of his sungarb are two words woven into a label.

Dennis Quigley.

I look inside his pockets too. One has a rectangular thing in it. I discover a row of smaller, soft purple rectangles under the wrapper. They smell of fruit, same as the bubbles the boy was blowing. I pop a rectangle into my mouth but spit it out immediately. The rectangle definitely doesn't taste like fruit. But the prenormal thing is, it tastes like something I've eaten before.

I sit on the edge of the bed. And I swear I don't even touch the see-through thing wrapped around the boy's wrist. I don't say anything. I'm only looking, thinking, *What is that?* when the whole thing lights up. Words scroll along the front.

Welcome, Nathan Quigley. 3:07 AM.

Stop, I think, sort of automatically, as though I somehow already know what to do. And guess what? The lights immediately fade away. So I try it again. *Start. Stop.* Every time I think it, the thing around the boy's wrist either lights up or fades. The more I do it, the more I feel like I've done it before.

After the tenth time, the entire thing turns blue and a question scrolls across it. *Help?*

And right away I think, *Yes.*

I've probably never needed help more than I do right now. The thing turns white.

Another message. Select from favorites. Mail. Settings. Contacts. Chat. Lood.

Lood. What's that?

The thing is familiar, I have to admit.

A *doohickey*?

No, a *device*, that's what it's called. But I've never heard of Lood before. That I'm sure of.

The device changes again, only this time not to a solid color. Instead it shows a picture of this girl with the most ginormous tatas ever created. She's kind of cupping them with her hands at the same time as she licks her lips, which aren't the normal color but a bright, frosted pink. She lowers her eyelids.

"I'm waiting for you," she says. In a slightly different voice, not quite matched with her lips, she adds, "Nathan."

She opens her mouth and makes a little moan and the entire strip starts to quiver and buzz. Then her picture goes still and gray and some new words appear.

Want more Celia? Buy credit now!

But then, just as I'm sort of puzzling over what *Celia* and *credit* are, something new appears. A little square with a lot more words inside.

New chats waiting. Read now?

As soon as I think yes, the device is covered with words, tinier even than the ones on a screen of the Books. The boy (Dennis? Nathan? I guess the words are names, though I can't be sure which one belongs to the boy) grunts and rolls over, throwing the hand with the device on it across my lap. You know, sort of like he's inviting me to read it.

Stumpy00 - Joined 2/3/16

NatheMan, r u there?

That's what I read when the new chat opens. But I don't understand it at all, so I keep on reading all the earlier chats too.

FancyVividBlue - Joined 4/6/17

check this out please :)

bit.ly/clubnaturelle

Stumpy00 - Joined 2/3/16

wtf is this real??

FancyVividBlue - Joined 4/6/17

New "clothing optional" resort. Club Naturelle. The little red head kills it. Up for it imo.

Stumpy00 - Joined 2/3/16

Can I go stay? Where is it?

FancyVividBlue - Joined 4/6/17

Outside of Woodend.

NatheMan - Joined 3/16/18

Stumpy u cant afford it!!!

FancyVividBlue - Joined 4/6/17

haha break in. Free to perv last time I checked. Look out for big guy with dreads if u go. He's a stoner for sure if u want to get in on it.

Stumpy00 - Joined 2/3/16

Are u serious? U see the gate?

FancyVividBlue - Joined 4/6/17

I cld pick that lock any day.

NatheMan - Joined 3/16/18

I'm there.

Stumpy00 - Joined 2/3/16

U r a horny beast

FancyVividBlue - Joined 4/6/17

Niceeee!

Stumpy00 - Joined 2/3/16 - Posts 76

U r never going to get in NatheMan.

That's when the device starts to make a noise, a shrill, screeching sound that splits the air inside the empty hut. The tiny words disappear, replaced by new, bigger ones: *Mom calling.*

I don't know how to stop the noise. I mean, I don't know if I know. And if I do know, I don't want to think about how.

The longer the sound goes on, the louder it gets. I grab a pillow and shove it over Dennis's arm but the device goes on making the noise, a piercing scream in the prelight. So loud someone's definitely going to hear if I don't stop it pretty much immediately.

So I do the first thing I can think of. I yank the device from Dennis's wrist and throw it on the floor. Then I stomp my heel down on top of it until it's totally crushed and completely silent.

My mouth is dry but my hands are wet, like all the moisture from my body has collected there instead of staying where it should be.

I have to leave the hut. Right now, I want to be anywhere but here.

13

I NEED TO BE somewhere quiet. The orchard is about the only place in creation anyone would roam all by herself this early in the day, when there's hardly any light at all. So that's where I go.

Although the device is crushed and gone, the sound it made still rings in my ears. Plus, I have to find something to do with my hands, which just won't stay still. I end up stuffing my pockets with fruit. Pretty soon my sungarb is so full of peaches and lychees and mangos and melons that it's dragging around my shoulders. There's way more fruit here than a person could ever eat. So much of it that if anyone else sees me, they're definitely going to want to know what I'm doing picking so much and why I look so precalm.

And I don't have an answer. Or not one that I want to tell anyone, anyway.

I should get going, I know that. Drag myself back to the hut, clean up the broken device, check whether the test boy has disappeared or at least start figuring out how to make that happen. But the orchard goes right up to the fringe, and now in the weak, pearly light, something makes me walk over to the tree line. I stand with my toes curling into the grass that divides the garden from the beyond.

Where Dot lives.

Or, if I listen to the boy, the grass that separates us from a place called *Woodend*.

Not that I would ever listen, obviously. There's no such thing as Woodend. The fringe is just trees — endless trees — and the only way you can get through to the other side is when you're soaring through the air on your way to meet Dot at the end of your life.

That's what I believe.

Scratch that.

It's what I *know*.

But no matter how many times I remind myself of that, I guess the boy even being here has done something to me. As in, it has lodged the teeniest, tiniest question mark in my head.

What if the trees aren't endless? What if there really is a Woodend on the other side?

There isn't.

But maybe . . .

Then an idea comes to me, already perfectly formed.

Find out.

Right here, from where I'm standing, it would only be one more little step into the fringe. I could take that one step, then another and another and another until I knew for certain.

When I think of it like that, it sort of sounds easy. I mean, it's only *walking*.

I swear I'm trying, really trying hard, to shut those thoughts off. But when I look down, I see my right foot lifting off the ground all by itself. Slowly, slowly it moves downward into the fringe like the ground is pulling it. I try telling it to stop, but apparently my foot isn't even slightly listening because now it's almost there, almost in the fringe . . .

No!

I practically scream the word out loud. *This* is what the boy wants. *This* is the whole point of the test!

If I walk into the fringe now, it'd be an instant fail. I'd be going against Dot's word. I'd only be proving I really am as predotly as she seems to think.

I yank my foot back and plant it on the ground. I won't do it. I will not fail.

I want to love Dot, maybe even be chosen on completion night. I want to be Fern's best friend and Jasper's latest hook-up and even just ordinary Wren with the red hair who likes to climb, who everyone approves of. I want to fit in and be just like everyone else. I don't want to be alone. I . . .

"You're up early."

Brook. Right there behind me, a coconut under one arm and the knife in the other hand.

"Oh my Dot! Don't do that."

I check my foot. On the ground. Good. Very, very good.

"Don't say hello to you? That's a little predotly."

He's been talking to Gil. Do they know? About the boy and the test, I mean? Is that even possible so fast? They must know. Why else would Brook choose the word *predotly* out of nowhere like that?

"Of course *speak* to me. Don't sneak up behind me, that's all I meant."

"You're the one sneaking." Brook looks around. "All by yourself in the orchard so early."

Brook and I just stand there. There's hardly any sound, just this little *ping-ping-ping* as Brook gouges the dirt from under his fingernails with the tip of the coconut knife.

Eventually I say, "Okay, so neither of us is *sneaking*. I came for something to eat, the same as you."

"Way over here?" Brook looks down at my feet, and I can see him noticing they're almost, but not quite, in the fringe. "Interesting place to pick fruit."

Brook is already tall, but now he kind of draws himself up so that his shadow swallows me. I try stepping around him, but when I move so does Brook until it ends up like some completion night dance that's really, really not working out. So finally I stop.

I can't help myself blurting, "Is everything okay? Are you prehappy with me about something?"

That gets Brook's attention. "Why?" he asks. "Should I be?"

I can't answer him quickly enough. "No. No way. It's just . . . in the gazebo . . . when me and Gil —"

Brook laughs a single note. "I don't want to hook up with Gil, if that's what you mean."

Relief pumps through me. I guess he doesn't know about the boy or Dot's test or anything.

"With *Gil*?" I laugh, all shrill and prenormal. "Gil's into girls."

"I'm aware." Brook's jaw is set so his chin juts forward and two knotted bunches appear on either side of his cheeks. "I don't think Gil should be going off with anyone at the moment, that's all."

Brook swaps the knife to the other hand and goes on scraping away at his fingernails. "He's the only one who can hear her. Right now, he needs to be listening."

Brook is watching for my reaction. I wonder if he can hear the ringing, whistling sound inside my head.

I feel my lips moving and hear my voice asking, "What do you mean, '*right now*'? What's Gil supposed to be listening for?"

Brook fixes me with a look that I can't read. Part of me thinks he's wondering how one of Dot's creations could possibly be so presmart. Another part thinks maybe it's something else completely.

But all he says is, "More signs." Like that much should be obvious to anyone.

"There's going to be more?"

Signs like, say, a crushed wren? Signs that will let everyone know exactly who Dot is testing?

"Gil thinks so."

"Signs of . . . signs of what, though?"

"You hooked up with Gil. He told you, I'm sure. You know what the signs are telling us."

I swallow. I try to act like I'm not sure exactly what he's talking about.

"You mean . . . the stuff about people turning predotly?"

"Exactly." Brook folds his arms and smiles. "Gil believes Dot's trying to tell us who they are. Do you think so too?"

"Um . . . if you guys say so."

Brook doesn't know about the test.

Correction: he doesn't know *yet*. And for one wild moment I think maybe I should tell him. I even get the idea that Brook and Gil could help me make the boy disappear and pass the test. They're close friends of mine, after all. It's just possible they'd understand. And maybe . . . maybe that's even what Dot wants!

She wants to see how much I trust the others and how much they care about me. It could be she's waiting for me to throw myself onto the ground or against Brook's chest and just blurt everything out right now. Then Brook would tell Gil and then *he* would . . .

An image jumps into my head.

The wren.

Its mangled wing.

Gil's white hands crushing it.

That flare as its little body hit the flames.

When I stop and think about it, I realize I literally have no idea what Gil would do if he knew about the boy. I decide I'd better stick with my original plan. I have to fix things before anyone finds out. All by myself.

"So, are you eating that coconut or what?"

Brook looks at the coconut like he doesn't even know how it got under his arm. "It's for Gil," he says. "He likes fresh coconut water in the morning."

"He can't get out of bed and get it himself?" I'm careful to say it like Wren would. Wren the way I always was, before the boy and the prenormal dreams or whatever they are appeared.

"Gil's busy."

"What, sleeping?"

"Watching." Brook's eyes skate up to the sky. There's a heaviness to it, like it's full or weighed down or something.

The sun's climbing. It's almost over the fringe now but the clouds are low, and so the air is only getting hotter, steamier, thicker.

"Better go give it to him, then."

"What?" Brook's sort of staring into my eyes, and definitely not in a hooking-up kind of way.

"Um, the coconut? Didn't you say Gil was waiting for it?"

Brook's staring *at* my eyes, I realize now. Taking in the shrinking circles at the center, I'm sure. But he doesn't say so.

He just says, "Tell me if you notice anything predotly. Any signs."

"Me? I haven't seen anything." The whole time, I'm looking away carefully.

"Sure," Brook says. He's smiling, but I'm not sure he believes me.

* * *

There's this banging sound coming from inside the empty hut. It's loud enough to hear from the path and so is the voice saying, "Work, you stupid thing." Around the back of the hut I can still hear it.

The boy is awake. Dot's biggest ever test is crashing and banging around, and if I don't go in right now, someone's going to find him.

I use the window around the back of the hut instead of the door, which obviously is right on the path. You know, where anyone could see me going into the empty hut, now that it's light. I guess the boy doesn't hear me hauling myself inside because he stays where he is, down on the floor picking up the scattered pieces of the device. It's only when my feet hit the floorboards that he gets up. With just one set of shutters open, it's pretty prelight in the hut. I can see the purple mound on the boy's head though, oozing in places, but also now crusted with black.

"I'm going to make you disappear," I inform him. Like I know exactly how to do that or something.

For a little while, the boy just stares. Then, in a voice that sounds all puffed up and confident, he says, "You won't get away with it."

The way he squeaks at the end of the sentence makes me wonder if I've made the boy precalm. I should have chosen better words. The boy might be just a test, but that doesn't mean I want to scare him.

"I didn't mean to —"

"You can't just kill me, you know."

Kill.

The word is nowhere in the Books, but I somehow know what it means. At least, I'm pretty sure *kill* is a really, really prenice thing to do to someone.

"Nathan Quigley's my big brother," the boy says. "And he could get you really bad if he wanted. He's probably going to anyway because of what you did."

The boy — who must be Dennis — looks at the pieces scattered on the floor. "He's definitely going to get me for taking his device."

"Wait," I tell Dennis. I try to touch him, just on the arm or whatever, but as soon as I get closer he shoves me away. "I don't want anything prenice to happen. I only want you to go away. It's what Dot wants."

"So that's why you wrecked my brother's device?"

"I didn't wreck anything."

Dennis holds up the only part of the device that's still in one piece. The transparent strap, all mangled and dented. "Yeah, right."

"It was making a noise. I couldn't stop it."

"This noise?" Dennis makes a sound then, exactly the same one the device was making when I smashed it.

I'm nodding but shushing him at the same time.

"It was ringing. That's how it sounds."

I know, I think. I've heard the noise before. But at the time it made me feel precalm, and now it makes me feel precalm just thinking about how I might know what a ringing device sounds like or what a device even is.

Dennis's eyebrows and eyes squish together. "You'll have to pay to get it fixed."

I guess I look as blank as I feel, because then Dennis asks, "How come you don't know anything about anything?"

He scans the hut, looking at the butterflies hovering around the window frame and the ones carved into the ceiling, the portrait of Dot on the wall, the bed, the furniture, and the row of colored sungarb hanging in the closet.

"Is everyone at Club Naturelle like you?"

"Club Naturelle?"

Dennis rolls his eyes. "Don't you even know where you are?"

"I know where I am. The same place I've been since Dot created me."

"Aren't you all on vacation or something?"

Dennis touches the spot on his head carefully with his fingers and makes a face. "You can't just stay here the whole time."

"Here is all there is."

To myself, I add, *See, Dot? See how faithful I am?*

"You think this is the only place in the whole entire world?" Dennis says.

I nod, even though I'm not entirely sure what he means by *the whole entire world*.

"Okay," he continues. "So then where does the gate leading out of here go?"

"There's no gate."

I shouldn't know what a *gate* is. The word *gate* shouldn't even exist.

"There is so a gate."

Obviously, he wants me to know all about it. "Pretty pathetic. It took me about one second to guess the passcode. Nathan's Internet friends didn't think he could get in here. But guess what? I got in, and I'm only nine. So there!"

Dennis is standing right in front of the open shutters. If anyone walked past right now, they'd see him.

"You . . . um . . . what?"

Dennis beams. "It was so easy! Now that I did that, Nathe's going to know I'm not a little kid anymore. He's going to let me hang out with him from now on, for sure."

I'm shaking my head when Dennis reaches for the door.

"Anyway, think whatever you want. I'm going. My mom is probably mad by now. And I want to get back to Nathe and tell him —"

"No!" I shriek. "Don't go."

Not now, in the daytime, when everyone can see you. Not that I know how I'm going to make Dennis disappear, even in the prelight. It's just, I'm sure that if he doesn't stay hidden until I work it out, then everyone's going to find out how predotly I am.

"Nah, I think I'd better . . ."

I go to the bed and let the fruit spill out of my pockets all over the red-streaked sheets.

"Look, I brought you stuff to eat."

Dennis's hand is on the doorknob, but I can tell he's sort of interested.

"What?"

"Come and look." When he comes over to the bed I say, "See? Plenty. Raspberries, peaches, mangos, everything."

"Is fruit all you have? No toast or Froothoops?"

Froothoops. I hear the word and immediately think of Julius, without even knowing why.

"If you don't want this, I can bring you other food. There are tamarillos. There are rambutans."

"No thanks," says Dennis, turning toward the door. "Yuck."

"Stay."

My arm swings out to grab him. I have him circled in creation's most awkward hug.

If he wanted to, Dennis could bust out of it. But he doesn't. He lets me keep talking.

"You have to. Just until prelight."

Dennis doesn't seem to know what I mean by this, so I tell him, "Until night."

Dennis steps away from me. He puts his hand on the doorknob again.

"Why should I?"

No one can see you, I want to yell. *Don't you get that?*

But instead I say, "There are animals out there, you know."

Dennis looks sideways at me. "Like cats and dogs?"

"Like lions and tigers. Bears too."

Dot's animal creations are as gentle and kind as Dot herself, it says so in the Books. But Dennis doesn't know that. And something tells me he wouldn't like meeting a bear. I'm not sure how I know that. I just do. It's the same way Julius would feel, I find myself thinking.

"If you wait, I'll take you to the fringe myself," I say quickly. "You'll be fine."

Dennis thinks about this. "Only as far as the trees?"

I look away then. I guess he wants me to say I'll take him to the gate. But there are a whole lot of problems with that. One, we're not supposed to go into the fringe. Two — and this is the big one — there should be no such thing as a gate in the first place.

So I decide to stall. I tell Dennis, "We'll see."

A gate should not exist. But then, neither should Dennis. And if Dot can create a real boy to test me, there's no reason she couldn't also create a gate. That's absolutely, totally believable, right? As far as going into the fringe goes, I'm going to have to think that one through.

Dennis looks around the hut. Finally he says, "Okay. I guess I'll stay."

I smile.

A smile flickers to life on his face too.

"But you can't tell Nathe I was scared of bears."

"No way," I tell him. "Promise."

14

WHEN FERN FINDS ME, it's practically prelight again, and I'm on the path outside our huts. Heat rises up from the stone, and there are all these ants turning in busy circles at my feet.

"*There* you are," she says. "You weren't at the lagoon."

Or the newfruit grove, or anywhere at the same time as everyone else. After I left Dennis's hut the second time, I filled my picking bag in the newfruit grove. Early, before too many other people arrived.

The rest of the day, I kind of hung around the empty huts without going in or anything. Sometimes I walked to the orchard, other times just up and down the path. Going too far away from Dennis made me feel all precalm. I mean, what if he suddenly decided he didn't care about bears anymore?

Behind Fern, the path is all lit up with torches rammed into the soil. The light from the flames turns Fern's hair into these long, pale, gold wires. She's switched on, charged up, the same way the actual air around us seems to be.

"Everyone's over at Gil's," Fern comes right up close, her smiling face kind of looming at me. "Something's happening tonight!"

"What do you mean, something's happening?"

A wind is gusting. There's a fizzing kind of smell, and the near-prelight sky is a heavy grayish-yellow.

"Who's everyone?"

"Sage," Fern says. "Luna, Jasper, Drake. You know, everyone."

All my friends, in other words. And not one of them realizing what's really going on with me.

"That's okay. You go. I'll just . . ."

Fern's bow lips mash down into a straight line. "Gil said to find you. He wants you to come. He's been wondering where you are."

Brook probably told him about the orchard this morning. Scratch that. Brook *definitely* told him.

"Are you going to hook up with Gil?" Fern asks, all jittery and excited. She's jumping around on the balls of her feet when normally she'd just be planted in one spot, still and serene. It's like she's soaking up whatever's going on up there in the sky somehow.

"Not tonight."

Fern squeals and grabs both my arms. "Oh my Dot! You hooked up with him already? How was it?"

I give her my *you-know* look, even though Fern doesn't know, not really, since she's never hooked up with Gil or any guy, for that matter. She doesn't ask anything else, though. Despite how huge she thinks me hooking up with Gil is, she's sort of distracted too. As in, her eyes are roaming all over the place. I guess that's how she spots the deer running out of the shadows around the base of my hut. It's this soft, brown color with white speckles on its flanks. Its eyes are so deep and brown and clear that they practically glow.

"How gorgeous!"

Naturally, Fern loves all of Dot's creatures, but she especially loves the furry, long-eyelashed variety. She practically falls down my stairs and stretches out for a stroke, but the deer is way too quick. It leaves my hut behind and disappears under Fern's, next door, its tail just a flash of white behind it.

* * *

Gil's balcony is totally packed. There are people lounging on the stairs, sitting on the floor, cross-legged on the path out the front, or curled up in the doorway. Gil himself is swinging in his hammock, one pale arm thrown over the side, those long fingers of his sort of stroking the wooden deck.

Sage has snagged herself a floor cushion. Fern gets onto it right beside her. There's no room for me, and anyway, Sage is already whispering in Fern's ear and holding her hand. So I'm left looking for somewhere to sit. It turns out the only free space is leaning up against Gil's balcony railing, right beside Brook.

"I saved this spot for you," he says. This would be prenormal even if it weren't for our meet-up in the orchard. I mean, Brook and I have always been friends but not, you know, *best* friends. "I haven't seen you all day."

"Yeah. Well. I've been busy."

"Doing what?" Brook asks.

Luckily the wind starts up then, which kind of removes the need to answer. On the palm trees, every single frond is churning, and the sky is empty. No birds, no bats, nothing. There's hardly a torch left alight, and when fat drops of rain start splashing down, the last of them go out anyway. Down on the path there's the smell of hot, wet stone even though the wind has turned cold enough to dimple the skin on my arms. It isn't going to rain the way it normally does, a quick downpour and then it's over and all of creation is washed clean. Whatever's happening now seems like a whole other kind of thing.

And then there's this flash. A branch of light cuts the dome of the sky in half. The branch is purple with a smell to it, like a fire just went out or something. Then the light disappears and basically everyone on Gil's balcony is screaming.

Nearby, someone says, "Do you think Dot's prehappy about something?"

A prenormal little flutter starts to work its way up my spine. The rain is really pouring down now, so heavy it makes all creation look white. Next, a crash. A boom, really, which has to be the loudest sound I've ever heard.

Dot's more than a little prehappy. She's so prehappy, I swear she must be tearing creation apart. Then more purple flashes light the trees and the roofs of all the huts, including the one with Dennis inside.

Dot knows he's in there, naturally. She's always watching. Maybe she thinks I'm not working fast enough at making Dennis disappear, that

I'm not taking her test seriously? And now she's whipping up all these rumbles and flashes just so everyone else will find out about him.

Over on the hammock, Gil's eyelids are flickering closed. Right away, Brook gets up and goes over there. He hovers around as Gil starts to rock, faster and faster until his whole hammock squeaks as it swings. He yells stuff out too, just like in the gazebo, the same stream of letters with only the odd, random word making sense. Gil throws his hands up to the balcony roof and tips his head back, tears rolling down his face as he screams out Dot's name and tells her he is listening.

Then there's another flash and another crash, practically on top of each another. Around me, everyone's talking at once.

What's going . . . Gil can hear Dot . . . did you know?

Suddenly, there's this wave of people surging across the balcony. Everyone decides they have to get close to Gil, all at exactly the same time. When the sky lights up again, I see Brook trying to calm everyone down. An elbow slams into my shoulder. From every direction there are faces coming toward me, sweating and squealing, teeth and the whites of eyes flashing in the prelight.

Then Gil stands up. Everyone on the balcony goes completely quiet, like the noise from the sky has somehow sucked the sound out of us. Gil holds up his arms, and a purple flash in the sky lights him from behind.

His eyes snap open, and he says, "Dot wants me to share something with all of you."

It looks like Brook is going to make some kind of comment, but the silence doesn't last long enough to let him. The entire balcony wants to know what Dot said.

"Some creations don't love Dot as much as they should," Gil announces.

I can hear people asking each other how that could even be possible. The concept of predotliness is totally new to everyone apart from me, Gil, and Brook.

"Dot wants us all to look out for predotly creations. Anybody who exposes one will be chosen on completion night."

My head has a floating feeling, like it's not attached to my neck correctly or something. Now the talk on the balcony is all about what predotliness is and how to find it.

Except I'm not saying anything. I'm focusing on getting off of Gil's balcony as fast as possible. There's this feeling kind of boiling up inside me. I can't identify it, not completely.

The sky flashes and rumbles overhead. Then the wind gusts. It rattles the roof of Gil's hut so that one whole edge lifts up, then crashes back down again. Gil's entire hut looks like it's coming apart. Any hut might, including the one with Dennis inside.

I find myself remembering that Dennis isn't much bigger than Julius. He's all alone in that hut, small and precalm too, most likely.

And out of nowhere I think, *Not again. I can't let it happen again.*

Fern comes toward me from out of the mass, her eyes big and glittery. She's talking to me, but I can't hear her. Or more to the point, I'm not listening. I'm trying to make sense of that last thought. Dennis, Julius . . . I can't let *what* happen again?

"Did you know Gil could talk to Dot like that?" Fern repeats. "Come over with me."

Something's telling me to leave Gil's hut right now. I have to get to Dennis. I guess it's because I want to help Dennis disappear. You know, before anyone finds out about me and him and Dot's test. Before I'm *exposed*. That has to be it, right?

"Wren?" Fern trills, her round face hovering so close to mine our noses are practically touching.

I push her out of the way, literally shove her aside.

"I can't now," I hear myself snap as Fern recoils.

"I'll come talk to Gil!"

It's Luna. She rushes forward, pulling Fern with her. Somehow Luna scrambles onto someone else's shoulders until she's right in front of Gil, kissing him directly on the mouth like the two of them are going to hook up right there on the balcony.

"I tasted Dot. I really did," she squeals.

Then everyone wants to kiss Gil, and Brook's trying to stop them all by making a barrier with his arms.

I force my way through and kind of tumble down the stairs. Out on the path, the rain is coming down sideways, but I don't even care. All I want to do is run and run and only stop when I make it to Dennis.

15

At least when I'm running, I'm not thinking about why I'm running in the first place. My feet slide everywhere on the slick path, but all that matters is putting distance between me and Gil's hut, and getting closer to Dennis. Until somebody comes up behind me.

Brook, I think, turning around. He has this way of popping up right when I'm feeling my most precalm.

Except it isn't Brook. It's Blaze, grabbing onto me so I have to stop running.

"I went to Gil's," he says.

I give my arm this big shake but apparently not hard enough for Blaze to let go of me or anything.

"Brook said he saw you run off."

Brook misses nothing, I swear.

There's a flash and a roll, still close together. The wind has turned quiet things noisy. Shutters slam, roofs creak, and huts groan and shudder on their stilts.

I have to shout so Blaze can hear me. "And you care because?"

Since the pond, I've had zero interest in talking to Blaze. I've done everything I could to avoid it. And then came the whole falling out of the hammock thing and our little encounter after. *That* made me want to act like the guy was never even created.

Blaze, all intense and quiet with his goodnight rhymes and prenormal eyes. Blaze, who acted funny when I suggested hooking up, which is something Dot created us to want. Just being close to him makes me feel prehealthy in the stomach.

Then, straight out, Blaze says, "You see things. I know you do."

Another flash. Another roll.

Blaze is leaning in toward me now. Between the rain and the clouds and the whipping wind, I can hardly see him. But I can feel him, right up close, breathing on the top of my wet head.

"Tell me what you see."

He makes a grab for my other arm, and I'm all caught up trying to pull away. There's this crack as a branch shears off a tree and circles through the air.

Then, gentler, Blaze says, "Come inside."

"I'm not going back to Gil's."

"No, my hut."

"I need to be somewhere."

"Now? You know storms are presafe."

Storm.

Now as Blaze says it, I remember the word. There hasn't been a storm since we were created, and there's no mention of them in the Books. It's just one more word I shouldn't know, and yet I do. I'm not telling Blaze that, though. I can hardly admit it to myself.

Anyway, there on the path in the rain, Blaze and I are stuck. We can't move because I won't come to his hut and he won't let me *not* come. According to him, it's not safe to go anywhere or do anything now there's this storm. I'm in the middle of wondering whether we're going to stay like this all night when an even bigger gust of wind blows. This time it's so strong that it snaps an entire tree. There's a creaking sound, and then, I swear to Dot, the palm on the edge of the orchard comes crashing down on top of the empty huts. Wood splinters. Two, maybe three, roofs have split.

Dennis's? It's too wet, too prelight, too precalm to see anything.

All I can do is feel things and hear things, like the rain stinging my face and chunks of wood colliding in the air.

Blaze grabs me again, and this time I'm totally sure he's not going to let go.

"Come to my hut," he yells.

"No." Rain runs in thick rivers down both our faces. "I have to do something first."

"Okay," Blaze says. "Then I'm coming too."

* * *

I couldn't tell you which one of us is less enthusiastic. Maybe Blaze, when he figures out we're running toward the wrecked huts instead of away from them. In fact, he calls me prenormal and presmart and pre-pretty-much-everything-else-you-can-think-of. I don't answer, and I don't stop.

Now that I'm about to tell him about Dennis, now that there's no way I can get out of it, I just want us to get there.

Naturally, Blaze doesn't want to go inside Dennis's hut. He stands on the path shouting his head off, but I just barge past him up the stairs. I guess he has to follow me then. Inside, the shutters are banging in the wind, and the rain's coming in. Dot's portrait is on the floor in pieces, but the roof is all there, intact, above our heads.

All I can see of Dennis is his face, a pale circle in the prelight. It's streaked with dirt and what looks a whole lot like tears.

There are a lot of things it would make sense for Blaze to do right then. Like go over and check if Dennis is real, for one. Turn to me and say, "Where did he come from?" or "How did he get here?" or "What's going on?" Anything, really, except for what he does, which is step out of the way and wait for me to go over to Dennis.

Dennis wipes his nose with his sleeve and draws a long, deep, ragged breath. I'm pretty sure he's going to start crying again. "I'm not scared," he says. "Only little kids are scared of storms."

I tell Dennis what happened with the tree and how the huts next door might be wrecked, but the hut he's in is completely okay. He thinks about it. Then he straightens out his rumpled sungarb and smiles.

In a low voice, I say to Blaze, "He's leaving. He's going to disappear."

But Dennis walks over to Blaze and sticks his little hand out in front of him. I guess Blaze doesn't do the right thing, though, because Dennis suddenly grabs Blaze's hand in his, and then he sort of pumps Blaze's hand up and down.

"Pleased to meet you," Dennis says.

Blaze laughs, but in a nice way.

Dennis goes, "What? Don't you know that's polite?"

"Yeah?" says Blaze. In typical Blaze fashion, he doesn't seem to have a clue what to say next. Finally he manages, "You're . . . um . . . you're smart to know that."

"*Everybody* knows that." Dennis kind of pauses then, like something's only just hitting him. "I've figured it out. You're aliens. You're from outer space."

I have no idea whether Blaze knows what Dennis means by *outer space.*

"Could be," Blaze says. "We're not sure."

I don't know if Dennis gets Blaze. I wouldn't blame him, because I don't either.

Dennis gives him a puzzled look and says, "Well, maybe you're not aliens. But you're definitely not like anyone else in Woodend."

"That's where you live?" Now Blaze turns to me. "You found him?"

"Last night, over by the lagoon."

"Have you told anyone?"

I shake my head.

"No one?"

Another shake.

"Why not?"

"Because it's my fault he's here. I mean . . . it's because of me."

Blaze is probably losing half of what I'm saying since I'm pretty much whisper-blurting it straight toward the floorboards. "I'm not predotly, I swear. At least, I'm trying not to be. But I think what's happening is . . . I think Dot's testing me. I don't know, maybe I . . ."

I trail off and sneak a glance at Blaze. What's he going to think about Dot's test? What's he going to think about me now that he knows Dot is testing me?

I clear my throat. "Like I said, it's a test. Plus, he's going. Tonight. Then everything can just go back to the way it was."

"Won't happen."

"It will. I'm going to make it. I'm going to pass Dot's test and show her that I —"

Blaze is fully grinning now as he interrupts me. "If he's here, then the Books are wrong."

"Don't say that. It's not true. That's what this whole thing is all about. Dot sent Dennis to test how much I believe in her. I'll never pass if you go around saying the Books are wrong. I'm not going to let you. It's not even —"

"Stop."

"Why should I? I don't want to fail. Otherwise I'll be predotly, and I'll never be chosen and —"

Blaze shakes his head side to side really slowly. "The Books aren't real. Maybe even Dot herself isn't."

"Don't you get it? That's what she's testing!" Then something occurs to me. "She could be testing you too."

I fold my arms, thinking maybe that's going to change his mind. But it seems like nothing's going to stop Blaze. Apparently he hasn't heard one single thing I've said.

"It's made up. The whole thing."

That's when I know for sure what I'd pretty much already guessed. "You aren't going to help me, are you?" I ask. "You're planning on making everything worse." I can feel my eyes narrowing, daring Blaze to disagree with me.

Not that Blaze seems to notice or care. He just says, "We have to tell everyone."

I'm struggling to comprehend this suggestion, to imagine myself announcing to the rest of creation how Dot's testing me, but how, in Blaze's mind, that means everything we thought was true just so happens to not be.

Blaze seems to be handling the whole concept just fine, though. He's gone from not knowing how to talk to Dennis to raining questions down on him. You know, like where we are, and how exactly Dennis got here.

Once Dennis gets over the fact Blaze doesn't know where he is, he tells him that what we call "creation" is actually Club Naturelle. "It's like a resort," he says. "For weirdos. For people who want to walk around with their clothes off. Nudists. That's what it said on the computer anyway."

Then Blaze wants to know who's in charge of Club Naturelle, which is when I have to interrupt.

"Dot's in charge," I remind Blaze. "There is no one else."

"It doesn't work like that out there."

"Oh, like you know so much about *out there*?" In a rush I add, "If there even was such a thing."

Blaze doesn't exactly meet my eyes.

Suddenly, I get the feeling that Blaze has seen a whole lot more of *out there* than me. Or he thinks he has, anyway. He hasn't seen everything, obviously, because he didn't know about the hand thing Dennis did. But a lot.

Part of me is wondering exactly what sort of things he has seen in his head, and how long he's been seeing them.

But I don't ask. That would mean telling Blaze what I've seen. That would mean admitting it out loud.

Dennis has no idea who's in charge of Club Naturelle, anyway. He only found out about it on something called the Tech Specs forum. According to him, he logs onto it using something he calls a *screen name*. Not his, but Nathan's, which I can tell from how he's acting is something he shouldn't have done. From the way Dennis describes things, I'm guessing it was the Tech Specs forum I was reading when the device started to ring.

"I could search Club Naturelle for you," Dennis goes. "I'm awesome with the Internet."

"Yeah," Blaze says. "Search it."

It's clear even to me that Blaze doesn't really know what this means.

Dennis's proud smile collapses. "I can't," he says. "She wrecked Nathe's device."

But Blaze doesn't give up when he finds this out. Now he wants to know who wrote about Club Naturelle on the forum, and exactly what they said. He tells Dennis even that information might be useful.

"Some of it had to do with her," is all Dennis will say, looking at me.

He studies Blaze for a minute, his big build, twisted hair and red-brown skin. "And maybe you."

He tells Blaze exactly what was written there, about how I'm the redhead who was *up for it*, and how the big guy with the *dreads* looks like a *stoner*.

For some reason, Dennis seems to find it difficult to tell us.

Blaze just goes on asking questions. Next he asks who told Dennis about Club Naturelle.

Dennis says, "I only know the screen name. Someone who never posted before."

"What name?" Blaze asks. "What was it?" He's talking quickly now, quicker than I've ever heard him talk before.

"FancyVividBlue. I never forget that kind of stuff." For a second, Dennis looks pleased with himself. But then he says, "I'm not really supposed to . . . Nathe would kill me if he knew I was posting on his forum."

Blaze turns to me. "FancyVividBlue. That's where we start. Dennis takes us out the gate, and we look for FancyVividBlue, whoever that is. Maybe they know something."

Inside my head, I'm practically screaming. What is Blaze even talking about?

Aloud, I say, "I can't stay here."

"Inside the fringe? Me neither, not now that we —"

"No, as in, this hut. All this, it's . . ."

"Don't say predotly."

"Why not? That's what it is."

"There's no point saying 'predotly' if Dot doesn't exist."

"She does. Dot created us. How else would we even be here?"

Blaze is perfectly still, perfectly steady. "Let's find out."

"I can't believe we're even . . . *obviously* there's a Dot," I say. "There has to be. This Dennis thing is a test, and I don't want to fail it."

"Say it isn't a test. Say Dennis is real and Dot isn't."

My entire body is jittering.

Dot's listening. She always is. And this is it, my big chance to show her my faith is never going to flag.

"No."

Without Dot, there would be no way to know what to do or how to act. No Books. No fun. No kindness. No chosen ones. No way to know what is good and what isn't. No anything that means anything. Just this huge hole where Dot is supposed to be.

"Just try and . . ."

"You're serious?" I ask. "You literally think there's no Dot?"

"I want to know for sure. I want everyone to."

"No."

N.O. I think. *Nonononononononono.*

If I fail this test, then I'll never be dotly again. Maybe no one could be. Has Blaze ever thought of that? If one of us starts doubting Dot, then we all might end up doing the same. This thing with Dennis is like a single drop of water in the waterfall crashing down the escarpment. But you don't get just one drop in a waterfall. There are always going to be other drops until the whole thing is gushing out of control.

Is the ground underneath me moving? It really feels like it. All creation's kind of tilting and shifting and whirling around us. Nothing is fixed. Around me, colors blur and blend until everything looks like one big, brown mess.

Blaze takes a step toward me. His arms are stretched like he's about to try to hug me or something. The thing is, he doesn't know where to put his arms. I put my hands up, as if I can hold him back physically as well as stop all the stuff he's been saying.

But naturally, my hands don't do a thing. It's way too late. Already about a bazillion thoughts are forming inside my head. Merging into each other in one huge unstoppable, formless glob.

. . . what if there is a Woodend what if the books are wrong where do we go when we go beyond or don't we even go beyond do we just stop that's it over what are the rules then how do we act what's the point of us who's watching over us if Dot isn't who's going to love us for always no matter who we are or what we've done . . .

"She's lost it," I hear Dennis say at the same moment I use my raised arms to shove Blaze out of my way. I'm out the door of the hut, already soaked and practically at the path before Blaze reaches me.

"Come back."

I still have my arms up, only now they're kind of twisted in front of me and I can't do anything to stop them. My breath is coming in these little gasps, and in between those are *yip-yip-yip* sounds that I don't even recognize as my own.

"It was like this for me too," Blaze tells me.

I want to shut Blaze up, but he doesn't stop.

"I was precalm too. You get used to it."

Never. No way.

I never, ever will.

If Blaze happens to be right, then we're all alone. No one is looking after us or helping us or loving us. Even if a person could get used to that, who would ever want to? Not me.

Blaze sighs. "Do you remember if you've ever been to the beach?"

I stare blankly at him. "I was little when I first went," I say. "There were other kids there. Splashing and laughing, all of us trying to drag each other in. I used to dig my toes into the wet sand. I was happy, you know? In the waves, I was happy."

I swear, tonight Blaze has probably said more than he ever has since he was created. Over the roaring sound of the rain, he asks me, "What have you seen?"

"Nothing." I'm thinking about Julius and his fuzzy sungarb warm against my leg, his springing curls.

"Right. Everything's just like it says in the Books. Dennis isn't real. All this is one big test designed just for you."

When I nod, Blaze turns for the hut. But suddenly, he spins back around. "Why would Dot test you?"

I say, "Why is the sky blue? Why does that one pond glow? Why does Dot do anything she does? We're not supposed to know. We're too presmart."

"Why *you*, though? You've never done anything pregood. And isn't Dot supposed to love you?"

"She does." I falter. "I guess . . . um . . . she just wants to make sure I love her back."

But even as I'm saying this, Blaze's words are hooking into me, a burr in my skin.

Yes. Why me?

Blaze is saying, "The others can make their own decisions. I'm telling everyone about Dennis, first thing."

"You can't. He's disappearing tonight. I'm helping him."

We're locked like that, me on the path and Blaze on the stairs.

"Maybe the others don't want to know," I say. "Normal people just want to have fun. Do dotly things. Hook up. Be happy."

He shakes his head. "You can't be happy about something that isn't true."

"But if you don't have Dot, there's no possible way of even being happy. There just *isn't*."

16

I SEE JULIUS and me again, and it's more than a jumble of images this time. Now everything feels way more real. As in, I don't just see a little scene unfolding. I can feel it, smell it. Taste it practically.

This time, we're standing on some gritty-soft yellowy stuff, and at our feet water is curling and rolling its way toward us. It's hot, but it's a dry heat — nothing like here. There's the smell of salt, and way out in the water I see creations with slick black backs and wet heads bobbing up and down.

Surfers.

"Viva, can I get ice cream?"

I'm wrapped in a towel, trying to wriggle out of one set of sungarb and into another, something impossibly small and red and stretchy. For some reason it really seems to matter that no one sees me without my sungarb on.

"We just got here."

"Please?"

Julius is grinning so wide that I start smiling too.

"Okay."

Then Julius and I climb a huge, long staircase fixed to a kind of rock wall that reminds me of the escarpment. We go to this little hut thing with a window in the side. We come away with cool, frozen blocks on sticks that melt all over our fingers.

"Lick it. It's getting all over your clothes."

Julius's mouth is ringed with brown. His pink tongue circles the frozen block.

"I love the beach," he says.

"Yeah," I tell him. I bite into my own frozen block, sweet like the ripest mango. "Me too."

* * *

When I come out of it, I'm inside Dennis's hut. I'm sort of paralyzed, lying there in the prelight shot through with silver from the moon. I can make out Dennis's sleeping shape on the bed. Blaze is curled up on the floor, asleep too. His chest is rising and falling, and his eyelashes make crescents on his cheeks.

Did I mention Blaze's eyelashes? They're really long and just a little curly at the tips.

Studying them, I wonder why Dot would bother giving someone like Blaze lashes like those. Blaze with his questions and theories. Blaze who hardly talks but then won't drop a subject when you want him to. Even now I keep hearing what he said to me last night: *but why you?*

I'm pretty sure of the answer.

Dot's testing me because I'm predotly. I must be, otherwise I wouldn't enjoy those scenes with Julius the way I do. I mean, they're unsettling, but they're sweet and tender too. The feel of his little hand in mine, the thumb dry from too much sucking. If I'm being really honest, I like it.

The whole time I've been awake, I've sort of been plucking at my thighs. You know, just above where my sungarb ends, without really realizing it. Now I take a fingerful of skin and I twist. Hard. I figure it's only what I deserve for being predotly.

The skin turns white, then red, and it stays that way as a hot, sharp feeling rises up all around the pinched part. It sounds prenormal, but that small jab makes me feel a little better, at least for as long as it lasts. It's comforting and, even though I've never done anything like that before, it's kind of familiar too.

The only thing is, the feeling wears off too quickly, which means I have to keep doing it.

I twist.

I'll never be a chosen creation.

Another twist, a harder one, and then I try clawing my skin too. Bright red welts appear, which has to be good.

Maybe I can rip this predotliness out of myself. I like that idea, so I claw myself a second time, drawing blood out from under the skin.

I'll make it better, I swear. More clawing, more blood. It feels prehealthy and precomfortable, but good too, if that makes sense. This way, Dot has physical proof of how much I want to be good. How much

I care about being chosen when completion night comes. It could be that this twisting, clawing thing is the only way Dot's going to realize I'm serious.

It's only when my legs are meshed with lines and streaked with blood that I realize I've taken it too far. If anyone sees my legs, they're going to know something's up. I jump up and wash myself off with water from the jug.

Then I fold my legs under me, curl up on the floor, and try to sleep.

17

WHEN I WAKE UP, the sun is already climbing in the sky. It hits the shutters at just the right angle to send this shaft of light stabbing into my eyes. I have to get moving. I should have done something last night but I was too shocked, too unsure, too full of prehappiness to know it. Now I don't have a whole lot of time.

Dennis is still asleep on the bed, only a few steps away. If I wake him up now, maybe we can make it to the fringe and to the so-called gate before anyone —

"Leaving?"

I guess the pressure of my feet on the floorboards was all it took to wake Blaze. He's sitting up now, getting ready to scramble to his feet.

"Just going for a walk. You know, if that's okay with you."

I straighten my sungarb over my scratched-up legs. No way am I letting Blaze see that.

"You were going to take Dennis."

Does my face look as hot and red as it feels right now? Is there any way in creation Blaze will believe my best casual "no"?

A snore rumbles from Dennis's nose.

"I'll come for a walk," says Blaze.

"You're not telling everyone already, are you?"

"Not yet. When they're up."

I go to the back window, but naturally Blaze uses the door. I mean, what does he care if anyone sees us? He wants everyone to know about *out there*, about Dennis and FancyVividBlue.

No one sees us, thank Dot. All over the place there are towels and chairs and Books and sungarb, still scattered where the wind and rain dropped them last night. The hut next to Dennis's is totally crumpled. Where the roof should be there's just a big, wet, jagged hole.

The roof, or half of it anyway, is rammed into the grass beside the path. Something's underneath.

On its side, trapped by the back legs, is the little spotted deer Fern and I saw last night. The deer's not skittering around anymore, obviously. Pretty much the exact opposite. Its front legs are splayed out, and there are trickles of blood from its soft, pointed ears.

When it sees us, the deer starts howling, eyes rolling and head dipping so that its stubby horns spear the air.

At the noise, doors open and people appear. Some are alone but most are in twos, holding hands and everything. Plenty from Gil's hut too, people who probably decided it was raining too hard to go back to their own huts last night.

My mouth is open, and my throat feels raw. It's funny how I don't even realize that it's me making those sounds I can hear. I just watch everyone crowding around, asking each other what happened and whether this has anything to do with that stuff Gil was talking about.

Fern comes up beside me, and I think of her trying to stroke the deer last night.

Now she says to me, "Are you okay, Wren?"

The deer goes on moaning and yowling and kicking as Gil comes pushing through the crowd. He's going to tell everyone we need to show Dot how kind we are, I'm totally sure of it. We're supposed to look after all Dot's creatures. Book of Kindness, Chapter 1, Verse 1. It says so right there.

Gil will know the right way to lift the chunk of wood from the deer, and how to help it.

Gil smooths his hair back from his eyes as he walks toward the deer, saying hello to everyone and smiling. Then he crouches down by the deer and looks into its rolling eyes. When he lifts his head, he looks happy still.

"Dot wanted us to find this," he says, like there's no doubt about it at all. "It's quite an obvious sign. If we discover anything predotly, it must be crushed. Just like this deer."

"How do you know?" someone asks. "I mean, it's just an accident."

It's only when Fern says, "Wren!" right into my ear that I figure out the person talking is me.

Gil whips around. His blue-brown eyes study me, flicking their way across every little part of me, my dotmarks, everything. His hands are on his narrow hips. The same hands that, a couple of nights ago by the pond, were in my hair, on my skin, and everywhere else too. "I know because Dot told me."

All over again I think of the wren with the mangled wing, how Gil tossed it onto the bonfire, and how the little body made the flames flare up. Suddenly I'm pretty certain he won't be lifting the roof and helping the deer.

Gil's gaze shifts so that he's looking nowhere in particular. "Who found the deer?"

"Wren did!" says Fern. And she whispers to me in a voice frothy-light as spray from the waterfall, "Oh my Dot. If you found a sign, you're going to be chosen on completion night for sure."

Brook is right there at Gil's elbow, like he always is.

"I'll do it," Gil says.

Brook shakes his head. "Let me," he says.

Then he disappears in the direction of the orchard and comes back holding the coconut knife. Its long, paddle-shaped blade sparkles in the early morning sun as he tries to pass it to me.

"Wren? You need to finish this." Brook watches me, waiting for my reaction.

I shake my head really fast. As in, hummingbird-wing-fast.

Brook's eyes never leave my face. "Dot wants you to. This is Dot's work. Unless you don't —"

I jump in before he gets the chance to say anything about predotliness or believing or whatever else might be about to come out of his mouth. I blurt, "You know what? I wouldn't know how. Dot didn't create me strong enough." Then I let out this little laugh.

Then, thank Dot, Gil says, "This first time, you can watch."

He steps back, holds out his arms, and kind of sweeps everyone else back too.

Everyone but Brook.

Brook crosses between the crowd and the deer. He drops to his knees. Then, all swift and strong, Brook hauls the deer upward and grabs its neck, anchoring its body down with one knee.

I'm pretty certain the deer knows what is about to happen. Its hooves, sharp as the coconut knife, gouge huge chunks out of the ground. The deer thrashes in the grass, trying to roll itself away from Brook, planning on setting itself free, I guess. It opens its mouth to wail, and inside there's a row of barbed teeth, one snap away from Brook's arm.

Brook doesn't stop. He raises the knife and plunges it into the deer's warm throat. The front legs are now flying in every direction all at once. Brook pulls the knife out and blood streams from the cut. Still the deer goes on bucking and twisting, and even Brook, strong as he is, can hardly keep it pinned against the ground. He slices through the skin underneath one side of the deer's jaw, then saws the blade until he reaches the other side.

The deer shrieks. I blanch. Blaze looks away, and everyone else watches with their big eyes and their slow, heavy, dazed smiles. And when the whole thing's over, Brook drops the deer's heavy, soft body onto the ground. Steam rolls out of the deer's cut throat. Brook's arms are wet and bloody up to his elbows, his sungarb is torn, and his is face all red and sweaty.

Jasper starts clapping, and it isn't long before everyone else does the same. Clapping and cheering and whistling like we've just finished dancing to the best-ever dottrack on completion night.

Even Fern. At the same time though, her face is shiny with tears. "It's so . . ." She studies the deer, which is still sort of jerking on the ground. "Isn't it beautiful, doing Dot's work?"

Brook eases the deer out from under the crushed roof of the hut. Fern doesn't look away at all, not even when he slits the deer's soft belly, puts a hand in and pulls out the slippery blue and brown and purple innards. She totally watches the whole thing, until at last Brook gathers up the two front hooves and drags the deer away, leaving this long, slick, sticky trail behind him as he goes.

* * *

The two of us are the last ones left at the huts.

Blaze says, "Still want to pass Dot's test?"

I tell him that I do, obviously.

"Gil's dotly and you want to be like him?"

"Gil's trying to be good. He thinks he's doing what Dot wants. He's just . . ." I realize I have no idea how to finish that sentence. Plus, even to me my voice sounds wobbly. I breathe in and out, carefully, through my nose. "Obviously I want to be dotly. One of the chosen ones and all of that. That's what we're all supposed to want. It says so in the Books."

The mess on the grass is drying black. Already, it's starting to smell.

Blaze starts, "If Gil finds Dennis —"

"If Gil finds out Dennis is here because of me —"

"He isn't." Blaze sighs. "There is no test."

"Okay, so why else is he here, then?"

"To impress his brother, sounds like."

"Brothers don't exist," I tell him, trying to squish down the picture of Julius that keeps popping into my head when I say the word *brother*.

Blaze doesn't even bother answering.

So I say, "Go to the gate, then. Get Dennis out of here. Take him to Woodend if you're so convinced it's real. You can go looking for FancyVividBlue. Do whatever you like."

"I will. Tonight."

"Fine."

"You're not coming?"

I'm not. I don't need to. Not now that Dennis has Blaze to protect him from the bears. I say, "Even if I did believe in a gate, which I don't, Dot's creations aren't supposed to go through the fringe." A fly buzzes past my face. "It says so in the Book of —"

"The Books say Dot created this place and only this place." Blaze lets his eyes slide to the mess on the grass. "They also say Dot's creations are kind to all creatures."

I get what he's implying. It's just I still don't want to talk about it or know about it or have anything to do with it.

"Why do you care if I come? This is your little obsession. You don't need me."

The way he acts, it's like Blaze doesn't need anyone, ever.

Blaze digs his toe into the ground, turning up divots of bloody, sticky grass. "I'll come back once I find FancyVividBlue. When I know what's going on. I'll get help."

"I'm fine, thanks."

"You're not. You believe something that isn't true." Pause. Huge pause. "At least, you say you believe."

"Do whatever you want," I say. "Just leave me out of it. Leave us all out of it."

"The others have a right to know. It's presafe to tell them outright, now that Gil's . . . you know. But we could go out there, find out how to fix them —"

"Everyone's fine. We don't need fixing. And there is no *out there*. We're all good."

"Because everything's so dotly in the garden," Blaze says. "There's nothing prenormal about Gil and Brook? Everything they say, you believe."

"I know I believe in Dot."

And the thing is, I want to. I'm *desperate* to, to be totally precise.

Except there's something else that I'm only just figuring out.

The Dot I want to believe in is *my* Dot. You know, the beautiful, peaceful, happy version, smiling down from the silky banners in the gazebo.

Only now I'm wondering if Gil and Brook believe in a completely different Dot.

18

THE KNIFE IS BACK where it should be, hanging from its nail on the coconut palm in the orchard. The blade is bright silver. So clean, you'd never know what just happened if you weren't right there to see, hear, and smell the entire thing.

I cut a pineapple, a coconut, and a couple of mangos, green-skinned with an orange blush. When I get back to the huts, I guess everyone's in the newfruit grove because it's really quiet. The empty huts have their shutters closed, apart from Dennis's. One of his is partway open, and through it I can see a sliver of Dennis's pale face and one wide-open eye. His expression tells me that Dennis saw exactly what Brook and Gil did.

When I get inside the hut I tell Dennis, "I brought you something." Even for the old Wren, my voice sounds way too cheery. "Pineapple! It'll be super awesome."

As I start slicing into the fruit, the knife blade flashes in the gloom. I try handing Dennis a thick circle, but he won't take it.

I cut myself a slice. "Sweet," I say.

I make a big deal of licking the juice from my fingers. I try again to offer Dennis some, but he doesn't even look at it. His eyes never leave the knife. It might not have been my best ever idea to bring it into the hut with me.

"You saw?" I ask.

I put the knife on the ground and give it a kick so it slides all the way over to the other side of the hut, the blade circling.

"Yeah," Dennis says. He folds his arms, and I can tell he's about to start sniffling.

"That deer. I know it seemed like a prehappy thing to happen."

Dennis studies the floor, but I plunge on.

"But it really wasn't," I say, trying very hard to mean it.

For some reason, Dot wanted Brook to cut that deer's throat. That must be true, even though it's the opposite of how the Books say to act. Thinking anything else would be predotly, and I definitely don't need to be doing anything predotly right when Dot is testing me.

It doesn't matter that I don't understand Dot's reasons. She has them, and that's all I need to know. That's what I keep on telling myself, anyway.

Dennis mumbles, "So how come that pretty girl was crying?"

It takes me a second, but I figure out which girl he means. "Fern was *happy*. Really. If you got to know her, you'd realize she's always happy, pretty much." Then I hear myself saying, "Fern is totally fine."

I slice into a mango, releasing its dotly smell into the hut. But Dennis is even less interested than he was in the pineapple.

"So, guess what. You and Blaze are leaving tonight."

"Me and Blaze?"

I can hear this rising note in my voice. "Um, yeah. You and Blaze."

"But you said you'd take me."

I sigh. "It's predotly to go into the fringe. But Blaze doesn't care. He wants to leave. I don't. So he's taking you."

"You said there were bears." Dennis's eyes are really filling now. No matter how fast he wipes, he can't hide his tears.

"Blaze can protect you."

Dennis's lips jut out. "You *promised*."

I try smiling an *it's okay* sort of smile at him.

No go.

"I'm only going if you come too," says Dennis.

"But Blaze is a great guy," I say, while inside me everything is sort of collapsing.

Because here comes a huge dilemma.

It's not right to go into the fringe — the Books are totally clear about that. But if I don't go, Dennis won't disappear and I'll fail the test Dot sent me. Whatever choice I make, there's no way I can come out of this one-hundred-percent dotly.

If I didn't know that Dot was wonderful and perfect, I'd think there was something not quite fair about this whole scenario. The only way I can see to save the situation is to bend the rules.

I strike a deal with Dennis. "If I promise to come with you, then *you* have to promise that you won't leave the hut until prelight. You can't let anyone see you."

"As if." Dennis looks at me like I'm the most prenormal person in creation. "There are bears *and* guys with knives out there."

* * *

The newfruit trees are barer than I've ever seen them. On the upper branches, the rain has turned practically all the fruit to pulp. Down lower, close to the trunks, the newfruit are mostly whole, although their thin silver skins are dented and pocked. They're about as far from perfect dotly newfruit as it's possible to get.

I choose a tree on the edge of the grove, away from everyone else, and climb onto the lower branches. When I look down, Blaze is heading over to me. I drag my sungarb around my scabby legs as he hands me a bag. Somehow he's managed to nearly fill it for me, even though there's hardly any dotly fruit left in the grove.

I jump down from the tree.

"Dennis saw." I can't quite bring myself to add, *what Gil did to the deer.* "He wouldn't eat. He's trying to act normal, but I think he's pretty precalm underneath."

"I've heard some people do that." Blaze does his mouth twist. "Act like everything's fine when it isn't."

I ignore that. "He promised not to leave the hut until prelight. He said he wouldn't because of Gil and Brook."

Which is exactly when Gil's voice says, "Did I hear my name?"

"Nothing important," Blaze answers.

His picking bag is full. Mine is too, almost, because of him. So now Blaze strides off through the grove, away from Gil. I start walking after him, moving too fast to sling my bag over my shoulder the way I normally would. Instead, I bunch the top together in one fist.

Not that tightly, I guess, because when Brook says, "How did you fill your bag so quickly?" I fumble and the whole thing falls to the grass, spilling newfruit all over the place.

I crouch down and start piling newfruit back into the bag. But my fingers don't seem to be working the way I want them to. The fruit keeps rolling back out again.

"Careful with that," says Gil. "We don't want to do anything predotly."

I haven't forgotten. Not even slightly. It's sort of impossible to forget something like *anything predotly must be crushed* when you're the predotly thing in question.

"I wouldn't. Never."

But a single newfruit has rolled out of my reach, and I can see from here that the underside is squished and bruised. It's not exactly the way anybody dotly wants to thank her creator.

Don't let them notice the squashed one, I think. *Please don't let them.*

By now Blaze has turned around. Gil looks at him, then lets his eyes settle back on the pile of newfruit at our feet. Blaze kind of lunges for the squashed newfruit, scooping it in one hand at the same time as he grabs three perfect fruits with the other. Down on his haunches, he starts piling fruit back into my bag. The squashed one he doesn't put in. I don't see for sure, but I guess he stashes it in the pocket of his sungarb, which today is the brightest shade of peacock blue.

19

FOR THE MILLIONTH TIME that night, I wiggle my fingers into the slats of the shutters.

"They're still on," I say.

"Wren. Stop looking."

I let the slats snap back into position, which gives a pair of butterflies hovering just outside the window a pretty gigantic surprise. They rise up into the air and resettle themselves on the railing around the balcony of the hut.

"I want to get going, that's all."

Blaze says, "I worked that out."

He's sort of smiling at the same time, though. I guess Blaze thought I changed my mind about *everything* when I told him I'd changed it about coming to the gate. He doesn't know I promised Dennis I'd come, and I'm not going to fill him in.

A moment later, I'm working my fingers back into the slats all over

146

again. I'm totally precalm for a whole number of reasons. For a start, there's going into the fringe. Then there's the whole issue of the gate. I want for there to be a gate created by Dot so that Dennis can disappear through it.

But then, if there is, I can't figure out what's going to happen next. Go through it, and I'd be failing Dot's test, surely. Stay behind, and I'd have to find a way of telling everyone where Blaze has gone. And explain how it's even *possible* that he's gone.

"Wren!" he's saying, noticing I'm at the slats again.

But then I notice. "The lanterns are all off. I guess everyone's asleep."

Right away Blaze shakes Dennis, who has fallen asleep, balled up on the bed the way he's been since I turned up at the hut and told Blaze I was coming with them after all.

"Time to go," Blaze tells him. "You're almost home."

Even though the entire garden's prelight and quiet, we don't go out the door. After the deer, not even Blaze wants to do that. He goes out the window first, landing silently in the grass on his bare feet. Dennis is next. Soon I'm sliding out the window on my stomach.

Halfway in and halfway out, I'm working on swinging my legs through the window so I can make a clear jump to the ground. I've got it covered, obviously. I mean, I can climb and everyone in the garden knows it. But maybe because we're hurrying or maybe for some other reason, Blaze reaches up and lifts me right out the window. He kind of gathers me into a U-shape and holds me so that my legs dangle over one of his arms and the rest of me is right up close against his chest. We're only like that for a moment, although even that might be longer than the whole window operation really requires. The only thing I'm sure of is it's enough time for my sungarb to slither up my legs. In the moonlight, the purple bruises and red welts on my legs show up as dark streaks on my skin. Blaze looks at them and at me with his mouth open to say something. But he doesn't.

He just puts me on the ground and holds on until I'm absolutely, definitely steady on my feet.

Then we're ready to run for the fringe. Blaze at the front, Dennis in the middle, and me behind both of them.

"Clear?" Blaze is saying.

Inside me, everything is sort of lurching around. It's because of what we're about to do, I figure. You know, run to the orchard and then into the fringe, where Dot's creations should never, ever go.

All that's more than enough reason for the warm, squishy, prenormal feelings inside me. Nothing whatsoever to do with Blaze and the window or the look on his face when he saw my legs. Obviously, that was just surprise.

Not *tenderness* or anything like that. I wouldn't want it to be, because Blaze is not my type of guy and we're way past hooking up anyway. Even if I felt like it (which I definitely don't), I know for sure Blaze wouldn't want to.

At least, he didn't back in my hut that other night, so I'm guessing that's still the way things are.

"Did you hear me? I said, are we clear?"

I scan around behind me and off to the sides. "Um . . . yep. We're good, I'm pretty sure."

It's then that I hear it. Just a soft sound, but one I definitely recognize. Footsteps on the path, around the front of the hut. Blaze is already running, about to leap from the cover of the hut toward the orchard. I literally have to lunge after him. He has his red sungarb on tonight, and his silver bag is slung over his shoulder, packed to leave creation behind.

I grab Blaze by the neck and drag him and Dennis under the empty hut, down where the trapdoor spiders make their nests. We crawl across the dirt to the very middle of the shadows underneath the hut. I can only see a pair of feet but it's enough to know who's out there, prowling between the huts.

Brook.

Dennis starts to say something, but Blaze jams a hand over his mouth. We have to stay still. Still and completely soundless.

At that exact moment, something drops into my hair from overhead. The first thing I want to do is scream. Loud. But I swallow it, and the scream sticks in my throat like some fruit I've eaten way too fast. My hands fly to my long, thick hair.

I feel a spider there, big as my hand. I knock it from the top of my head, and the spider scuttles down the gaping neck of my sungarb. Its fuzzy legs are all over my skin, every place at once.

I want to squirm and flap and brush it free, but I don't. I can't.

Out on the path, Brook's feet have stopped moving. They shuffle toward us. There's a cracking of knee joints as Brook squats down. I flatten myself to the ground, like the lower I make myself the less visible I'm going to be.

The spider works its way onto my back. I swear I can feel all eight of its legs. As the spider crawls along my spine, I keep my hand cupped against my mouth to trap any sound that might escape.

And the whole time, Brook's totally still, just listening, while the spider roams all over me. Back, shoulders, neck, face. Everything.

Then there's another sound. A sort of scuffle as something low and brown and furry shoots across Brook's bare foot. A mouse, maybe, or a possum. Brook immediately draws his foot back and stops to listen. He waits for a while. And then, finally, he gets up. I guess he figures it was the furry brown thing he heard moving under the hut.

He starts walking again, away from the orchard, back toward his own hut.

Blaze goes, "Now?"

"Now."

We squeeze out from under the hut. We have to run. As in, this second. I know that, but there's something I need to do first. I stand there shaking and shaking until the spider runs out of my sungarb. It scuttles across the grass, and I start to bring my foot down on top of it.

I want to twist and turn and grind the spider into the ground. But I don't do it. It says not to in the Book of Kindness. Then I remember Gil and how the Books didn't stop him from doing what he did to the deer. And Dot loves Gil, or she seems to anyway. So, for a second time, I bring my foot down toward the spider. But I stop myself again. I don't want to be like Gil, not really.

So I'm just standing there, foot in midair, confused — frozen practically.

Blaze grips my arm and hisses urgently into my ear, "C'mon, Wren. Let's go."

* * *

"Ready?"

We're on the edge of the orchard where the fruit trees meet the fringe. I can hear this kind of rushing sound in my ears. There's nothing making it that I can see. There's only what's going on inside me, my entire body trying to cope with the idea of what we're about to do.

That somehow loving Dot means stepping into the fringe, going against the Books and everything I've ever thought was true.

"Wren? Are you —"

"No." I practically bark it at Blaze. "I'm not ready, and I'm never going to be, so let's just get it over with."

Instead of letting Blaze pull me into the trees, it's me who goes in first. Holding my breath and everything, but definitely stepping into the fringe and finally doing what I have to do to pass Dot's test, even if it feels like a totally pregood way to act.

Inside the fringe, the trees are so close that their leaves all knit together. It's way cooler here than anywhere else in creation. Every one of the trees is alive with some kind of bird or little animal with yellow-green eyes.

"Creation didn't collapse," Blaze says. "So far."

I'm pretty sure he's attempting a joke, which shows how happy he is to be doing what we're doing right now. Unlike me, with my quick little breaths and sweaty skin.

"Sure you know the way?" I ask Dennis.

"I made it all the way here by myself, didn't I?" He gives me this look, a hopeful, pleading kind.

Approve of me, it seems to say. I figure it's the same look he's used to giving his brother Nathan. It's one I bet has been on my own face a whole lot recently.

Pretty quickly, our little line of three turns into a triangle, with Dennis up front. Dennis leads us through the trees, away from the lawn and the huts and everything that's familiar.

The whole time we walk, I'm humming a dottrack, "We Belong 2 Dot." I guess in my mind it's protective or something. My way of saying to Dot that even though I'm in the fringe, it's only because I love her and want to pass her test.

"What's that song?" Blaze asks.

Clearly, it's been a long time since he paid serious attention in the gazebo.

"It's the same one she always sings," Dennis says. Which is about when he stops. He spins around.

Out of the prelight comes his triumphant voice. "There. Told you I'd get us here."

Ahead of us, the trees in the fringe thin out and give way to more grass, soft as the lawn we walk across every day. Rising up from that, all silver-shimmery and opaque, is a wall, five times as tall as Blaze.

I walk over to it, and in the light it gives off, I can see it's patterned with a swirling design made up of hooks on these long sticks, all linked together. There are words there too, in these big, blocky letters.

RESTRICTED
AUTHORIZED PERSONNEL ONLY
TRESPASSERS WILL BE PROSECUTED
HAZARDOUS MATERIAL

In its own way, the wall looks sort of beautiful, all glimmery. And the second I see it, I know I was right all along about the test. Dot made the wall and Dennis just for me. Dot created everything around us, so obviously she can create something as simple as a wall.

We keep moving, following the wall until the words stop and there's a blank section, no design or words or anything. Nothing apart from a little rectangle with the numbers zero to nine on it.

The gate.

Blaze can't stop staring at it and neither can I. I mean, it's impossible not to see a real-life gate for the very first time since you were created and not wonder what's on the other side.

According to Dennis, it's a place called Woodend. But I wonder whether Dot would really bother creating an entire place just to test me. Maybe there's nothing at all there, just swirling mist or clouds or something. We're going to have to open the gate if we want to know for sure.

Dennis is blabbering. "I know the passcode off by heart. Same as I remembered FancyVividBlue."

"Show us," says Blaze. "We want to see."

He looks at me sideways, checking on me, I guess, wanting to see if I'm as excited as he apparently is. Standing there, one of his arms brushes my shoulder, but he doesn't move it away or anything. Clearly Blaze has no idea that I won't be coming with him if there's anywhere to go on the other side of the gate.

Dennis goes over there. It feels like I'm floating, kind of like I'm watching myself watching Dennis. With the tip of his finger, Dennis touches the numbers and each one makes a soft little sound, starting low and getting higher, like a kind of song.

When Dennis is done, he swings around to us with this huge smile on his face. He steps back. "It's processing. It's going to open in a sec. This part takes a while."

For a long time, Blaze and I stare at Dennis's striped back. One and six. Sixteen.

Finally, Dennis turns around again. This time, there's a different expression on his face. He's still smiling, only now he also looks unsure.

"The number's right. It's so basic, no way would I forget it."

"Try it again," suggests Blaze.

So Dennis goes through the whole thing all over. The numbers beep again, only this time they don't sound so much like a song. And then, guess what? The gate stays exactly where it is.

"It's right. I know it. One–two–three–four–five–six–seven."

"Try again. You could've pressed the wrong one accidentally."

Dennis puts the numbers in all over again, but this time I don't think any of us actually believe the gate's going to open.

"They've changed it." It seems important to Dennis that we understand this. "I don't get it. If they've changed the passcode, they must know I'm here."

The part that really seems to bother Dennis is why no one is looking for him, if whoever is in charge of Club Naturelle knows that someone broke in.

I stop listening. The thing is, nothing Dennis says makes any actual difference. Dot created a gate, but it's shut, and it's staying that way. Which means Dennis won't be disappearing through it. Dot's test isn't over after all. She's asking something more of me.

"So climb it," I say.

The gate might be sheer and high, but I'm one of the best climbers in creation. Dot made me with special skills, so maybe now is when I'm supposed to use them. Anyway, between the three of us there has to be a way to get Dennis over. Blaze too, if he wants.

"There's no way," Dennis says.

"It's okay. I'll help you."

Dennis shakes his head at me in this precalm way. "Listen."

When Dennis says that, I actually do hear something. As well as shimmering, the gate is making the softest buzz. Dennis picks up a twig. He throws it toward the gate. But instead of bouncing off, the twig bursts into blue and red and orange flares, at the same time making a crackling *zzzzt* sound.

"It's electric."

Blaze asks, "What does that mean?"

Dennis grabs a whole lot more twigs and throws them at the gate. Each one sparks and crackles. Dennis grabs huge handfuls of twigs and grass that he hurls at the gate, watching it all hit and fall smoking to the ground.

"We're locked in," says Dennis. Over and over and over.

"Dennis?" Blaze's voice is soft and gentle. "Here, put this on."

Blaze takes a peacock-blue sungarb from his bag and hands it to Dennis. It's only then I notice the dark, damp stain spreading across the front of Dennis's own sungarb.

Dennis lets out this shrieking, wild kind of laugh. "I'm not wearing a dress. If he ever found out, Nathe would —"

"Just until your other sungarb dries out."

"Clothes," says Dennis, angry. "They're called *clothes*. And dark is *dark*, not prelight. Precalm is scared. Prenice is bad and —"

"We'll get to Woodend some other way," Blaze interrupts calmly.

But Dennis just keeps on talking in this high, thin voice. "And prenormal is weird and sick and horrible. Just like everyone in this place, whatever it even is."

20

WALKING BACK THROUGH the fringe, both Blaze and Dennis are silent. As we walk, I get this picture of myself cross-legged on a bed. Not the one in my hut and not in Julius's, either. Somehow I know that the bed belongs to me. On the wall above it, there are all these posters of creations like me turning what I recognize as *backflips* in the air.

There's a figure too, kind of framed by the doorway.

Mom.

She's in crisp white sungarb with a thin red stripe, a neat bag over her shoulder. But her face looks pinched and exhausted. Even in a fragment of an image I can see that.

"How was it today?" She steps toward me to smooth the curly hair on my unwilling head.

"Okay."

"Really?"

"No."

The next thing I see, I'm holding one arm out to her. Strapped around it is a device exactly like Dennis's. The other thing I can't miss is the thick, white material wrapped around my arms and shoulders.

Bandages.

I see Mom's eyes flick across the tiny screen of my device. I can't read it, because the words are too small and things are shifting and splintering the way they do when I see things. But I can hear what Mom says.

"I don't know, Viva. It sounds very drastic."

My mouth moves and lets loose this barrage of words that I don't understand. Even in these images I'm a blurter, I guess. The odd phrase floats to the top.

"I'm the perfect candidate. This is going to fix things . . . if I don't like it, I can have it removed."

There are tears sparkling in Mom's eyes, still there even after she tries blinking them away. In this tiny little voice she says, "Please don't tell me you're seriously considering this."

"I've already applied. I'm sixteen. You can't stop me."

"Stick with the counseling a little longer."

"It's not helping. It's never going to."

Mom sighs. "No one blames you. You believe that, don't you?"

I see myself reach for something buried under my pillow. It's a piece of fuzzy red fabric balled-up in my hand. I start to stroke the fabric.

"Who else is there to blame?" I say.

21

BLAZE HAS DENNIS'S DEVICE upside-down on the table in my hut. He pulls it apart, one crumpled piece at a time, his fingers almost too big to pick up all those tiny squares and rectangles. He lays each piece on a folded-up sungarb and sort of stares at it, like he's hoping the device is going to reassemble itself.

Dennis wants to get the device working as much as Blaze. He keeps talking about working out where we are. Maybe it's not Club Naturelle after all, he says. He wants to know who's in charge, what it's for. He even wants to find a picture of all creation from above, the way Dot would see it.

A *satellite photo*, he calls it. Not that it would really help, Dennis says. If the *electric fence* goes all the way around, there's probably not going to be a way out. According to Dennis, that's the way someone wants it.

I don't bother telling him the answer to all his questions is Dot.

Blaze says he'll sort out the pieces, just keep trying until he somehow manages to put the device back together. That's his plan. It's just, to me, the device looks even less like something that's ever going to work again than it did when Blaze started.

Anyway, Dennis wouldn't quit asking Blaze when it would be fixed, so finally Blaze had to take him back to Dennis's hut before returning to work on the device in my hut.

"Wren?"

There's no pause before the door of my hut opens. Brook is standing on my balcony. Blaze gets up, and in one movement, sweeps the pieces into his pocket.

Brook stares into the hut. "What are you two doing shut in here by yourselves?"

Blaze shrugs. I guess the best answer to that question is not to answer at all.

Brook goes, "Everyone's at the gazebo." He doesn't need to add, *And you should be too.*

With the door open, I notice how the early morning air is damp and thick and solid. There's a smell to it too — one I don't recognize.

There's charcoal in it, but something else too. It's a rich, fleshy, fatty kind of smell. Already the smell is working its way into my sungarb, my hair, and even my skin.

Getting up, I ask, "What is that smell?"

"An offering to Dot," Brook says, in this *of course* voice.

Out in front of the gazebo, there's a ring of people. Over their shoulders I can see they're standing around a fire with a kind of big cross-bar built on top of it. There are two forked sticks rammed into the ground and another one resting between them horizontally. Speared onto the stick in the middle is a charred shape with three spindly legs sticking out.

There are no white spots and no soft little tail, and the head is completely gone. Still, it's pretty obvious what it is. Or what it used to be, anyway.

Brook goes, "Eat something."

"We're not hungry," Blaze says.

"Eat," Brook repeats, as smoke drifts past him. "Dot did what she did to the deer for a reason. It wouldn't be dotly to waste it."

He watches us carefully, clearly wanting to know exactly how his words are sinking in.

It doesn't matter how prehealthy the idea of eating the deer makes me feel. Or how, for whatever reason, being so close to the fire suddenly makes me super-aware of my dotmarks.

I'm just going to have to ignore the way they seem to stretch and pull and drag at my skin.

I have to eat some deer if that's what Brook and Gil want. It's possible what they want isn't the same thing Dot does. But until I figure out how to make Dennis disappear, the best thing to do is not to stick out.

So I tell Brook, "We'd love to try some."

"Really?" Brook's pretty interested in this.

Gil is by the fire, and the deer's fourth leg is on the grass at his feet. He picks it up, tears chunks from it with his hands, and passes the dripping pink flesh to Blaze and me.

"All of Dot's creatures should be honored. Even the ones Dot uses as a sign."

"Where in the Books does it say that?" Blaze asks, like he's really interested to know. As though he thinks the Books actually do say something about eating Dot's creatures.

Gil's mouth is ringed with glistening fat and streaks of charcoal. He ignores Blaze.

"Go on. Eat."

The deer flesh is still warm from the fire. I think that maybe if I hold my breath, I won't be able to taste it as strongly as I can smell it.

I open my mouth and feed in the first piece. It's a solid lump, chewy with little strings that refuse to dissolve in my mouth the way fruit does. Next to me, Blaze chews and somehow manages to swallow.

But the deer flesh won't go down my throat no matter how desperately I try to force it. Actually, forcing makes things a whole lot worse. Now the flesh coats my tongue, and I feel my chin go all wobbly and my mouth fill with a thick, burning liquid.

I can't let anything prenormal happen. I have to swallow the deer. Does Dot want me to? I don't know. But I'm sure if I don't, I'm going to look majorly predotly in front of Gil and Brook.

"Now that we've got the taste for it, I know Dot will want us to go on eating the flesh of her creations," Gil says. "Don't you think, Wren?"

The hot liquid works its way to the front of my mouth. I clamp my hand over my mouth to keep it back. I can't have the deer flesh and the hot liquid splashing out in one big sticky mess all over Gil's bare feet. I turn away from the fire and suck in air through my nostrils. Anything to get rid of that rich, greasy smell. Sweat cools my skin and makes me shiver.

One last intake of breath, and I manage to swallow a tiny lump of flesh.

"There," Gil says. "I knew you'd love it."

There's still a little string of deer flesh caught in my throat, and I'm coughing and gagging, my mouth filling with liquid all over again.

"Take some more."

Gil watches me bite and swallow, bite and swallow, my throat bulging with each fleshy lump that goes down. And it's then, right when I'm wondering if I'm going to have to eat the entire rest of the deer, that Gil notices the bird.

Bird, that's what Gil calls it anyway. And okay, it definitely is up in the sky, but that's really the only way this thing is like any other bird in creation.

The sound it's making is like no bird I've ever heard. It comes toward us, making a jagged whirr, this kind of *whoomp whoomp whoomp* noise. It doesn't fly straight or anything, either. It banks and swoops, dipping down, then rising up and repeating the whole thing over and over again. It churns the air as it heads for the gazebo, rippling the grass and swirling the leaves.

Now it's close enough for me to see its shiny white body and the circle-shaped blur on the top. I've seen one of those things before, except not here. In Julius's room, on the front of that book.

Hector the Littlest Helicopter. And so I think, *That must be the word for this thing, then. A hector.*

By now, everyone else is looking at the hector too. I mean, they're really gawking. Obviously they are, because this thing must be pretty extraordinary to anyone who's never seen one in a book.

The hector sweeps across the garden, left to right, all over the place.

Leaves and dirt, dust and grit circle through the air and into our eyes. The entire lawn moves in waves the way the lagoon does on windy days. The sound gets louder until it's directly above us and low enough to read the single word in blue letters on its belly: POLICE.

Everyone's shouting at Gil, wanting to know what the thing in the sky is. Somehow, over the top of all the noise, Gil comes up with an explanation. He decides that Dot must've sent a gigantic bird with huge talons on the bottom to scoop up anything predotly in the garden.

Animals. People, even. Because naturally, anything predotly must be crushed.

Everywhere, people start to scatter, exactly like ants before a big storm. The hector banks left, heading for the huts, and now I can see there's another circling blur at the tail.

Jasper and Luna run past, shouting that they're going to the gazebo, that everyone's going there to talk to Dot. The crowd streams past me, and everyone's going in the same direction. I'm right in the middle of the heaving, screaming, gritty swell of bodies.

I want to run in the opposite direction, but I can't seem to move.

Two arms close around me. They lift me off the ground and drag me sideways onto the lawn. I stumble and fall to the grass, and people trample my hair and hands and body in their rush to get to the gazebo.

I feel myself sliding across the grass, pulled by my feet, and I open my eyes and it's Blaze. He lifts me to my feet and shouts above the noise, "That's not a bird!"

I nod. He's right. It's a hector, sent here by Dot so I can complete my test. Now is my chance. I can show Dot I'm not going to be tempted by Dennis and his stories about Woodend. All I have to do is make sure he gets on board that hector.

"It came from out there," Blaze goes on. "It's looking for Dennis."

I don't admit to him that I know what hectors are, or how I know. I don't say he has the wrong idea about why the hector is here.

It's so noisy, that's part of it. But mostly it's because I'm too busy imagining Dennis inside, soaring higher and higher until he vanishes from creation, leaving everything happy and golden again.

* * *

Through the fringe — that's the quickest way to get to Dennis. Now that I know I'm close to passing Dot's test, going in again is a risk I think I can take.

Over our heads, the hector makes this whipping, whirring sound, close and then farther away. On top of that, even in the fringe, I can hear people shouting and the sound of my own breath in my ears. Ahead of me, Blaze's footsteps are heavy but fast.

We make it through the fringe and into the orchard, with its thick, sweet smell of fruit. On the edge of the orchard is Dennis's hut. The hector is right above us, dipping low, sending blossoms spiraling into the air. We pass the coconut tree with its empty nail. It doesn't matter where the knife is now.

The hector is so close, there's surely no way Gil or Brook can get to Dennis before we do. I mean, the hector is going to have to spot us soon. And then this will all be over.

We run for Dennis's hut. Up the stairs, because there's no time for the whole thing with the window. I'm heaving for breath as Blaze opens the door and we stumble through it, plunging from the dazzling sunshine into the still prelight of inside.

"Dennis?" calls Blaze. "Come on."

But Dennis isn't on the bed, and he isn't looking out through the shutters. He's not under the bed or inside the closet or at any of the other places we search, tearing open doors and knocking sungarb to the floor with a clatter of hangers.

The hut is empty. Apart from his striped sungarb, still damp from last night, there's no sign of Dennis.

At the same time, Blaze and I both head back out Dennis's door. Around us, animals are circling, darting underneath the huts, looking for shelter from the hector. And the two of us are just as clueless, pretty much. Shouting Dennis's name and everything.

Both of us are desperate for a flash of peacock-blue sungarb.

We head down the path toward the lawn in the middle of creation. I check my hut. I pound on the door of Fern's. We tear open every door and check all the huts, without knowing why Dennis would be there.

It doesn't even matter because there's no sign of him. Creation is big, and Dennis is small. He could be anywhere. Anyone could see him. He could miss the hector altogether, and I could fail Dot's test.

I yell his name again, but there's no reply — only the sound of the whirring coming toward us from every direction at once. Gil has probably found him by now, or Brook. They must have, I think, and about a million pictures light up in my head.

Dennis with his sungarb all damp between his legs.

The gate, shimmering and impassable. A sparking twig.

Steam from the deer's cut throat.

The empty nail where the coconut knife should have been.

Dennis's device and those things that FancyVividBlue wrote about Blaze and me.

A butterfly circling.

Brook.

And Gil, always Gil, smiling just slightly as he says, "Anything predotly must be crushed."

22

I SEE THEM FIRST. Poking out from under Dennis's hut, there they are, ten white toes, each one ringed with dirt. I run to the hut, and Blaze follows right behind me. The white toes are attached to white feet. Those are attached to skinny white legs, which are covered with a peacock-blue sungarb. The legs aren't moving, and underneath the hut, the body is still.

Blaze passes me, lunges for the hut so fast he ends up falling and sliding toward it on his knees. He grabs Dennis by the feet. It takes no time at all for Blaze to pull Dennis out, but somehow it's long enough for me to imagine what we're going to find. Sticky blood on Dennis's chest, a slit in his throat? Who knows what kind of pregood things Gil imagines Dot wants him to do to Dennis?

Then Blaze yanks again, and the whole of Dennis appears, unhurt as far as I can see.

Dennis's eyes screw up against the burst of bright light. A smile spreads across his face, sweet and breezy as a towel unrolling beside the lagoon. His tongue swipes his lips.

Blaze leans in and uses a thumb to pry apart Dennis's drooping eyelids. Dennis's eyes are usually gray, but they don't look that way right now. The colored part is basically covered by the black circles in the center.

Huge black circles, just like Gil's eyes and Brook's and Fern's. Like mine used to be, before the dreams.

"Hey, you guys. What's up?"

Blaze doesn't answer. He bundles Dennis up until he's just a bunch of legs and arms. Then Blaze runs with him and I follow, heading for the orchard, for an empty patch of Dot's creation where the hector might be able to land. The harder we run, the more Dennis laughs.

When Blaze deposits him on the petal-flecked grass in the orchard, Dennis's head flops to one side.

"Why do you have to be so intense the whole time?"

Blaze ignores Dennis. He starts shouting, like the hector can somehow hear him. I'm listening for the sound to build, the way it would if it came swooping toward us again. The same sound it'd make as it flew away with Dennis on board, leaving me in the orchard, test passed, free to be as dotly as I want.

But the hector doesn't come near us. I don't want to believe it, but it sounds like it's flying away. Soon the hector is tiny in the sky, the *whoomping* noise getting quieter.

"It can't leave!" I shrill. "He has to get on! If he doesn't, then . . . then . . ."

"Too late," says Blaze.

He looks first at the sky, then down at Dennis. Not that Dennis even realizes what's going on. He's laughing still, and I catch the smell of his breath.

Honey, vanilla, sunshine, frangipani, and freshly washed sungarb — the blissful smell of the dotliest fruit in creation.

Dennis has eaten newfruit, I realize. And suddenly the test is about as serious as it's possible to get.

"Any more of those silver things?" Dennis says, feeling in the pockets of the sungarb, "I could go for another one."

His voice comes out blurry. "Nathe would love these."

Dennis curls into the grass. His eyes are glazed. His mouth curls into a grin. That look. I've definitely seen it before.

* * *

A new picture. I see a flash of an image, this time a guy. The gorgeous one from the park. He's beside me on a bed. He's looking up at the pictures on the wall of the room we're in. Backflip pictures. I recognize this as my bedroom.

"I should take all those down." I stand up, wobbling a little on the bed. "I don't even know why they're still there." I begin to rip the pictures off the wall. "It's been months since I . . ."

"How come you gave up gymnastics?" the guy asks.

"I don't know. I just . . ."

"You should keep doing it. Gymnasts are sexy."

My hand stops on one of the pictures, mid-rip. "You think?"

The guy sort of ponders this. "They're okay."

Still, my hand hovers over the posters.

Then he smirks. "Not as good as ballerinas, though."

And I tear the picture from the wall.

I guess he doesn't really care about gymnasts or ballerinas, though. Already he's onto the next topic.

"Found these in your mom's desk." The guy pulls a little rectangular bag from his pocket, clear, with two capsules inside.

He holds it up. "As soon as I heard your mom was a doctor, I knew she'd have something good lying around."

"Are they . . . isn't that kind of . . ."

"Relax, Miss Just-Say-No. Your mom's a doctor, right? They're not street drugs or anything. These are safe."

"Mom thinks drugs mess with teenagers' brains."

"That's kinda the point."

"Aren't they going to . . . you know . . . wipe me out? I'm supposed to be responsible . . . I mean, Julius is asleep, and Mom's not going to be back for a really long time."

"You're still going to be here. We'll stay all night. You'll just be more chill than the average babysitter."

So I close my eyes and stick out my tongue. The guy lays a capsule on it, and I swallow. Then he takes something else from his pocket. A box. He flips the top open and takes out a short white stick. He puts it in his mouth, lights one end and sucks on the other end, his eyes narrowed.

He blows smoke from his mouth like there's a tiny bonfire inside.

Cigar? No. Cigarette.

The guy holds it between two fingers and pops a capsule into his own mouth. He swallows and starts to laugh. "You look like someone's about to die or something." He passes me the cigarette. "Here."

"No, thanks. I don't smoke."

"One drag."

I take the cigarette and put it in my mouth. "Okay."

"There's a pool here, right?" the guy says. "Let's go skinny-dipping."

And as I watch him watching me smoke, I see his eyes widen and darken. On his face, there's a big, blissed-out smile setting in, same as the one I feel creeping across my face.

23

I'M CRUSHING BLAZE'S HAND. I guess I grabbed it when the hector flew away. You know, about the time it sank in that my big chance to make Dennis disappear was gone.

Really, truly gone.

Blaze is just letting me do it. He's probably thinking I wanted to leave in the hector, the same as he did. We're like that, holding hands, just looking at each other dumbly, when behind us someone speaks.

"Wren? What's going on? I heard laughing."

At the same moment, Blaze and I turn.

Sunshine is streaming down, turning the person standing there into a black silhouette edged with light. It's a familiar shape, the same completely adorable one I've loved since I first fell from the sky. A short shape, soft and round and sweet.

Then Fern's voice says, "Oh my Dot. Who's that?"

I can still see the outline of grass pressed into Fern's arms. There are even some stalks in her hair. Her sungarb swings from her left hand. In her right, the coconut knife. She must have been harvesting in the orchard and then fallen asleep in Dot's sunshine. Probably flat on her back, sungarb in a silky puddle beside her, her soft, round tatas pointing up to the sky.

Fern would have to be the only person in creation who could sleep through the sound of a hector.

Fern's eyes fix on Dennis, the black circles in the center of her eyes almost the same as his.

"Wren?" Fern looks from me to Dennis. "Who is that?" Her nose wrinkles. "Why is he so small?"

"He's no one. He's . . . um . . . I mean . . . I don't exactly know."

Nice one, I tell myself. *Great answer.*

"Get Gil." Fern's still smiling, but I can tell her expression is just about to crack. Then it does, and she looks at me and says, totally precalm, "Don't touch him. It. Whatever. Anything predotly must be crushed. That's what Gil said."

At this point, Dennis opens his eyes. When he sees Fern, he sits up, and then *bounces* up to standing, practically. But when he gets close to Fern, he can't seem to figure out what to say. "You're the pretty girl," he finally manages.

It's like Fern is some beautiful newfruit blossom. Dennis kind of gapes at her in wonder.

"We have to get Gil," is all Fern says, and she doesn't look dazed or sleepy or dreamy or sweet anymore.

"Could you hug me?" Dennis asks. "Just once. Please?"

Fern looks from me to Dennis, then back to me again. "You're not moving. Why aren't you getting Gil?"

She steps closer to Dennis. She's holding the knife out in front of her like it's not connected with her body, even though it is. It definitely is. At the end of Fern's hand, the coconut knife is basically the sharpest, shiniest thing I've ever seen.

Dennis seems all pale and exposed, like something from the lagoon that's lost its shell.

"Fern, you're going to cut someone."

I drag Dennis away from her, my arm around his shoulder. In my head, a prenormal set of words rings out. *Not again, no way. I am not letting something bad happen again.*

"Listen," I say.

But Fern mashes her lips together and shakes her head at me.

Beside me, I can hear the smooth in and out of Blaze's breathing.

"Tell her, Wren," he says. "You have to now."

"Tell me what?"

"Okay, all right. If you stop right there, I'll tell you."

Fern doesn't come any closer, but she doesn't let the knife drop, either.

"This isn't what you think. His name's Dennis. He's . . . um . . ." I look at Blaze, who gives me just the tiniest little nod and smile. Except I don't say what Blaze is expecting me to. Instead I blurt, "Dot sent him. Did you see that big huge bird just now? The bird dropped him."

I can't tell who is staring harder at me now, Blaze, Dennis, or Fern. I'm guessing none of them can believe what they've heard.

"Wait," says Fern. "What?"

"He's . . . he's a new creation."

Fern's round face wrinkles. "There's nothing in the Books about Dot creating anyone new."

"I know, but . . . Dot's trying it out. Just temporarily. To see if creation is ready for new people. Small ones."

"Really?"

"Of course!" I tell her. "Just because something's not in the Books doesn't mean it can't be real." As Fern thinks this over, I go on. "It makes sense, when you think about it. What else are all the empty huts for?"

That gets Fern nodding. And now that I've started, words begin to tumble from my mouth, unstoppable. It's the blurt to end all blurts, basically. "Dot wants you to look after Dennis."

Fern starts to lower the coconut knife. "*Me?*"

"Of course *you*. Why not? She loves you. She's thinking of choosing you on completion night, if you take care of Dennis well enough. It's . . . it's sort of like a test."

A grunt from Blaze. But whatever, because now Fern's smiling.

"She's choosing me? For real? What do I have to do?" Fern asks.

It's kind of prenormal how quick Fern is to believe everything I say. She *wants* to believe me, I can tell, because believing is the easiest thing to do. I understand that. Believing is how you get to keep things exactly the way they are, all nice and calm and happy.

I tell Fern, "Nothing much. Just make sure no one finds out about him. Dot . . . um . . . she doesn't want anyone to know she's testing you, in case the others start wondering why they're not being tested."

"That's all?" Fern brings her hands together, and I kind of shrink away from her.

She has totally forgotten about the knife she's holding. She's actually clapping.

"For how long?" she asks. "Just until completion, I bet. That's when she's choosing."

Completion night. As in, two days away.

"Um, right! Just till then. Dot's going to take him back to the beyond and make some others just like him."

Fern looks down at Dennis. She angles her head to one side. "How do you know all this?" she asks me.

"I never told you, did I? I can hear her. She told me Dennis was coming."

"Wait. Oh my Dot. You're like Gil?"

I shake my head. "Gil's like me."

I'm surprised how easily all this is coming out of me. The only problem is I can't stand to look at Fern while I'm saying it. Or at Blaze. *Definitely* not at Blaze.

"Gil's mixed up," I go on. "He thinks he can hear her, but I'm the only one who *really* can."

"Oh my Dot, Wren. Seriously? How lucky are you!" Fern laughs and hugs me. She jumps up and down on the spot, squealing, "You'll be chosen for sure, then. We'll be chosen together!"

"I guess."

"Maybe Gil thinks he caught it when you guys hooked up or something! That's hilarious."

She shakes her head, and her blond hair falls across the brown skin of her tatas. For a moment, I wonder whether Dennis will ask Fern where her clothes are. But Dennis can't even seem to form words.

"I know," I say to Fern. "Pretty funny."

The entire time I can sense Blaze, standing silent beside me.

"So everything he's been saying about predotliness, is that —"

"I don't know where Gil got that stuff from. Everything's one-hundred-percent normal. I mean, deep down we all know there's no such thing as a predotly creation, right? Why would Dot make someone like that?"

"Totally!"

Which is about the point Blaze turns his back on me.

* * *

Inside Dennis's hut, the air is trapped and still and stale.

"Thanks for your help carrying him," I tell Blaze when I finally make it back with Dennis, who won't stop laughing and flopping all over the place.

I was thinking Blaze wouldn't even help Dennis through the window, but it ends up that he does. He even offers *me* his hand. When he puts it in mine, it feels wooden as the hut itself. Once I'm inside, I know he's going to say something to me about what happened with Fern. I also know I'm not going to enjoy it even slightly.

I kind of wish Blaze would just get started, but he doesn't. Instead he spends ages pouring Dennis water and looking in his eyes and all this other stuff.

Finally I say, "Are you ever going to talk to me again?"

There's a little bang from one of the shutters and Blaze goes over there, paying a ton of attention to it, making sure it's really closed and everything.

Then, when there's no more closing to do, Blaze kind of sighs. "You're pretty imaginative."

"Not a compliment, I'm guessing." I slide into one of the chairs beside the table. "I had to say something to Fern."

"You're best friends. How about the truth?"

"All that stuff about Woodend and FancyVividBlue? Dennis never got the gate open, remember? You don't even know if that is the truth."

"What you said definitely isn't."

"If I told her Dot thinks I'm predotly, she might have . . . she was holding the coconut knife, in case you missed it."

Blaze doesn't even bother denying that Dot thinks I'm predotly. He just says, "How about you? Do you think Woodend's real?"

"I came to the gate, but I never said I thought you were right." Even to me, this sounds lame. "I haven't stopped believing in Dot. All along, I knew she was testing me."

Blaze stays quiet. He doesn't believe me, I can tell. Then he says, "How about Dennis? The way you ran through the storm to get back to him? You were looking after him. Don't tell me you didn't think he was real."

Those same words flash through my head. *Not again, I can't let anything happen, never again . . .*

"I was making sure I didn't fail the test, that's all."

Around the other side of Dennis's bed, Blaze is running his thumb over the bristles on his chin. Now he comes over to the table and sits down beside me. "I want to know why."

There's hardly any sound in the hut, just the flutter of butterflies' wings outside the shutters.

"Why do you think you need Dot so much?" he says.

Really, what I want to do now is shake Blaze. Or if not that, then scrunch my hands into fists and pummel them on his broad chest. Anything to stop him from just sitting there, all big and still, like he's been *planted* or something.

"Dot is why we wake up," I say. "She's the reason we pick newfruit and have fun and *everything*. She's the answer to any question. Obviously I need her. Dot's the point of the whole thing."

There's a tapping sound from the shutters. One of the slats starts to wiggle its way open, so Blaze slaps it closed. But he's hardly taken his hand away before the slat starts moving all over again. This time a butterfly squeezes underneath, bright purple wings all speckled with stars. I've never seen a butterfly act that way before. I mean, this butterfly is persistent.

"Maybe there is no point."

The purple butterfly loops once around Blaze. Then it finds me and starts circling, like I'm some flower all sticky with nectar and it hasn't eaten in forever. I mean it *buzzes* at me, flicking my hair in my face and fluttering its wings in my ears and eyes.

Batting it away, I come up with the presmartest retort in all creation. "There is a point. There just has to be, okay?"

The slats are moving again, two at once now. Blaze flips them closed, but another butterfly pushes its way into the hut, its fuzzy red wings striped with orange. I watch Blaze tip his head to the side as he tries to figure out what is going on with these butterflies. But even as he stands there, a third butterfly appears. And then all the other shutters start tapping too.

Suddenly it seems like the space above my head is full of butterflies in every color and every pattern Dot has ever come up with. Spots, stripes, and swirls. There are iridescent blue ones, bright green, pink, and yellow — even butterflies with translucent wings buzzing so fast they are just one big, pearly blur. The butterflies land on my shoulders and in my hair. As fast as I brush them away, new butterflies appear, and by the time I've swatted them, the original ones are back. They're in my ears, on my lips. Somehow, they're even working their way underneath my sungarb until I can feel their fuzzy, tickling wings all over me — everywhere at once.

The shutters are open now, all four of them, and the butterflies are streaming in. So many butterflies that I think surely there's no more room in the air for them all. But somehow there must be, because they don't stop coming. I'm wheeling my arms around, trying to brush them off, but there's no way I can move fast enough.

I'm covered in butterflies, swamped.

"Must have disturbed a nest or something," Blaze says. He's halfway to the door, ready to get out of there. "That's if butterflies have nests," he adds slowly.

Right then, I'm so not thinking about butterflies' nests. And I'm definitely in no state to go running anywhere. All I can think about is what Blaze just said and how badly I hope he's wrong.

So I get down on the floor next to the bed and cover my face with my hands.

"Wren?"

"Everything is easier when someone's telling you what to do," I say from underneath my fingers. "It doesn't matter if you make mistakes, because you know Dot's going to be there, no matter who you are or what you've done."

I can feel Blaze beside me down on the floor now. Somewhere above my bent head, the shutters are slamming open and closed.

"What mistakes have you made?"

Then, randomly, I see Julius. I hear the sound of his voice, really softly, calling out my name. There are all these other sensations too.

Lights flashing. Someone screaming. Smoke that smells so real I actually start coughing.

"That's the whole thing. It doesn't matter. If I can pass her test, then Dot's going to approve of me again. She's always going to love me, whatever I've done."

"You're so prenice that only someone imaginary could ever love you?" he asks.

When Blaze says that, I'm suddenly sure. Without understanding how or why exactly, I know that I *am* prenice. Pregood. Prelovable. Pre-everything-there-is. I want to cry then, just burst out howling.

But I don't. Somehow I stop myself.

Instead I say, all muffled into my hands, "Dot's not imaginary."

"You don't think that," Blaze says. "You're just good at pretending."

"I'd rather do that than think like you. Have nothing ever mean anything. No one to love you. Just on and on until . . . what? You don't even get to go beyond. If there's no Dot, then this is all there is."

"That's right," Blaze says over the sound of beating butterfly wings. "That's why we shouldn't waste it."

24

THE GAZEBO STINKS of flowers. The smell is so strong, it's like the air is sticky. The dottracks seem louder, and on top of that, there are all the colors. Purple and orange and blue sungarb, meshing and clashing and sort of vibrating against each other everywhere I look.

There's Dot's picture rippling on the silky banners dangling from the roof. Even the bubbles are colored, slicks of queasy yellow and sickly pink swirling all over them as they float away through the lattice. I follow them with my eyes until each one bursts, leaving nothing but foamy dribbles against the bright blue sky.

Fern whispers from behind me, "I came up with the best idea."

"Yeah?" I don't turn around because Gil's at the front of the gazebo with his fingers laced, watching everything that's going on.

"I'll make him a garland!"

Gil is looking right at us now. Whatever Fern's talking about, I'm thinking it'd be way better if she told me later.

"The design's either going to be random multicolors or stripes. What do you think Dennis would like better?"

"Honestly? Um, both sound pretty awesome."

Fern isn't giving up. "But which would he —"

Gil says, "We're talking to Dot, not to each other."

"Oh my Dot." Fern giggles. "He's so positive he's going to be chosen, isn't he? He doesn't even realize that it's really you and me who are the ones . . ."

At that point, Fern's voice kind of melts into everything else in the gazebo, and it's impossible to tell one bright, happy, glossy thing from another. I get up from the cushion that Fern and I are sharing and navigate my way to the door of the gazebo.

If I could just breathe one single, fresh breath of air, then I'd be fine again, I know it. I get as far as the door.

Brook's there, blocking my way. "You don't care what Gil has to say?"

From the front of the gazebo, I hear Gil speaking. "I've checked everything in the garden, and I'm pleased to announce none of Dot's creations are missing. No animals and no people, either."

He pauses here so everyone can laugh. "In time, Dot will tell me why she sent the bird. Until then, we should all stay dotly and make sure others are too." His eyes roam the crowded gazebo. "Including you, Fern."

Fern's eyes are closed. Inside her head, I imagine there's nothing but garlands.

"Fern?" Gil repeats.

Finally, Fern opens her eyes but only when Luna turns around to poke her.

"Can I go now?" I ask Brook.

"No one is saying you have to do anything." He takes a step sideways and lets me through.

A breeze rolls across the lawn, and I stand there with one hand on the lattice, gulping down cool air and watching the animals on the lawn. A pair of flamingos at a fountain. Some low-slung type of cat with tassels on the tip of its ears, yawning in the sunshine. A gazelle too, only not feeding on the grass or anything like that. The gazelle is staring straight ahead, shifting its weight, steadily and repeatedly, side to side.

You'd think it was dancing until you saw its dull, glazed-over eyes. How have I never noticed those eyes before? They're how I know the gazelle isn't dancing.

As in, not at all.

* * *

I had no idea it could take Fern so long just picking flowers. First she wants to go to the orchard to look for vines, but she'll only pick the ones with little curls of green springing off them. On top of that, the leaves have to be perfect and glossy without one single speck of brown. The actual flowers need to be the most vibrant, fragrant, and succulent things Dot ever created.

When I ask her how much longer until she has what she needs, Fern only says she isn't sure. "It has to be dotly, Wren. I want to look after Dennis. I really, *really* want to be chosen."

If her arms weren't full of leaves and flowers, I'm one-hundred-percent sure she'd be trying to hug me now.

"I figured."

Fern does a couple of mini-jumps as she chimes, "We're going to be cho-sen."

Then she goes off into a big long ramble about how amazing completion night is going to be, about the party on the lawn and the colored lanterns in all the trees and dancing and hooking up . . . By the time she gets up to wondering exactly how Dot's going to let us know who's chosen, I've kind of blanked out.

Once, I liked to think about whether Dot herself would appear before us on completion night or send us some kind of message or exactly what. Now that it's nearly here, my head is full of too many other things.

Dennis, Julius, Gil, and Brook.

And Blaze, especially Blaze, asking me, *Are you so prenice only someone imaginary could ever love you?*

When Fern's finally ready to weave her garland, she decides she wants to work in the orchard. She chooses a peach tree and we sit down underneath. Her face is speckled with light and shadow as she makes the base, a twisted circle of vines. She's really concentrating, rolling two stems together, binding them with a thinner stem, then carefully knotting the whole thing into a circle.

As Fern works, she hums dottracks. She looks so completely happy, sitting there poking flowers into the circle of vines, testing out the effect, trying out every possible combination of colors as she yammers on and on and on about being chosen and what her special, super-secret purpose might end up being.

Fern's my best friend. She has been since we were created. But for the first time ever, hanging out with Fern is giving me a pregood feeling.

It's nothing Fern has done. I mean, now that she doesn't have the coconut knife in her hand, everything about Fern is lovable as ever. It's just, Fern looks so sure of everything around her, so effortlessly happy.

It's exactly how I used to be, and I want to feel like that again. Plus, it makes me prehappy to be keeping this huge secret from Fern, the one about which one of us is really being tested. It's way too late to go back, though. Way too late for the truth.

When Fern eventually finishes the garland, I tell her it's beautiful, which it is. So beautiful, it kind of hurts to look at it. The garland's a perfect circle with a ring of blue flowers attached. On top of that, paler blue flowers, then paler again, until the very top circle, which is made of about a million tiny white daisies. We've been sitting under the peach tree for so long that I'm sure we've grown roots or something.

But Fern springs up just fine. "Let's go give it to him!"

It took a lot to convince Fern she didn't have to spend the entire day in the hut with Dennis. It took ages to persuade her Dot's version of looking after Dennis basically only means not telling anyone he's here. But now Fern has the idea that she wants to see him, there's nothing I can do to talk her out of it.

On the way there, Fern wants to talk about who's going to hook up with whom on completion night. She tells me how she still likes Sage, but Luna's also cute. Then she asks, "How about you?"

I make a sort of *mmhmph* sound, hoping Fern will let the subject go. As if.

"There has to be someone."

"I don't know. Drake, I guess."

She squeals. "Drake's your number one?"

"He's okay."

"I know who likes you."

She waits for me to say *Really?* or *Oh my Dot, who?* The way anyone else would. The way *I* would've once. When I don't, Fern keeps going anyway.

"It's so obvious. You can tell by the way he looks at you. Blaze!"

Right away, I feel as prehealthy as I did in the gazebo before. The combination of the words *Blaze* and *Wren* and *hooking up* aren't sitting right with me.

"Blaze never hooks up," I say to Fern, laughing her off.

Not with me anyway. Especially not now.

My answer doesn't dull Fern's sheen, not even a little. She just moves straight on to considering my options, like one person is completely interchangeable with another.

"So, you hooked up with Gil. That means you could be with Jasper again."

"Jasper," I say. "Sure. Why not?"

* * *

"Shut them!" Dennis grumbles, his hand over his eyes. Apparently, it's not so fun once the effect of eating newfruit wears off. "It's too bright."

I wriggle the rest of the way into the hut and swing the shutters closed behind me. The hut is cool and shadowy now, hardly even light enough to see Dennis, or Blaze at the table with the pieces of the device spread out in front of him again.

"Better?"

"No," says Dennis. "My eyes hurt. Everything hurts."

He looks up at me from under low eyebrows, which is when he sees Fern standing behind me. His face uncreases. Suddenly, he's smiling. In fact, it seems like there's light beaming directly out of his skin. "You came to see me!"

Fern bounds over to the table where Dennis is sitting. "As if I wouldn't! Don't you know you're the most important thing in creation right now?"

Dennis tries patting his hair straight, but it springs back right away. His eyes never leave Fern. "Am I?"

"Totally! Dot's coming to take you back tomorrow night. That's completion night," she reminds him. "And I'm going to be a chosen. I'd say that makes us both pretty special."

Tomorrow. If I don't work out how to make Dennis disappear by then, Fern's going to know all the stuff I've been telling her isn't even slightly true. And then she'll probably tell everyone about Dennis and me and the test. That'd be the dotly thing to do, and Fern's totally dotly.

But right now, Fern's holding the garland behind her back. She pulls it out and says to Dennis, "I made you something."

Dennis takes the garland. "Flowers?"

It's pretty obvious he has no clue what he's supposed to do with it.

"You wear it," I tell him, wondering if Dennis is going to say *no way!* Like he did with Blaze and the sungarb.

But he doesn't. He just lifts the garland onto his head and sits there with his neck and back all straight, making sure it doesn't fall off.

"Not now," Fern says with a laugh. "On completion night!"

Dennis won't take the garland off, though. He even gets up to look at himself in the mirror.

Fern stands behind him and drapes her arms around his neck. "I'll see you later. I'm going to the gazebo."

"You're going?"

"I want to thank Dot for making you look so good in your garland."

Dennis goes, "You don't have to do that. You could stay."

But Fern's already at the window, getting ready to slide out like she's been doing it ever since she was created. Dennis closes the shutters behind her, his hands on the window frame Fern's just touched. Then, instead of sitting back down at the table, he goes over to the bed. He lies face up, his garland tipped sideways, staring up at the ceiling.

Now there's a space for me at the table, next to Blaze. That's actually the only place for me to sit. But when I go over, Blaze doesn't even look up from the device.

"How's it going?"

"Still busted."

"You put those two pieces together, though. So if you keep going you're definitely going to . . . or probably you'll be able to —"

"Fix it before tomorrow. That's what you mean."

"That would be —"

"So Dennis can leave on completion night, and Fern won't know you made that whole thing up?"

At this point, there's really nothing I can say.

Blaze goes on, "You're not leaving with me, even if I do fix the device. You were never going to."

"I'm . . . I guess I'm . . . you know. Still thinking about it."

It seems better than telling him no outright. But Blaze gets up from the table so fast that his knees bang against it, sending the pieces of the device skittering across the floor.

At first I want to get up too, just walk out of the hut and go. But when I really start thinking about that, I'm suddenly not so sure. Outside the hut is the orchard, Fern and her garlands, and the sticky sweet gazebo with the dottracks worming their way inside my head.

And the only place to go apart from that is my own dank, shuttered hut.

"You two need some of those silver things," Dennis says.

"What, so I can feel as prehealthy as you?" I say.

On the bed, Dennis rolls over onto one elbow. "You'll feel good for a while."

"As in, how good?"

"Really good."

"She can't eat newfruit," Blaze says flatly. "Wren won't do anything that isn't in the Books."

25

THE SMELL OF NEWFRUIT is all around me, a big thick cloud of it. The newfruit trees have started to blossom again after the storm. Pretty soon every branch in the grove will be loaded with young fruit, but for now all that's left to pick is the stuff that's pocked and bruised.

Am I really going to do it? Here in the grove in the middle of the night, there's no Gil or Brook, no Fern or Blaze to see me.

But someone is looking, of course. Dot. Whatever I do, she's going to see it.

I take a newfruit in my hand and kind of cup it there. A quick twist, and it'd come free from the tree. I could bring it up to my mouth, eat it, and — if Dennis is right — feel better straightaway.

More than better, even. Amazing, awesome, completely incredible.

I'd also be doing one of the most predotly things a person could ever do. A way bigger deal than going into the fringe, for example. The times I did that, it was always to pass Dot's test. If I ate the newfruit now, it would be purely because I wanted to. Nothing to do with becoming dotly again.

I let go of the newfruit again like it's hot or something. I do this scratchy little laugh, all by myself in the prelight.

What am I even doing here? I can't eat a newfruit. No matter how prenormal things get or how precalm I feel, I could never, ever do that. I should just go back to my hut, try to sleep, and try not to think about Fern or Blaze, Gil or Julius.

But the idea of that is so heavy it might as well be physically pressing down on me. All by themselves, my legs fold under me and I find myself sitting on the ground underneath the newfruit tree. And there, half-buried in the grass, is a single, dropped newfruit, right beside my hand.

I pick it up. I place it in my open hand and look at it.

Eat it. Go on. Right now. Beyond that, I don't really think about it. I mean, if I were thinking, what happens next wouldn't happen. I lift the fruit to my mouth and take a bite.

I wait for something gigantic to happen.

Is the sky going to flash? Will the ground open up or the grove tear itself in half? The trees should start churning. Or a wind should blow up, or maybe Dot's hand will reach out from the beyond and squash me the way I wanted to squash that spider.

But those things don't happen. Not one of them. I've just done the worst thing a creation can do and guess what? Absolutely. Nothing. Happened.

My mouth floods with the flavor of newfruit. It's lame to say it's indescribable, so I'll give it a try. At first the newfruit tastes like berries, tart on the front of my tongue. Then it dissolves into honey, only a thousand times sweeter. It ends up tasting like what I imagine a fresh pink flower would taste like. Or — and this is going to sound really prenormal — a dragonfly. Kind of bright and sparkly and fresh, if that makes any sense at all.

Literally right after I've finished the first newfruit, I decide I'll have another. I'm already as predotly as I can get, so why not?

I'm definitely craving the taste, but more than that, I want more of the feeling that eating newfruit has given me. The feeling of knowing the rules but breaking them and following my instincts instead, no matter how confusing they happen to be.

I guess you'd call the feeling *freedom*.

I jump up on my feet, tweak a newfruit from the tree and pop it into my mouth whole. I spit the pit out, then I pick another and another, stuffing them into my mouth so my cheeks have a matching bulge on each side.

It's about then that a whole different feeling kicks in. I start to imagine I'm in midair, falling, but not plummeting or anything. More like drifting downward until I feel myself land in a gigantic pile of feathers.

I harvest more newfruit. I totally strip two or three trees, but even then I'm not sure I have enough to keep the feeling going.

But there's not much fruit to begin with. I fill my pockets. I only stop when the newfruit I'm trying to cram into them start rolling back out.

I drop some newfruit in the chute, then get down on my hands and knees and yell directly into it. "Hel-lo, Dot? Can you hear me? Are you there? Is anyone there?"

Then I work out that I'm treading on all the newfruit I dropped on the ground. The fruit squashes and splits under my feet in a way that seems hilarious to me.

So I stomp around, laughing, with my head tipped back to the sky, as newfruit squishes between my toes and blossoms shower down from the uppermost branches of the trees.

When I'm sticky all over, literally dripping with juice, I get the idea to go swimming. I run to the lagoon, still and glittery with those pinpoints of silver light way down on the bottom.

I take off my sungarb, and the moment before I dive in, I see my face reflected in the surface. My eyes are just like Fern's and Gil's and everyone else's again. Huge black circles in the center, covering the green.

I'm starfishing in the water, staring up at the sky, when the sensations swamping me switch direction without warning. Now instead of floating, I'm plunging downward. Arms and legs flailing, everything inside me loose and unhinged.

And then another idea jumps into my head. It fixes itself there until I find myself planning the whole thing out.

I'm going to climb the escarpment. I could jump from up there, I think, but not even aim for the water the way I do when I'm jumping from the rocks. Instead I'd point myself at the rocky edge of the lagoon and deliberately smash my head so I'd have to go beyond.

I wonder if I'd even get to meet Dot, now that I've eaten newfruit? I need to tell her how much I wanted to pass her test and be dotly. I want to understand why I couldn't seem to do that and why exactly it is I am so pregood in the first place.

I have so many questions to ask, and suddenly it seems pointless to wait when I could choose to go beyond and ask them right now.

I splash to the edge of the lagoon. Tears and water mix together on my face as I run to the escarpment. My fingers find the first crevice easily. I dig my hands right into the crack in the rock and use the strength in my arms to lift myself clear off the ground. With my feet, I steady myself on a lip of rock. I wiggle my fingers out of that first crevice, then reach higher for the next crack and the next, until I'm ten or more whole body lengths above the ground, right over the lagoon, high as the ledge Blaze pointed out to me on the first day things started going prenormal.

Up here is where the climb's going to get really interesting. Higher up, the crevices are way farther apart and the rock is all slippery from the waterfall.

There's a wind blowing sideways across the rock, and it whips my sungarb around my wet skin and splashes spray all over the place.

I swing my arm over my head and find the next handhold, then I look down to work out where to put my feet. There's a perfect little crack for my toes, but it's too far to reach. So I hang on with my fingertips and kind of kick my legs so my whole body swings toward it. Loose stones go rattling down the rockface and plunk into the lagoon below.

But I don't stop climbing. I keep going until I'm almost at the top, reaching a hand out for the lip of the escarpment and hauling myself up and over the rock.

I did it.

I am on the edge of everything. In a few seconds, life down there, the sunshine and the fun, the testing and the doubt, all of it will be over.

I want that, I tell myself. I've convinced myself I want to end all that right now.

I take one last look. Creation has kind of unfurled itself below me, the lagoon with its silver lights and the huts all black, apart from one with a lantern on, which has to be Gil's maybe, or Brook's. Owls and bats circle while the daytime animals sleep.

I look straight past it all, over to the fringe, where between the trees I can just see patches of the wall shimmering in the prelight.

Beyond that, on all sides, the ground rises sharply upward to rocky hills as tall as the escarpment.

It's only from this high up that I can see over the top of them and down the other side. Right there are a whole lot of huts. Tons of them, way bigger than ours and all lit up in whites and oranges.

Inside those huts are people like Dennis who've never heard of Dot. People who weren't created by Dot and don't believe in her and who just go on living in those sparkling huts of theirs.

The Books, Dot, and all creation . . . it's just like Blaze said. Not real. Maybe I've always known it, even if I wouldn't let myself admit it.

It's the most prehappy knowledge there could possibly be, and after all this time dreading it, I feel the truth breaking over me. I'm standing there on the edge of the escarpment, and I know right now I have to decide.

I could jump and never have to deal with knowing there is no Dot. Or I could climb down, get out there, and find out what's really in the beyond.

I watch the lights for a while. Some of them are moving, some winking on and off. Spread out in front of me like that, they're really kind of beautiful.

And maybe, if the images inside my head are real, one of those lights could be shining down on Julius.

It feels like the newfruit are changing course inside me yet again. All I know is the urge to jump fades away and something else replaces it.

Suddenly, I'm full of ideas about exploring the beyond, finding Julius and Mom and even FancyVividBlue. I plan on doing those things with Blaze, the guy who thinks I don't need someone imaginary to love me.

And I realize I'm leaving Dot behind up here because I've found something better.

Hope maybe? Love? Or is it some combination of the two?

I don't know.

* * *

If you like to run, I'll tell you it's even better in the prelight after lots of newfruit. Especially when you're somewhere no person you know has ever been before, and you're not wearing sungarb. On top of the escarpment, across the smooth cool rocks, that's when running gets truly awesome.

Arms out to my sides like wings, I'm circling around laughing when it hits me that I should run to the wall and back again, just to see how far away it is from here.

I run and run until my bare toe hooks something metal, hammered into the rock. I pitch forward and land with a crack that sounds like it should feel really prehealthy but somehow totally doesn't.

Eye level with the ground, I see there's more than one metal thing in the rock. There's an entire row of them, strung together with a wire that has little tags attached. Words are printed all over them.

Shepherd Corporation Shepherd Corporation Shepherd Corporation

I lift my face from the rock just high enough to see that ahead of me are more lights, only these ones are rushing past and making a kind of *whooshing* as they go. And between me and them, there's nothing apart from a thin, straggly row of trees.

26

I FIGURE I'LL TELL BLAZE right away. But things don't turn out like that at all. When I turn up on Dennis's balcony, Blaze doesn't even let me speak. He steers me inside, checking all around in case anyone saw me standing out there in the open.

I ooze down into the chair he's pulled over, and when I'm sitting, I realize how much I needed to be doing that exact thing. Blaze's chair is across from mine — close but definitely not so close that we might accidentally end up touching.

"Guess what?"

The silence that follows isn't a long one, but it's enough time for me to decide and undecide and re-decide a million times.

Tell him, and he'll want to leave immediately. Don't tell him, and he'll stay for a little longer, and I'll have a little longer before everything turns completely upside down.

"What?"

But instead of words, what comes out of my mouth is a jet of liquid complete with half-chewed newfruit. I guess you'll understand what state I'm in when I say the sight of Blaze's dripping legs and feet actually makes me laugh. "Sorry! Oh my Dot . . . I mean . . . sorry!"

Dennis has been awake this entire time, and he's laughing too. Loudly. "How many did you eat?"

"Um, a lot. You were totally right about them."

Blaze is over by the closet. I can see him maneuvering out of his stained sungarb and sliding on a fresh one, managing the entire thing without showing me more than the quickest glimpse of skin. He sponges off his feet and the floor before he sits down again.

"What were you going to say?"

The smile on my face feels loose and sloppy. "Hang on. Just wait."

I blink while the hut whizzes around me. Too late. My mouth is filling all over again. I'm going to . . .

Blaze jumps up. His chair clatters.

Dennis is laughing so hard he's literally curled up in a ball.

I release more chewed-up newfruit, but this time Blaze is out of range. By the time it's over, I think Blaze has forgotten I had something to tell him, but he hasn't.

He asks me again, "What is it?"

"I know how to get out."

I hear Blaze telling Dennis to get up and make room for me to lie down. It sounds like he's a long way off, under the surface of the lagoon or something. He has to lead me to the bed. Well, he half carries me, to be totally accurate. I roll myself into a ball.

Blaze brings me water and sits down beside me, and I tell him about climbing the escarpment and what's at the very top. Or really, what *isn't* there.

"There's no wall," I say.

"Sure about that? You're not thinking too clearly, you know."

I stifle a belch. "Swear to Dot."

"No need for one," Blaze says, seemingly to himself. "Not if we all believe we're not allowed to climb too high."

Then he turns to Dennis, who is sitting at the table, listening. He's as ready to leave as Blaze is.

"How far away is Woodend?" Blaze asks.

"It's close. You can walk. It's easy to find. There's nothing else around."

"Those sounds she heard —"

"Probably just the road."

"Cars," Blaze says suddenly.

In my head I immediately get a picture of a long, straight, black stretch filled with *cars.*

"So, um, we can leave whenever we want," I say.

And right away Blaze asks, "Who's we?"

"You, me, and Dennis. Tomorrow. As soon as it's prelight."

Blaze holds the glass up to my mouth, and I take a drink.

"You're coming?"

"I'm coming."

Tomorrow night is completion. The dotliest night in all of creation, the one I've dreamt about for three-hundred-and-sixty-four days. But now, all my little plans — wearing one of Fern's garlands and maybe being chosen for a special purpose — seem to be pointless.

And instead of going to creation's biggest party, I'll be leaving my entire reality behind. I guess I'm committed now.

I decide to tell Blaze everything. "I've seen the beach," I say. "I only said I hadn't because . . ." I take another sip, sideways, so a dribble of water runs out of my mouth and onto the sheets. "I don't know why. Anyway, it's this boy and me. Julius. He's my *brother*, I guess. We're walking down these really tall wooden stairs and they're so hot. We're holding sticks with cold sweet stuff on top."

From over at the table Dennis says, "Ice cream. It's called ice cream."

I know that, I think. *I already know.*

"We lick it really fast, but it still drips all over our fingers."

"That happened to me too!" says Blaze.

Dennis is laughing. Now that it looks like he's going home, Dennis is happy again. Plus, it seems that to him two people not understanding ice cream is prenormal.

"Did you surf?" asks Blaze.

I tell Blaze I don't know that word. Instead I describe Julius and me, side-by-side on the edge of the water. The whole time, my brother and I are holding hands.

Just once I look back at the sand, and there's Mom in a hat, sitting on a towel and hugging her knees. She calls out things like, *Be careful!* And, *Have you got your sunscreen on?* But she's smiling too.

"And the other thing is," I tell Blaze, "Julius doesn't call me Wren. No one does. When I see things outside, everyone calls me Viva."

"Viva," Blaze repeats. "Suits you."

Then he sticks out his hand, and I take it, and we pump them up and down. It seems hilarious to me, maybe because the last of the newfruit is still hanging around inside me. Although even Blaze is laughing.

"Pleased to meet you, Viva. I'm Luke."

Luke.

It's a better name for him than Blaze. Luke sounds calm and quiet and, you know, sort of sweet. As soon as we get outside, that's what I'm going to call him.

"Okay, here's a question for you. Do you think there's ice cream in Woodend?"

Blaze doesn't answer in the normal way. I mean, he doesn't use words. Instead I feel his hands in my hair. He draws it all away from my face, brushing the sticky strands off my face. He holds it in a bunch at the back of my head.

Then suddenly, with one fingertip, he touches the back of my neck. He keeps doing it.

I guess maybe there's a scratch there, or a freckle. Something Blaze has never noticed before, anyway.

After that, he lies down beside me, and the two of us curl up together like bananas in a bunch.

* * *

At least the hut walls have stopped moving. Now when I open my eyes, the problem is everything is too bright. Sounds make me feel prehealthy too. A bird singing first thing in the morning splits my head.

"Happy completion day," says Blaze.

I'm pretty sure he just made a joke. Which just might be Blaze's first-ever joke — that I know about at least.

I beg him for water, and he gets up to bring it.

He's in a shining mood. Everything he does and everything he says seems to really mean, *We're doing it. We're leaving, together.*

Last night, in my state of newfruit bliss, the whole thing seemed like such a brilliant idea to me too. It's just now that it's morning and everything's stark and clear, I'm going to have to get used to everything all over again.

Beside the bed there's a set of drawers, the way there is in every hut. I open the top one and there inside is a Books unit, just as I'm expecting. All the huts have them, including the empty ones. Anyway, I don't know if it's a good idea or the opposite, but I switch the Books on and start to read.

The Book of Fun. The Book of Kindness. The Book of Acceptance.

Written down like that, our life sounds so amazing. You know, like something that really should be true.

I scroll through every page of each book from the first to the last. Sort of saying goodbye, if you can say goodbye to a bunch of words on a screen.

Then I notice some words I've never seen before, right down the bottom of the last screen. The letters are so tiny I have to zoom way in just to read them.

© SHEPHERD CORPORATION 2018

I cover the words with my finger. When I lift it again, guess what? They're still there.

"Dennis?"

He looks up from the chair where he's as asleep as anyone can be sitting upright.

"What's Shep-herd Corporation?"

Blaze has been lying on his back, looking at the roof. He asks, "Did you see something?"

I'm about to say no out of habit, I guess. Then I remind myself we're leaving together and that means we tell each other things. I show him the tiny words at the very bottom of the very last screen of the Books.

"There was something about Shepherd up on the escarpment too," I say.

Dennis says, "Shepherd is this big company."

"Anything to do with nudist resorts?" Blaze asks.

"Nah, they make medicine. Like, for sick people and stuff. You know, drugs."

Drugs.

The exact same word that the gorgeous guy in my vision used when he gave me that capsule. I tell Blaze an edited version. And I share everything I know — or think I can remember — about drugs. Some are like medicine. Other drugs people just take for fun, to make them feel happy or whatever.

The way newfruit made Dennis and me feel.

"Drugs can be really freaky," Dennis adds. "I saw this guy on the news once who thought he had worms under his skin."

Now Blaze says to me, "So a drug could make you believe something that isn't true."

I get it. He's talking about Dot. He thinks one of Shepherd's drugs could be why we believe.

"For this long, though? Don't drugs wear off?"

Blaze shrugs. "Might depend on the drug."

"If any company could make a drug that powerful," says Dennis, "it would be Shepherd. They're so important, they practically run the world."

* * *

Later, the whole thing with Gil happens.

It starts when I hear Gil out on the path, thumping up and down the stairs of all the huts, heaving the doors open and shouting at whoever's inside.

He yells, "Everyone out. Right. Now."

On top of that, there are the crashes of chairs falling and tables splintering on wooden floors.

Brook's voice comes next. "I can do this. You shouldn't be . . ."

"You took them!" By now, Gil's shout is a bawl. "I can tell from the look on your face."

Shutters bang, and a girl's voice cries out.

"I didn't!" It's Luna.

"You put them down your sungarb and hoped I wouldn't notice." Gil again.

"No. I'd never!"

Something smashes. A jug? A mirror? Then the door slams and soon Gil's stomping down Luna's stairs and into another hut.

"There's newfruit buried under all these flowers. Fern? Isn't there?'

"They're my garlands. For completion. Don't, Gil. Be careful."

Blaze and I are standing up by now. It's all too fast for me, too loud.

There can't be anything left inside of me to bring up, but that doesn't stop me from trying. I keep on dry heaving as I figure out what's happening and why.

The stripped newfruit trees. The trampled fruit on the ground. Gil and Brook noticed. I mean, of course they did.

"Oh my Dot," is all I can think to say.

Dennis goes, "Shit." He looks sideways as though someone might tell him not to use that particular word. "Nathe always says 'shit' when things go wrong. Mom says he shouldn't but . . ."

"Shit, then," I say. "Shit shit shit shit shit."

Farther down the path, another door bangs.

Gil's voice demands, "Wren?"

I guess he's on the balcony of my hut, where I should be.

"Gil's not coming down here to the empty huts," I say to Blaze, as if saying it will make it true. "I mean, there's no reason for him to —"

Brook's voice sounds from outside, cutting across me. "Hut's empty. Wren's not here."

Then comes Gil. "Find everyone. Look everywhere until every person and every missing newfruit is found."

"Let's go."

The way Blaze says it, it's like we can just stroll out of the empty hut and tell Gil and Brook that actually yes, we have seen the missing newfruit, since he asked. In fact, I ate it.

Oh and by the way, have they met Dennis?

"Go where?" I ask him.

The escarpment? Now? Even if we went through the orchard and then the fringe, we'd never climb all the way up there without someone seeing Dennis and chasing us down.

Then I think of something.

"The roof. I've climbed the roof of my hut before. We'll go out the window, around the back where they can't see us from the path."

There it is, our whole plan, thought up in approximately two seconds. Then there's this kind of flurry as the three of us scoop up everything that's ours.

Sungarb, Dennis's device. Anything that might tell Gil and Brook exactly who has been inside the so-called empty hut.

I go first.

I forget about my foggy head and shove open the shutters. With both hands on the window frame, I haul myself up until I'm standing on it. Next I grab the lip of the roof. Another big lift, and I'm lying flat on the sloping roof panel facing away from the path, my body pressed against the wood, already hot in the morning sun.

Blaze's head pokes up over the edge of the roof about the same time as Gil, out on the path but much closer now, says, "Check the empty ones."

Blaze's entire head and shoulders appear, followed by his legs.

"Okay, Dennis," I whisper down. "You go."

"I can't."

"You can," I tell him. "Just put your feet on the window sill first."

Doors scream open and bang hard against the sides of all the empty huts.

"Nothing. Nope. Empty," Brook's saying.

I can see the top of Dennis's small head. He's on the window frame at least, which would be wonderful if Gil's feet weren't already on the balcony. Our balcony.

"Grab the edge," I say. "That's it. You've got it."

A straining noise comes out of Dennis. Hands on the roof, he's trying to lift himself from the window frame. Trying and not quite managing.

"I'll check the last ones," Gil's voice is clear and loud, like he's standing right next to me.

Blaze and I each take one of Dennis's hands, and somehow, between us, we lift Dennis off his feet onto the roof just as Gil prowls toward the door.

"The shutters." Blaze dips down and lets his right big toe kiss the shutters closed the second before Gil opens the door.

Underneath us, we hear him take a few steps and sniff. Then he goes back to the door and calls, "Brook? Come in here."

The chewed-up newfruit is right there on the floor, but Gil tears the hut apart anyway. They don't find anything else, or nothing that isn't in all the other empty huts too.

Until Gil says, "Look."

"Where was that?"

"Under the pillow."

On the roof, Blaze and I look at each other. Neither of us has a single clue what might have been under the pillow.

"Dennis?" Blaze mouths.

But Dennis just mashes his cheek against the tiles and won't say anything at all.

27

NATURALLY, EVERYONE IN CREATION has a theory about the newfruit and the empty hut. Gil has all of us crammed into the gazebo talking to Dot, pleading with her to lead us to whoever or whatever took the fruit.

But when everyone's finished talking to Dot, Fern won't leave. She just stays on her cushion staring up at Dot's portrait, winding strands of her blond hair around her index finger. She twirls so hard the hair snaps off halfway up.

"Stop doing that," I tell her.

"There's no way she'll choose me now."

Fern lets go of one clump of hair, picks up another one, and starts the whole twirling and tearing thing all over again.

"What are you talking about?"

Fern twists more savagely, exactly how I tore at the skin on my legs. For roughly the same reasons too, I'm guessing. "Dennis took them, didn't he?"

"Fern, no, he —"

"You know he did. Because I didn't do what Dot wanted. I didn't do a good job of looking after him."

"You did! No one found Dennis, right?"

Fern looks uncertain, so I push on, "You totally kept the secret. You were trying. Dot knows that."

There's a tiny flash of a smile on Fern's face. "Did she say that?"

I look away. I have to. "Um . . . no," I say. "It wasn't exactly that."

"I don't deserve to be chosen anyway."

"You're one of the nicest people in creation," I say. "Even if she tried for a million days, Dot couldn't create anyone sweeter and dotlier than you."

Fern turns to me, that prenormal smile now fixed on her tanned face. "Admit it. It doesn't matter how many garlands I make — Dot wasted her time creating me."

I want to tell her the truth. Right now, the thing I want most in creation is to reach out to Fern, give her a hug, and explain how Dot isn't real. How it looks like we only believe in her because of something called a drug, maybe made by something called the Shepherd Corporation.

Most of all, I want to tell her that Blaze and I are leaving as soon as it's prelight. How we plan to find FancyVividBlue, work out the truth, and fix everything here. And how I'm going to look for Julius.

"Can you listen to me, Fern? This is sort of complicated. Dot didn't waste her time creating you. Not at all. She doesn't —"

Fern shakes her head, swishing her long hair. "I'm going to try talking to her again. Apologize and everything."

"Fern, seriously . . ."

"If it's okay, I think I would rather be alone with Dot right now," she tells me.

So I end up having to leave Fern there, chattering on, really believing everything she says is floating up to Dot inside a bubble. Maybe that idea soothes her.

But to feel soothed, Fern has to believe in the rest of the story too, and that makes her think she's this really prenice person. There's no point explaining it to her, not yet. Blaze and I are going to need a whole lot more information to convince her and everyone else.

That's the thing about the pretruth. Once enough people believe it, it's almost impossible to change their minds.

* * *

Ever since we made it down from the roof, Dennis has been hiding in my hut. And the entire day, he's been wanting to know what Fern's doing. How long it's going to be until Fern gets here. Whether Fern's coming soon.

Then, when Fern actually turns up all ready for the completion party, Dennis doesn't seem to know what to say. He just keeps looking at her in her melon-colored sungarb, her hair swishing down her back, a garland of pink flowers circling her head.

"I love your garland," I tell her, giving her a hug. "You look so . . . um . . ."

The word Fern's expecting me to use is *dotly*. Except right now I can't quite bring myself to say it.

"Everyone loves them." She's smiling as she says this, but I can tell she's really working hard to do it. "People are saying the garlands are the dotliest things they've ever seen."

Then she asks Dennis, "Why aren't you wearing yours?"

For the first time since Fern walked into the hut, Dennis looks away from her.

"The flowers wilted, didn't they?" Fern asks. She seems to be expecting this. Her smile completely disappears. To her, Dennis's garland wilting probably seems like one more way she isn't dotly enough.

Fern takes her own garland off and starts unwinding flowers from it. She shapes them into a rough circle and puts it on Dennis's head. The garland sits there on Dennis's fluffy hair, thin and withering already.

Looking at it, Fern's practically in tears. "It was supposed to be perfect. When she collects you, I wanted her to see it."

"Sorry." Dennis can hardly talk.

Fern goes over to him and kisses him on the cheek. She leaves her face there for a while, her smooth cheek pressed up against his small, sweaty one. "You haven't done anything. *I'm* the one who didn't make it right."

It's obvious she's close to bawling.

"Should we go?" I ask.

Way off in the gazebo, I can hear dottracks playing, turned up loud enough to dance to. The air is warm and moving just enough to carry the sound of people shouting and laughing. I don't know if the completion night party is the best thing for Fern right now, but I guess I don't know how else to distract her.

"I just have to pick up Blaze on the way past."

That part gets Fern's interest. "Sure you two aren't into each other?"

"Totally, totally sure," I tell her, even as I'm wondering if we ever could be or maybe if we already are.

"Okay. Whatever you say."

Then Fern says goodbye to Dennis. She hugs him, just in case Dot comes for him while we're at the party. Dennis's face crumples, and he doesn't even pretend not to be crying.

"Keep the shutters closed till I get back, okay?" I tell Dennis.

Dennis nods. Really softly, so Fern can't hear, he says, "Are you definitely going find a way to help her when we leave?"

"We're definitely going to try."

"Don't try. You really have to do it."

I know that, I want to tell him. I'm just not sure if we can. I'm not sure about anything once we climb the escarpment and push our way through those straggly trees.

So I just say to Dennis, "Don't look out or someone might see you."

Not that Dennis is paying a whole lot of attention. I can feel him watching us, or Fern anyway, the entire time we're walking away.

28

Completion night.

It doesn't feel like it, but it's here. And when Fern, Blaze, and I get to the party, it's just the way I'd always imagined it.

Lanterns glow in the trees, and people dance on the lawn. Everyone is circling and swaying in one huge, hot mass. The dottracks are so loud I can feel them as much as I can hear them.

In the crowd, the first person I spot is Sage. She already has her sungarb off, and the lanterns turn her big, pale body all kinds of different colors. When she sees us, Sage winds her way over and grabs onto Fern. She sinks back into the crowd, taking Fern with her, leaving Blaze and me just standing there next to each other.

Apparently there's nothing either of us can think to say or do that isn't awkward.

"Dance?"

I have to suggest it. Without something to distract us, it's going to be a seriously long night.

We've already agreed we can't leave for the escarpment until the party's really going. Our strategy is to make sure everyone sees us so that later on it'll take them longer to figure out we're missing.

"I don't dance."

"It's not hard, Blaze. Anyone can do it."

"Not me."

"You so could, if you tried."

"I don't work that way," he tells me. Then he adds a kind of full stop by sitting down on the grass.

I'm partway through lowering myself down next to him when someone comes up behind me. A pair of arms closes around me, and I feel warm breath in my ear.

"Stop right there," comes Jasper's voice with a laugh. "Don't even think about sitting down. You're dancing, Wren. Right now."

Blaze turns his head so he's looking back toward the huts. In the opposite direction, basically, from me, Jasper, and the patch of lawn where everyone is dancing.

"I can't."

"You have to. It's completion night. Someone's going to be chosen! Maybe it'll be you if Dot likes your dancing."

I try to act normal so I tell Jasper, "I've got some new moves. I'm just saving them for later."

"What's wrong with your old moves? I always liked them." Jasper slides closer, his hand tugging on mine, "Come on."

Even though Blaze isn't saying anything and Jasper's saying way too much, it's Blaze I'm noticing. New leaves, snapped green twigs, cool running water. That's what he smells like tonight.

"Go," says Blaze to the air. "If you want to dance, go."

"See?" Jasper tells me. "Thank you, Blaze."

"I don't want to."

"It's happening. It's decided. Come on."

The crowd of dancers opens up and sucks us in. It's sticky-hot in there. All around me, people are smiling and waving their arms in the air, smiling completion night smiles. It's hard to breathe, impossible to hear. In my ears, there's nothing but pounding dottracks.

I belong 2 Dot, U belong to Dot, we all belong, forever and ever, we belong . . .

I guess some people are singing, but I can't actually hear their voices over the music. With their mouths gaping open, it kind of looks like they're screaming.

Jasper keeps on pushing through the crowd. Being Jasper, he wants to be right in the middle of things. That's where Brook is, and Sage too.

But Fern's nowhere.

I wave at Sage and mouth, *Where's Fern?* But she either doesn't understand or she doesn't know.

Before I can ask again, Jasper's pulling me back toward him, yelling into my ear to be dotly and start dancing.

"Have you seen Fern?" I yell back.

Suddenly I have to know where she is. If I'm going to dance, it's Fern I want dancing next to me.

My best friend, Fern, who thinks she's predotly because of something I made up.

Fern, who I'm about to leave behind in a place not created by Dot, but by something or someone called Shepherd.

I definitely don't want to be dancing with Jasper, with his loud laugh and flashing white smile.

But Fern's nowhere in the crowd of dancers. Someone's dragged all the cushions out from the gazebo and there are people lounging on them, but even there I can't see Fern.

"She's fine!" Jasper shouts. "She's having fun. Like we should be!"

"Tell me where she is."

Jasper laughs. "Only if I get a kiss." He looms up toward me, but I push him away.

"What?" he complains at the top of his voice. "It's completion night. It's the dotly thing to do!"

Anyway, I guess Jasper thinks I'm joking with my push, because he leans in again and then his face is mashed against mine, his tongue working its way between my lips.

I try pulling away, but this time Jasper's really holding me, his whole body up against mine so I can feel him, his willie and everything, under his sungarb. The only thing I can move is my head. When I turn it, there's Blaze on the grass still.

He's not looking at the huts anymore but right at Jasper and me instead.

"Fern went off with Gil. They're hooking up," Jasper yells, as the music fades down between tracks.

Brook looks up then. He seems pretty interested in what Jasper just said.

"Hooking up?" I repeat, trying to get my head around such a prenormal statement. "Fern's not into guys."

"She is now." Jasper's tongue is on the rim of my ear.

"Can you just get off?"

Jasper loosens his grip and right away I spin around.

I need to find Fern more than ever now. And I need to tell Blaze this thing with Jasper isn't a thing at all. So, using my shoulders and my elbows, I try parting the crowd, but it's hot and slow and sweaty.

By the time I make it to the edge of the grass, Blaze is already gone.

* * *

He isn't in his hut or any of the empty ones, either. So I go to my hut, thinking maybe Blaze is in there with Dennis or something. But Dennis is lying on the bed, Fern's garland still on his head. He's really interested to know what Fern's doing right now, if she's having a good time and everything. So he obviously hasn't seen her.

I cut him off to ask, "Have you seen Blaze?"

With a fingertip, Dennis touches the point of the coconut knife by his side. "Not since he brought this around."

I guess Blaze thought Dennis should have the knife with him, just in case.

It's then I think of one other place Blaze might be. I'm hoping he's there, because it could be sort of significant.

"If he comes here, can you tell him I went to the pond?"

Dennis spins a finger in one ear while he thinks about that. "Aren't there tons of ponds in this place?"

"Tell him the one that glows."

As soon as I say this, Dennis wants to know all about the glowing pond and exactly where it is and everything. I start telling him, but it comes out sort of blurty and I'm not totally sure Dennis even gets what I'm talking about. So in the end I just say, "Blaze knows which pond, okay?"

Out on the path again, I run-walk past Fern's hut and Gil's, both empty. I pass the blackened patch of grass still there from the bonfire we had forever ago.

Then I'm off the path, heading into that one particular clump of magnolia trees. I keep getting glimpses of the pond through the trees. Not the water, but the pale green glow coming off it as two long, solid legs kick the surface.

It's hardly any distance through the trees to the pond, but on the way I still manage to think up a million things I could blurt out. I could remind Blaze what Jasper's like, how it wasn't really a kiss. Or tell him it was, but not one that mattered because it only went one way.

I could even ask him why he cares so much.

If he cares, that is. But when I get to the pond and there he is, guess what? I'm not the one who starts talking.

"I worked something out."

I sit down. I put my legs into the water.

"There's no Dot."

I frown. As far as I can tell, Blaze had that figured out a long time ago. He pauses, but I don't get that precalm feeling I usually do, the one that makes me want to fill in any kind of silence. Instead I just wait for him to keep talking.

"But that doesn't mean there isn't a point. Going to the beach. Waiting for the waves to break. Eating ice cream. Everything we talked about, it's all good. But the point is doing it with someone else."

"Someone like who?"

"Maybe your someone is Julius." He kicks his legs, and the pond brightens, fades, then brightens again. "My someone is . . ." Blaze stops.

He shifts on the edge of the pond.

"Just say it. Whatever you're thinking, you can say it. It's only me."

But Blaze is literally squirming, so I tell him, "You know what? Turn around if it's easier. That way you don't have to say it straight to my face."

"I suck at this," he mutters, just as I hear people coming through the trees toward us.

Their voices are way too loud and way too familiar to ignore.

"I thought you were showing me something."

"Let's kiss first."

"I don't want to, though. I don't —"

"How do you know you don't like guys if you've never tried?"

"I just know. Really. It's how Dot made —"

Gil interrupts. "I know you took them. We found one of your garlands under the pillow in the hut."

"I didn't," Fern pleads. "You know I'd never eat a newfruit."

"Here, let me help you take this off."

"No!'

"It'll make you dotly again. It's what Dot wants."

"You're all mixed up, Gil. You think only you can hear Dot."

Those are my words coming from Fern's mouth.

Then there's this sharp little intake of breath followed by a single word.

"No!"

She starts to cry out, then her high, wavering voice stops altogether, replaced completely by Gil's.

"You'll make Dot cry if you scream."

* * *

I know exactly how it feels to have Gil's hands creep and slither all over you because you think it's what Dot wants you to do. And now those same cool hands are touching Fern.

"Relax," says Gil as Fern whimpers. "This is going to be so dotly."

I'm going into those trees. I'm going to stop Gil before anything actually happens and tell Fern about Shepherd. Make her listen this time.

I'm about to do it too, when I hear this howling coming from the trees. Or maybe screeching is a better word.

It's Dennis. Dennis with his wilted garland still on his head. "You're hurting her!"

I'm crashing through the trees now, Blaze close behind me. Gil still has Fern around the waist. Her sungarb's on the ground, all shredded and dirty. And in Dennis's hand, the coconut knife gleams as it catches the glow from the pond.

"I'm going to get you," he stammers.

But Dennis is shaking and crying so hard, he can't even swing the knife where he wants to. All he manages to do is nick Gil's forearm with the flat, sharp blade. He might be bigger than Julius, but in that moment, they're like the same person.

Both of them too young to look after themselves.

Both of them needing my help.

"Who's this?" Gil asks, not even flinching as he presses a finger over the cut on his arm.

"It has nothing to do with you." Fern's voice comes out tight and shrill. "It's between me and Dot."

Dennis is frozen. He's gawking at Gil's arm.

"I'm in trouble, aren't I?"

That's when Gil takes the coconut knife from Dennis. It's easy. Dennis is so spun out he just uncurls his grip and lets Gil wrap his own fingers around the handle. The blade arcs through the air.

A split-second before it happens, I realize what he's about to do. Gil drives the blade into Dennis's neck. Dennis stumbles back, so the blade doesn't go in as far as Gil would've wanted.

At first, Dennis doesn't doing anything. It's like he doesn't even realize. It's only when Gil allows his arm to return to his side that Dennis yowls and blood starts pumping out of the yawning red slash in his neck.

Dennis's hand goes up to the wound. While it's there, the gushing stops. But then he pulls his hand away and blood keeps flowing. Fern screams as Dennis's chin tucks into his chest. He wobbles on his feet, gasps for air, and then crumples.

He hits the ground and stays there.

Fern starts beating on Gil's chest with balled-up fists.

Somehow, though, Gil's speaking quite clearly. He even sounds happy. "Anything predotly must be crushed."

"He isn't predotly. You don't get it! *I* was looking after him. Dot wanted me to. She told Wren."

Wham, wham, wham. Gil sounds hollow where Fern hits him. His hand lifts, fingers firming up their grip on the coconut knife.

"Get back, Fern." I'm kind of surprised to hear my own voice.

She turns to me. Sweet, round face, half a garland on her head, and a butterfly dipping and fluttering around her. "I'm going to be chosen. Dot's coming down, and she's going to choose me." She says it firmly, like that will make it true.

"You're not. No one is," I tell her. "Look around. It's completion night, and Dot's not here." Softly, I say, "Why? Because there is no Dot."

On the ground, Dennis makes a rasping, gurgling sound. I want to kneel down and scoop him up, run off with him and Blaze.

Save him.

But I can't do that until Fern knows — really understands — the truth.

I work hard at sounding calm. "The Books are written by someone called Shepherd. It even says so on the last screen. I can show you."

Fern's face is just totally uncomprehending.

"Me and Blaze are leaving. With Dennis. We're going right now."

It's the most serious blurt I've ever had, and now that I need to make the most sense, I feel like I'm making the least.

"You need to come too." I grab Fern, and I can feel my fingernails gouging her soft skin. "You can't stay. Obviously. Not after what Gil just tried to do."

It seems like Fern's working hard to sort her thoughts into something resembling sense. "Oh my Dot," she says to me. "*You're* the one who's predotly. How come I didn't get that? I should have . . . I just never thought my own best friend would —"

Blaze says, "We need to go."

"Fern's coming. She has to."

Gil turns toward me. The coconut knife is pointed right at my chest.

"Fern, come on," I plead. "Come with us."

And then my best friend says, "Anything predotly must be crushed."

29

"WREN!" BLAZE YELLS. "Leave her! We have to go."

"No!" I practically spit it at him.

"Fern isn't coming."

I know that. Something inside me accepts that I'm going to have to work on helping Fern later, from the outside. But there's a bigger problem.

"Dennis. We're not leaving him."

Not again. I can't let it happen again.

Blaze grabs me and tries to yank me away. Doesn't he get it? Dennis is small. Dennis is hurt. He needs me. But at that exact moment, I feel cold metal on my skin. The knife.

I scream. My arms wheel toward Gil. My hands make fists and then . . .

If you've never felt your knuckles driving into someone's eyes, then seriously, I wouldn't recommend it. It's not the best. I don't mean that it doesn't work, because it does. For me, at least.

My knuckles find Gil's eyes, and there's this squelching feeling. The coconut knife falls blade-first to the ground. Gil's yelling and Fern's screaming. Dennis is still slumped on the ground, but I can't stop or do anything apart from run.

Blaze and I head for the escarpment. If I semi-closed my eyes and shut off everything inside my head, I can almost believe it's Fern beside me instead of Blaze. We could be running from the huts to the lagoon back on the day that everything changed.

Only Fern isn't beside me. I've left her behind, with Gil and Dennis. I'm running away, and nothing is right. Nothing is fixed.

The whole way across the lawn, Blaze and I seem to be collecting butterflies. I hardly register them at first, but soon there are a lot of them. As in, masses, moving together in one great big cloud exactly like they did that time in the hut.

From the completion night party comes the sound of more voices — people yelling, their feet hammering the ground as they run toward us.

Everything predotly must be crushed.

The words echo all around us. I don't stop or turn around to look. I don't need to. I can already imagine Luna's and Jasper's and Brook's faces, lit by the flaming torches they've ripped from the ground beside the paths. It's like I can read their actual thoughts.

Tonight is completion night. Catch the two predotly ones, and it could be me who's chosen. I could be the one!

Every tree shivers with birds lifting off the branches as we run past.

Deer and mice scatter, eyes catching the moonlight, giving them a split-second glow. The first rocks begin to pound into our backs as we reach the lagoon, exploding around us as our feet slap the rocky ground.

We start climbing the face of the escarpment. Me first, with Blaze behind me, just as the pale shape of Gil comes hurtling through the avocado trees. I haul myself up. I try to, anyway, but clinging to the rock makes my fingers feel too spindly-weak. I suddenly imagine my body sprawled on the ground, blood pooling around me. It's just like when I froze on the rocks by the side of the lagoon forever ago.

Fall from the escarpment now, and that's what's going to happen. And now I know for sure my head won't repair itself. Dot won't lift me up and carry me off to everlasting happiness beyond the trees.

My skull will be split, and that will be the end of it. As in, the end. Nothingsville. That's it.

A hunk of rock spins by me and clips my ear. I yelp as it smashes on the escarpment beside me. I look down to see shards of rock showering Blaze's head.

He yells, "Keep going. You can't stop." His face is straining, his whole body sweating, fingers and toes white with the effort of heaving his big body up the escarpment.

More rocks explode around us. I turn and see that it's Fern throwing them. Luna's beside her and Jasper too now, his white teeth flashing like an animal's in the moonlight.

I don't see Brook, but I guess he's somewhere nearby since Gil's directly below us now, reaching for a handhold on the face of the escarpment.

"Move," Blaze yells, and so I do.

I have to. There's no choice but to climb faster and not think about falling.

I reach the ledge with its scrappy bushes and loose stones. But as fast as we climb, Gil climbs faster. His silver head is just below Blaze's feet now. Gil's hands are almost grazing his heels. So I grab a rock from the ledge.

Just like Fern, I pitch it. The rock makes contact with Gil's head, and he grunts but hangs on all the same. I guess Gil thinks he has Dot on his side. The idea of it makes him strong.

* * *

Gil has Dot, but I have other things pushing me forward. The instinct to survive this, obviously.

Come back for Dennis.

Then there's Blaze and there's Fern. We have to help her. We have to get out and help them. All of them.

There's strength in my arms and legs as I propel myself up the rockface. I'm a good climber — not because Dot created me that way. I can climb because that's what I've worked at. Climbing is what I've chosen for myself.

It's all these things that get me up the rockface. Then I'm over the lip of the escarpment and on my feet, hurling rocks at Gil. One smashes into his cheekbone. He makes this barking sound and loses his footing. He slips. At least I think he does.

He yells out for Brook, who for once is nowhere around as far as I can see. It's hard to tell exactly because it's prelight, and there's still that cloud of butterflies circling around my head.

I slap the butterflies away, and my hand brushes this purple one. My fingers close around it, and its glowing eye shines a green light through my bunched fist. Its wings buzz and whirr against my skin.

I open my hand and just before the thing flies away I see there are words on its hard body, raised up so I can make out the letters with my fingers.

Shepherd Corporation.

Blaze's hands appear over the lip. He half-climbs and I half-lift him over the top. His face is smeared with sweat as he scrambles to his feet. We cross the cold, black rock and run for the tree line as the butterflies circle and angry voices rise up from the lagoon below.

Over the wire with its Shepherd Corporation tags.

Through the straggly trees, toward the moving lights and low rushing sounds of the cars.

Any moment, it's going to be official. We'll be out of here. The two of us are going to be free.

Only it doesn't feel the way I thought it would. There's so much unfinished. We've left way too much behind.

30

A VOICE CALLS OUT, "There!"

Light streaks across the ground, bends around the trees, and knifes me in the eyes. From beyond the tree line, two figures run straight for me. Their faces are covered, their sungarb stiff and black and heavy. Close by, dogs bark.

Then, a low, clear *pock* sound.

"Wren!" Blaze yells.

The warning is too late. My forehead stings. A cloud of white fills the air around me, and I can't see Blaze anymore. I can't see anything. My eyes are raw and burning at the same time. Sensation pulses in my head, radiating out and down from that one point on my forehead. Now I'm doubled over, clawing at my eyes and screaming.

"That'll do it," that same voice says. Heavy hands haul me up. "You with us, Viva?"

Whoever he is, he knows my name. As in, my dream name. Not that

I can answer him. I can't even talk. My entire face stings, and my lips are numb.

But the voice isn't bothered, not at all.

"This way."

And then I'm walking. Or trying to walk. My arms are heavy, and my legs can't seem to hold me. The figure from beyond the trees, one of them at least, is carrying me now. I hear these moaning, choking sounds from behind me, and I figure they must be coming from Blaze. They're getting quieter the farther we go, but I can't turn to see what's happening behind me.

I can't even scratch my face, which feels like it's crawling with hot, red, biting bugs or something.

A long, low building rises up before us. Doors open, and all this white light floods out. Framed in the doorway is a cluster of people in blue sungarb.

Even through stinging eyes I can see their sungarb. They're these prenormal loose things printed all over with the letter S and a design I've seen before.

A long stick with a hook at one end.

Around their necks they're wearing cords with white rectangles dangling from them.

One leans close to me, and I see his rectangle has a picture of a face and underneath that, some words.

Alexander Reynolds – Medical

"How many did you fire?"

Behind me, one of the figures from the trees laughs.

"At her? She only needed one. Cap hit her right between the eyes and she was like . . . *boom!*" His hands slam together with a cracking sound. "All over."

"The guy?"

"Two."

Another laugh. "Three, tops. He's a solid unit, that one."

"Viva, can you hear me?" the man with the thing around his neck says. His voice is soft. "I'll look after you now. I'm Alex."

He takes me from the figure who's carrying me, muttering, "Couldn't you do anything?"

"Such as?"

When Alex doesn't answer, the man carrying me says, "It's safe, right? Non-lethal. Designed especially for the Grace trial."

Together, we move through the double doors and into the light.

"Doesn't make it pleasant," Alex snaps.

The man mutters something like, "I did my best."

"Blaze!" I yell.

But I don't think it comes out sounding like that. And anyway, it's too late because the doors swing closed behind us, shutting out the prelight and the figures and Blaze too.

* * *

I'm in a long hall of light. Everything is stark. Footsteps squeal on gleaming floors. On the walls, a hundred rectangles of color dazzle me. *Monitors?* I can't say. I can't see clearly. I can't even *think* clearly.

Where's Blaze? Where have they taken him?

"There's going to be bruising from the impact," Alex is saying. "The gas will make you disoriented for twenty-four hours at least."

He doesn't mention the red-hot insects, my swollen throat, or the tugging feeling behind my eyes, as though someone's yanking them from the inside.

"You're just over here," he says as he opens another door and passes into a blue room beyond. Inside, I'm semi-aware of a bed and a chair.

Alex helps me to the bed. There are rustles and whooshes as he fills a tiny cup with water and carefully rinses my eyes. He gives me capsules and more water to drink, drapes something heavy and soft over me.

At some point, I guess he leaves. The one thing I notice for sure is the firm click of the door followed by three loud beeps.

* * *

I'm clinging to the escarpment. Underneath the cold rock, my fingernails feel brittle, and the skin on my hands is shredded and torn. I'm trying my hardest to climb, but I can't move. I'm stuck to the rock like a creature in a shell. Rocks pummel the escarpment all around me, cracking apart and showering me with dust and stinging pebbles.

I turn to see who's throwing them, and it's Fern.

"Stop it!" I yell.

But she won't. She's standing there laughing, Gil's arm around her.

I swing around again and continue climbing. Someone else is standing on top of the escarpment.

It's Mom. She's exhausted, prehappy, crying. "I told you not to get involved in this, Viva."

"I'm sorry," I yell. "Can you help me up?"

But Mom only shakes her head. "It's too late."

As she says this, two tiny figures slip over the edge of the escarpment. Hand in hand, they tumble through the air.

One in red fuzzy sungarb and the other in stripes . . .

That image fades, and then I'm on the beach, standing right where the water meets the sand. Tongues of waves lick my feet, and beside me there's someone digging his toes into the sand.

"We need to go now," says Blaze. And he walks into the sea. Water swirls around his ankles and then his calves and his thighs. He turns. "Are you coming or what?"

"I'm coming," I tell him.

Blaze laughs, twists at the hips, and opens his arms. "Okay, then. Let's go."

But it's like on the rocks by the lagoon. I can't seem to move.

"I'm trying," I squeak.

Blaze lifts his hand and waves. Hurry up? Goodbye? I can't tell. The sun is sinking behind him, lighting him up in a haze of gold.

"Don't leave me!"

But Blaze is already melting into the sunlight.

* * *

I'm sweating. Inside me, everything is pounding. I try opening my eyes, but the lids are all puffed and heavy. The most I can manage is a tiny crack.

I'm in the blue room.

All alone.

I immediately think of Blaze. Is he close? How much time has gone by since I last saw him? Since everything happened with Dennis? It could be a moment or it could be hundreds of days. I want to haul myself off the bed, charge through the door, and find them both, but my limbs feel liquidy, my head spongy, and my tongue swollen in my mouth.

It's a while before I even notice there are two people in my room, Alex and a girl I don't recognize.

"When were they exposed?" the girl asks.

Alex glances at a circular object on the wall.

Clock.

Here, beyond the trees, my head is suddenly filling with new but familiar words.

"Sixteen hours. Not even. They'll be feeling ugly still. That's my professional diagnosis, anyway."

Ugly. That's the exact word for the way my head feels right now. Kind of like it's going to burst.

The girl's oval face bunches. "But the gas is completely safe —"

"And specially formulated for the Grace trial," Alex says. "I think we can all see how well that's worked out."

The girl turns her back and starts fiddling with a transparent bag filled with dark yellow liquid that's attached to me by a tube. "You mean the boy? There was no way to know he'd trespass into a restricted area."

"They could have amped up the security," Alex is saying. "It doesn't bother you that a nine-year-old could get through the gate so easily? It's almost like they wanted him to."

An indignant sound comes from the girl's snub nose. "He was a technology nut."

"He was a kid posing as his big brother on some hack computer forum. That hardly makes him a genius."

And suddenly I get it. They're talking about Dennis.

The girl smooths her blond curls. Her lips are the color of figs. She and Alex are the only things alive in this box of a room with its stale, cool air gushing from the ceiling.

Unless you count me, which right now I don't.

"The helicopter didn't find him. That's not odd to you?"

Helicopter, I think. That's the word — not *hector*.

"Children go missing. They die. It's sad, but it happens." The girl taps the device around her wrist. "Don't you read the news?"

"I do. I just don't believe it most of the time."

The girl sniffs. "You sound like one of those Circle people."

If I ever had a grasp of this conversation, I've definitely lost it now. *Circle people*? I have no idea who or what they might be. Alex seems to know though, because there's a little smile forcing its way onto his face.

"You know a lot of them, do you? You hang out together all the time, I bet."

"You work here, Alex. You take Lainie Shepherd's money, which is a whole lot more than most intern salaries. That makes you part of the Grace project."

"One of Dot's disciples, you could say."

There's a silence, which isn't actually silent since it's filled with all these beeps and hums from the equipment in the room.

"Think they'll take Grace to market?" Alex asks.

"With these results? Of course."

"You count this as a good result?"

"It was a trial. No one projected one-hundred-percent efficacy. Hiccups are part of developing any new medication."

"Hiccups. That's one word for it."

From underneath my swollen lids I see Alex hold up his right hand and tap each finger in sequence.

"Side effects including everything from blurred vision to suicidal ideation. Two non-responders. One hyper-responder who, stop me if I'm getting the details wrong, attempted rape, then stabbed a child."

"You'd scrap the entire concept of Delusion Onset Therapy for a few statistical aberrations?"

The girl's head is still except for the smallest quiver of her curls. "Grace is going to be a game-changer," she says. "There are plenty of depressed and anxious people out there, people searching for meaning. And the world is ready for an update on the bearded old man in sandals model."

"Grace is going to be a game-changer for Lainie Shepherd's bank balance, so who cares about a few *hiccups*?"

But the girl isn't letting Alex get away with that.

"The Grace implant is near-perfect. You know that. If you exclude trial participants with unusual blips in their gene sequence, this is a flawless example of a drug-induced delusion. Participants even formed delusional memories, Alex."

Alex steps toward my blue-sheeted bed.

"Let's check in with our trial participant over here." It's like he knows I can hear him.

Through flickering eyelids, I see he's consulting the white thing strapped around my wrist. "Viva, a.k.a Participant F37, Clinical Trial 1 of 2018. The Shepherd Corporation values your feedback. How's Delusion Onset Therapy working out for you? Not so great, huh? Unexplained memories coming back? Check. Thoughts about killing yourself? Check. Unwanted sexual contact? Check. Bad luck your particular set of genes was less than compatible with our wonderful product."

"She is going to be fine," the girl says firmly. "The lab has already developed a new implant for both non-responders. They will re-enter the trial at Phase 2 to confirm that it's safe."

Another non-responder? It has to be Blaze.

She checks the clock. "Let's just get on with this check-up."

Alex shakes his head. He sticks his hand into his pocket. "I need a cigarette first."

"You're not supposed to —"

"What, are you going to tell on me?"

The curly-haired girl doesn't seem to be listening to Alex's scoffing. If she is, she isn't responding. She just opens up one of my eyelids with a thumb, shines a light into my eye, and makes a note of what she sees.

"Religion is the opiate of the masses," Alex says. "Heard that?"

"Everyone's heard that," the girl snaps.

"Lainie Shepherd was just the first one to use it as a marketing idea."

The girl drops her little light with a clatter. "Maybe she's one of the few people who knows the *whole* quote."

She studies Alex, kind of challenging him to tell her what it is. When he doesn't, she gives this long, labored sigh, like the whole thing is just so simple she can't believe Alex doesn't know.

"Marx also said, 'religion is the heart of a heartless world.' Believing gives people something to hope for; even he could see that."

"That's Lainie," says Alex. "Sprinkling her magical hope dust wherever she goes."

31

THIS TIME WHEN I WAKE UP, my eyes open almost the entire way.

The blue room is a whole lot less swimmy. I'd even say I felt more like me, if I knew exactly who *me* was. I mean, am I Wren, Viva, or someone in between? Did Dot create me? If she didn't, how did I get here? Wherever *here* is.

Then my door opens. Someone's coming into my room.

Blaze? I imagine he's found me somehow. That he knows where we are and how to get out.

But instead of Blaze, there's a man standing in the doorway with his hands on a kind of wheeled chair. He's all dressed in blue, just like Alex and that girl were, with the same rectangle on a cord around his neck. But this guy has hair on his chin, covered by a sort of puffy, gauzy mesh. The prenormal thing — the *weird* thing — is that there's absolutely no hair on his head.

"I know," he says, catching me gawking. "I'm a mess in this get-up. Health regs. Can't contaminate our participants with a stray beard hair." He pats the seat of the chair, "Ready for a little ride?"

I prop myself up on my elbow. Could I run for it? Vault out of bed, past the man, and away down that bright, white hall with its flashing screens? If I am still here, then Blaze must be around somewhere too. And if I can find him, then maybe we can go find Dennis. If it isn't too late.

The man's hulking, rounded shape takes up almost the entire doorway. The more I think about escaping, the more he seems to expand, blocking the exit. "Okay there, Viva?"

I'm mute.

"You're going to the executive wing." He hoists me off my bed and into the chair. "God herself wants to see you."

The man pushes me out of the blue room and into the long, straight hall. The entire way, my head moves to each door we pass.

Is Blaze behind that door?

This one?

I can't ask, because the man just keeps on talking. His name is Jordy, he says, and he's an *orderly*. At least, I think that's what he says, because the whole time we're walking, the screens all along the hall are blaring at me too. The effect is overwhelming, but I find myself listening to the voice from the screens.

Half of all respondents agree: shame and suffering are yesterday's news!

There are pictures on the screens. Two teenage boys holding hands. A girl slicing at her arms with a small knife.

Announcing a sexy new player set to shake things up. Grace — a fun, convenient, and modern way to fill that aching spiritual void!

Jordy keeps pushing but slower. He's still talking about something called a *wart*, which he just had frozen off of his toe, but it's like he doesn't expect me to listen. The screens on the walls show the newfruit grove.

Grace is all-natural. It's extracted from a super-fruit called newfruit, developed exclusively by the Shepherd Corporation, then concentrated many thousands of times.

A smiling girl holds a tiny object between her thumb and forefinger. She turns and looks at it with delighted surprise.

The Grace formula enters the bloodstream via a discreet implant in the neck. It targets the frontal lobe to create a powerful belief in a brand-new divine creator. It's called Delusion Onset Therapy.

I see words on the screen. DELUSION ONSET THERAPY. Then most of the words disappear, leaving just three letters.

DOT.

I guess I make a kind of gurgling noise, because Jordy says, "All right down there?"

I shake my head side to side. "Stop," I manage to croak.

And Jordy does. He parks me near a screen. I'm staring at it so hard my eyes practically drill holes in it.

> *DOT is the result of countless hours of consumer testing. A seamless blend of ethnicities, DOT is designed for maximum appeal to today's global consumer. DOT is the deity troubled folks will love to love!*

Now the smiling girl appears on the screen dressed in the kind of sungarb I recognize, bright purple silk with a silver trim. Her long hair swings down her back so her neck's all covered up.

> *One hundred eager volunteers are going to prove it. They'll live for a year in Shepherd's luxurious testing facility, modeled on the original Garden of Eden but brought into the 21st century with a lagoon-style swimming pool, declawed exotic animals, five-star accommodation, organic food, and inspirational music.*

The girl walks through a grove of trees blazing with multicolored blossoms. She pauses, picks a single, perfect silver fruit, and slips it into a picking bag.

> *Throughout the trial, simple, enjoyable tasks will give volunteers purpose. Otherwise, our lucky one hundred are free to enjoy themselves as they please.*

A guy walks into the picture. He and the girl join hands and wriggle off their sungarb.

Our volunteers will experience none of the usual prohibitions on natural human desires. No shame or sin or fear. We've even developed a whole new vocabulary, removing all negativity. Volunteers won't endure darkness; they'll revel in the prelight! And they'll never think of themselves as stupid, sick, or miserable. Instead, they'll never feel presmart, prehealthy, or prehappy — thanks to Dot! Plus, volunteers won't worry about physical attractiveness. Nudity is celebrated as the wonderful, natural state that it is. All bodies are beautiful according to the Books of Dot, our extensively focus-grouped manual for believers.

The couple disappears, and the rectangle changes to show a perfect cloudless sky.

In the unlikely event of a death during the trial, volunteers will pass away peacefully, believing totally in a blissful place beyond the trees, where life continues eternally.

A string of flashing words appear on the screen.

Grace truly is a total belief solution! The formula will soon be available nationwide. And while teens are the core target, the formula also works on adults and the elderly! In months to come, stand by for a new product in the Grace range, specifically designed for infants . . .

Jordy's voice snaps me back. "Moments away," he's saying. He starts pushing again. "Can't watch corporate propaganda all day," he explains. "God hates to be kept waiting."

We reach a thick set of doors. Jordy waves a card at them, and they open. He wheels me through, and the doors close soundlessly.

Beyond the doors, there's another door. And for a moment, Jordy and I are alone in this small, airless space. Now is the time to ask him. Ask him if everything on the screens is true. Ask him if he knows where Blaze is and what happened to Dennis.

But there's so much I don't know, I have trouble figuring out where to start. And before I can even open my mouth, the second door opens and a girl appears and ushers us through.

She murmurs into a tiny black thing clipped over her ear so it hovers just in front of her mouth. She nods at Jordy but apparently can't be bothered to smile.

The place beyond the doors is still and plush. There's thick, pale stuff on the floor.

Carpet. And instead of being glaring white, like the hall, the walls here are sky blue with a pattern of clouds. I don't notice right away, because it's so soft, but there's music playing too. Soothing, gentle, floaty sounds.

The little piece of fight inside me drains away, leaving behind a brand-new feeling. Awe, I guess you'd call it.

"Special delivery," says Jordy to the sour-faced girl. Before vanishing through the doors he tells me, "I'll love you and leave you. Good luck, Viva."

"Ms. Shepherd is waiting for you," the girl tells me.

She takes the handles of the chair, the same ones Jordy was holding, not really wanting to touch them, by the looks of it. She steers me through a billowing gauze curtain. Beyond that is a huge, pale, curved room with a woman at the other end, sitting on a golden, saucer-shaped chair.

I'm too busy staring at the woman in front of me, all alone in this strange curved space, to notice the girl disappearing.

Have I seen this woman before? Somehow I can see the two of us together, in a place as bright and white as the hall I've just come from.

Her hands are stacked neatly in her lap. She lifts one and leans forward, holding it out to me. Thanks to Dennis, I know what to do.

I grasp her hand, the cool, soft skin, and pump it up and down.

"Lainie Shepherd," the woman says.

She angles her face forward and down. She smiles, and I see an image, a flash of those lips forming a bunch of words.

You look worn out . . . no wonder, with everything you've been through . . . I have an idea . . . a trial . . . recruiting volunteers now . . . no, no, absolutely free . . . I'll send the literature to your device . . . talk it over with your mother . . .

Lainie Shepherd's sungarb is the opposite of any I can remember ever seeing. It seems soft like silk, but it's thicker, and black as the center of Fern's or Gil's eyes. It comes right up her neck, then rolls over itself again. Instead of loose and billowy, Lainie Shepherd's sungarb is fitted close to her. Over the top, Lainie Shepherd is wearing some type of shiny garland.

Necklace.

It has a silver chain, and from the exact middle point there's a sparkling hook with a long handle. The hook itself is silver, but the very tip is studded with a fat blue stone, glittering with different colored lights. The way those chips of light flicker and dance, I can't stop looking at them.

"It's a blue diamond. Very rare," she says when she catches me staring. "This particular cut is known as Fancy Vivid Blue."

She picks up the hook and turns it over.

"Or do you already know that? The technicians couldn't tell me how much information had broken through the delusion. The drug was intended to last the entire length of the trial! You non-responders were the exception. You and Luke."

She flips the hook again, throwing rainbow speckles all over my chair.

"In case you don't recognize it, this is a shepherd's crook. They're not usually diamond-set. This one was a little present to myself to mark Phase 1 of the trial."

There's a slithering sound as Lainie Shepherd uncrosses, then crosses her legs. Her legs aren't a normal skin color. They're tinted the same dark shade as her sungarb. That is because of her *tights*, I realize.

Lainie touches a fingertip to her shoulder. She picks at the fabric, trying to remove a spot of something that isn't even there. She smooths her already smooth hair, cut to her chin in a bob and glossy as newfruit.

"That might give you some idea of how important Grace is to this company. You and the other clinical trial participants are part of the greatest innovation in the treatment of depression and anxiety ever to go to market. This therapy is going to help millions of people just like you. Billions, potentially. Spiritual belief is one of the best predictors of a fulfilled and happy life. Did you know that? Only, our core target audience is just a little too savvy for any of the existing products."

On the chair beside Lainie, there's a small, round table. On top of that, a bowl of newfruit, which accounts for the honey-vanilla smell that fills the room.

"It's difficult to believe something so small could be so powerful, isn't it?" She takes a newfruit from the bowl, handling it as carefully as any of Dot's creations would, examining every one of its little silver freckles.

"Unfortunately, in your case, not powerful enough." Lainie smiles. "Thanks to our genes, we all metabolize drugs differently. Grace turned out to be less effective for you." She pauses. "Or, if you like, you were better at fighting it off. Information from your past broke through the delusion when it should have been totally suppressed. Just bits and pieces, I'm assured, but enough to create doubt and confusion."

She tips her head to one side and smiles again. "It must have been very difficult for you." Lainie gets up. Instead of windows, she has gigantic curved screens fixed to the walls, stretching all the way from the ceiling to the floor. Lainie waves a hand in front of them, and at once I see the old, familiar lawn. Even though I know I'm not there, it's like I'm looking across the rocky plain at the top of the escarpment and beyond that, into creation itself.

"You must miss it. You were happy there. At the beginning of the trial, at least." Lainie waves her hand again. Now the screens divide into thousands of smaller squares. Inside each one is a little Wren, dancing, swimming, laughing, hooking up. Everything I ever said or did in the garden is playing back in front of me.

"The butterfly drones capture footage twenty-four hours a day," says Lainie. "The Books are quite accurate when they say Dot is always watching. There's a complete library of footage of all trial participants."

When Lainie waves her hand again, I see she's right. There are pictures of the gazebo and the lagoon. People horseback riding and sleeping in their huts. And as well as all the ordinary, everyday stuff, there's me supporting Dennis on our first trip from the lagoon to the empty hut.

There's Gil smashing up hut after hut. Gil and his cool fingers all over Fern. Gil, Dennis, and the coconut knife. All of it, captured.

I utter my first words since getting here. "You knew Dennis was there the whole time?" It comes out in a whisper.

I'm still trying to catch up with what this Lainie Shepherd is telling me, with everything I saw on the screens. I'm still trying to understand how it could be true.

The blue diamond at Lainie's chest sparkles. *Fancy Vivid Blue*, I think.

Another thought occurs to me.

"You *sent* Dennis?"

"Not Dennis in particular," she says. "I simply seeded small amounts of information on several forums. It happened to be Dennis whose interest I piqued." Lainie is calm. She sits perfectly still in her golden chair. "The footage indicated that you and Luke were fighting off the drug," she goes on. "That's certainly how it looked. But we had to be sure. I could hardly interrupt a multibillion dollar clinical trial and just walk up and ask you, could I?"

"So you watched while Gil . . ."

"Don't be upset about Dennis. We believe he is fine, although he wasn't on-site when we searched."

"He was bleeding. He wasn't moving!"

"My actions seem wrong to you."

I think of Gil and me, of Gil and Fern. I think of twisting and clawing my skin until it bled. The time I almost jumped from the escarpment to make everything stop.

My head fills up with newly remembered words to describe Lainie's actions. *Hideous. Revolting. Sick.*

"This is overwhelming for you," Lainie says. "But you need to trust me. I created you — or Wren at least. Your happiness is my greatest preoccupation." She lets out a tinkling three-note laugh. "Even if it doesn't seem that way to you right now."

A billion questions pop into my head. Arguments might be a better word.

What about kindness? Dot's supposed to be kind to all her creations. What happened to Fern and Dennis? None of it was kind.

But Lainie Shepherd is so smooth and cool and perfect that it's impossible to ask.

Lainie's on her feet now. "Try not to let little inconsistencies bother you," she says. "Accept Dot's comfort, and don't upset yourself asking why things are as they are. There are reasons for everything, but they're for me to know. Everything's wonderful, truly. You'll see that. Have faith in me."

In the room, something chimes.

"Hear that? The newfruit harvest is in," Lainie says. "We're making more implants for Phase 2 of our trial. All thanks to the efforts of our wonderful Phase 1 volunteers!"

Lainie walks toward me. She perches on the arm of my chair and puts a hand on top of my head. She gives it three quick pats before saying, "I have some really wonderful news."

She waits for me to say something like *What?* or *Tell me!* But I keep quiet and look at the plush floor.

So Lainie goes on, "I'd like to show you something before I tell you what it is." She waves a hand at her screens and brings up image after image of all creation. The huts, the lagoon, the gazebo. Only this time, everything is deserted, empty. Everyone is gone.

Lainie smiles at the surprise on my face. She waves her hand again, and now I see where everyone is. Images flash up of Jasper, Luna, Sage, Fern, Gil, Brook, and everyone else, sprawled out on beds in blue rooms, exactly like the one I've been in.

I gasp.

Lainie laughs. "They're only asleep." She pauses. "Or comatose, if you like. The trial implants were designed to last a year. Our medical team has placed the volunteers in medically induced comas while their brains process the sudden shift in reality. After that, the participants will be released back to their old lives."

Their old lives? For the first time I understand that every one of Dot's creations has mothers, history, and memories. Like me.

"Phase 1 of the trial is over, you see. Completion night has come and gone." She laughs again. "You must be wondering why no one's been chosen."

I start to shake my head, but it doesn't stop Lainie.

"I *have* chosen, though. Can you guess who? It's you! You and Luke. Your unique physiologies mean you can help us test a new, stronger version of Grace. You see? You've been chosen to do Dot's work."

So it is me after all. Of all one hundred of us, I am one of the chosen.

This might sound prenormal — *strange* — but a little thrill passes through me, even with everything I now know. I can't help it, and I don't understand it.

All I can say is, it's hard reshaping everything you believe. Even when you think you've done it, your old ideas have this habit of popping up to make you doubt yourself.

Lainie scans my face. "You're not convinced."

Can she see the billion things I'm thinking of inside my head?

Blaze, who might disappear in a haze of light if I don't go after him.

Dennis, so small and scared, the coconut knife in his hand. Dennis, who has to be *somewhere*. Dennis, who I need to find and protect.

"No." I don't even know I'm going to say it before I do. And the word might be very soft, but it's also clear. "I don't want to."

"There's nothing to be afraid of. Shepherd's research chemists are excellent. The very best. They've already formulated a brand new version of Grace for you for Phase 2. We could use your help with the babies. Can you imagine all those empty huts full of children?"

"I don't want it. Unchoose me. I want to go —"

Where, exactly? Who with?

"There's an implant for Luke too. By tomorrow morning, your belief in Dot will be completely restored."

"Luke? Where is he? Let me see him."

Lainie reaches down and rolls up the sleeve of the floppy blue sungarb I'm wearing. She traces the outline of my dotmarks with her fingertip, then settles back on the arm of my chair.

"I assume you haven't recovered any memory about how you got these. Julius? The fire?"

I blink my answer. No.

"I understand a boy named Hunter Keogh was involved, if that helps jog your memory."

32

I WAKE UP COUGHING. I'm lying on the grass beside this big blue shape. It's just like the lagoon, except the edges are straight and the bottom is completely flat.

Swimming pool.

There are rings floating on the surface of it as well as animals — these squat blue and yellow things that kind of look like legless horses. It's hard to see exactly, because everything is completely wreathed in smoke.

There's a body laid out beside me on the grass. The gorgeous guy whose name, I guess, is Hunter. Next to him, a pile of sungarb — *clothes* — is all tangled together. A dry wind is blowing, and flakes of ash twist and float in the air.

Everything is lit up orange, and there's a solid heat coming from the big white hut thing on the lawn.

House.

Instead of shutters, the windows have shiny squares of glass in rows, one on top of the other. In the upper row, way off the ground, the windows are glowing from the inside.

I see myself, the version of me who calls herself Viva, standing there looking up at those windows.

Suddenly I'm shaking Hunter awake and shouting at him. "There's a fire! My house is on fire!" Like that fact isn't totally, completely, immediately obvious.

Then Hunter's on his feet, and he's groping for his clothes. At the same time, he's tapping the device around his wrist. "The whole upstairs," he says into it. "Yeah, the roof."

I shriek, "Tell them Julius is inside!"

But whoever Hunter's talking to, he's already giving them that information.

"Yeah, her brother. Like, six, I think?"

There's a bang followed by a shattering sound. Where there used to be glass in one of the windows, now there's just this big, jagged hole. Hunter is sweating. His face is streaked with ash, his hair plastered to his head.

He thinks we should go, that's obvious.

I ignore him. I cross the lawn toward the house, and soon I'm bent over, coughing, but I keep on moving. I see myself putting my hand on the door, then yanking it back because I guess it's hot or something. So I bump my hip and shoulder into the door and open it that way.

This shimmering, hazy whoosh of air blasts out, and I stagger backward. Outside, the night is starting to fill with a whining sound. It's getting louder, ridiculously loud, and Hunter's yelling at me to get out because the fire truck is on its way.

Obviously I'm not listening. I just get back up and go inside the big white hut. The house where I — Viva — used to live.

Inside, everything's black. But it doesn't matter because I have to close my eyes against the smoke anyway. I'm kind of feeling my way along, through this big open room with sinks and cupboards, then out into a hall with a staircase in it.

My feet are on the bottom step. The fire roars like some kind of big cat in the night, and there are all these shattering noises as the lights on the roof explode, raining shards of glass down on my head, sprinkling them in my hair. The entire time, the only noise I can really concentrate on is this little voice calling my name.

"I'm coming to get you," I yell back. "Julius, can you hear me?"

He doesn't answer, so now I'm not sure whether or not he knows I'm in the house, or whether it's even Julius's voice I can hear. On the wall above my shoulder there are pictures of Julius and me. The glass has shattered, and the pictures themselves are curling and buckling and blistering in the heat.

The two of us are disappearing.

"Viva! Veeeeev-va . . ." calls the little voice, which may or may not even be real. "Help!"

"I'm coming," I say.

I try putting my foot on the second step, but I can't do it. There's heat and smoke and flames pouring down the stairs, building a solid wall in front of me. All the way up the stairs, the lights and the pictures go on exploding, and from the way I'm choking, it's like all the air has been sucked out and there's nothing left to breathe.

And I guess it's around then a spark ignites my sungarb, the sleeves of this flimsy little button-up thing I'm wearing.

Watching myself on those stairs, I try to figure out when I decide I can't keep going. I mean, when exactly is it that I realize I'm too precalm — too *weak*, too *frightened*, too *pathetic* — to go up those stairs and save my brother?

At what point do I just let him . . . I search for the word.

At what point do I let him *die*?

Next thing I know, I'm slapping at my burning sungarb and wheezing and kind of choking on words like, "I can't" and "I'm sorry."

Then there are voices from the door behind me, and someone strides in dressed in shocking yellow sungarb. And just like that, I let myself be swept back out the door and onto the lawn. Hunter is gone, and in his place are a whole lot of strangers who seem to think they definitely need to be there.

"You're the sister?" someone says. "You're Viva?"

Then there are hands all over me, dragging me away from the fire. The weird thing, and the thing I remember the most, is how, the farther away I get, the louder I hear Julius's voice.

"My brother's in there!"

That's the only thing I can say. I find myself lying down as all around me voices are agreeing that everyone is trying to help Julius, trying their absolute best to get him out.

Cool blades cut through my charred sungarb.

"Have they made contact with the mother?" asks a voice.

I hear myself demanding no one calls her at work, not until they get Julius out.

"You don't understand," I sob. "She left me in charge. I'm responsible."

Something cool goes on my hot, red skin. Am I screaming? I guess I am. The next thing I know, we're rushing along the road, sirens blaring. There are people crouched beside me, telling me to hang on because I'm doing great, I'm doing so well.

Except there's also a voice saying, "Upstairs bedroom. Probably a cigarette."

And that's how I know for sure it's completely and utterly my fault that my brother is dead.

33

I'M IN THE CHAIR hugging my knees to my chest when a super smiley woman comes into the blue room. She explains she's a counselor. "My role is helping you transition."

Without asking, she sits down on the edge of the bed. "Would you like to discuss the news you've had today? It will help, you know, to explore your feelings."

"Sounds kind of pointless." I'm facing away from her. My left cheek is resting on my knee, and I don't even bother to lift it. "After I get the new implant, I won't even know it happened."

"What did happen, Viva?" she asks.

"It's Wren."

"Wren. Sure, if that's what you prefer. Can you tell me in your own words what happened to your brother?"

The story comes out of me in this kind of dull trickle. The entire time, I'm talking to the wall.

When I'm finished, the counselor says, "The death of a sibling is profoundly traumatic. In your circumstance, it's even more troubling. I'd think there was something wrong if you weren't feeling angry."

I can hear from her voice that she's still smiling, like talking about Julius is the thing in all creation she loves to do the most.

Never once does she use a word from the Books of Dot, though. She says *death* instead of *going beyond*. Which makes sense, because without Dot there's no way to pretty up dying.

Unless you believe in Dot, death is a one-way trip without anyone to meet you on the other side.

The end.

Bam.

Over.

And that's what happened to Julius, all because of me.

"You've made peace with your decision to go ahead with the second procedure?"

I nod. I start thinking about being back in Dot's garden. How just a few days ago I was all fired up about saving Fern and the others as well. Now I don't have to bother with that.

But even if the others were still in the garden, I don't think I'd want to save them anyway. I mean, freedom and truth and knowledge are all great and wonderful until you find out why you gave up those things in the first place.

Obviously, there are flaws to the whole idea of Dot. In Gil's case, major ones.

But the way I figure it, being without Dot is a whole lot worse.

"I'd have the procedure right now," I say to the counselor. "I'll do it myself if you want."

"What about any others your decision might affect?"

I think of Mom, waving on the beach. Dennis and his rasping, wheezy breath.

Right now, neither seem enough to make it worthwhile living without Dot.

And then I think of Blaze. I picture him a thousand different ways. Kicking his long legs in the glowing pond, curled up beside me in bed . . .

Tomorrow, he'll be a believer with a brand new implant, just like me. At least, that's how I hope it's going to go.

"I've decided," I tell her. "I'm ready."

The counselor seems satisfied. When she leaves, she closes the door especially softly behind her, like hearing the door shutting might push me over the edge or something.

I start crying right after she goes. I'm not sure why, but I do know it has nothing to do with the door.

The next time the door bleeps, I'm still in the chair with my face all streaked and the end of my nose bright red. The person who comes in is dressed in blue sungarb with that crook pattern all over it. He even has a cord around his neck with the little white rectangle dangling from it.

Only the person standing in front of me isn't Alexander Reynolds like it says on the rectangle.

This time my visitor is Blaze. For the first few seconds after I realize who it is, I get all oozy. I feel like jumping up, going over there, and squeezing Blaze really hard. And then I remember Julius, and I know it doesn't matter how I feel about Blaze because he's never going to feel the same way. Not once he knows what I did.

And I can tell without asking that he doesn't know. It's so obvious by the way he sits down on the arm of the chair and puts his hand on my leg. Something he'd never do if he knew I'd killed my own brother.

"How come you're dressed like Alex?" I ask, and it comes out all choked.

Blaze stays quiet. He lets me fill in the blanks for myself.

"You're leaving?"

"And you're coming."

He gives me this *look* that's so tender and sweet that it makes me feel prehealthy to see it.

Scratch that. I find it physically painful.

He even offers me his hand, to help me up from the chair I guess, but I don't take it.

His words come faster now, all urgent and practical and everything. I guess he realizes for the moment this thing between us has stalled. "It has to be now. They're going to notice his pass is missing pretty soon."

I shake my head.

"It isn't optional, you know. Being chosen."

"You said no to the new implant?"

"I tried. They didn't like that idea much."

I want to explain to him how leaving seemed like the best thing to me too, until I found out about Julius. Now nothing seems like a good idea. All I want to do is forget. Forget what I did, and believe someone loves me unconditionally.

"They're going to launch this drug soon, you know. Even after what it did to Gil," Blaze says.

I lower my eyes. "Gil is just one example. It worked fine for pretty much everyone else."

"They're testing it on kids next."

"Lots of people decide what their kids should believe," I mumble at the floor. "Ever heard of a christening?"

Blaze's hand is kneading my knee. Hard. Like he's trying to wake me up from one of those deep, numbing sleeps. "What about Dennis, then? Don't you want to find him and make sure he's —"

"I can't help Dennis. I wouldn't trust myself."

"Why not?"

I have to tell him now. I have to close off the way I feel and just let the whole story about Julius unfold.

So I do. I try to imagine Blaze is someone I've only just met, someone I don't have any kind of history with. When I get to the part about Hunter Keogh, I go on talking like the information's irrelevant to Blaze. I figure it's going to be soon enough anyway. After tomorrow, I'm not going to remember anything about Hunter and his cigarette and the capsules that I guess made me forget to put the cigarette out all the way.

I get to the part where I'm on the stairs, and there's that little voice and the pictures curling on the wall.

Blaze tries to touch me then. He says, "Viva, I'm really —"

But I shake him off and tell him that my name is Wren.

"I'm not calling you that."

"Why not? That's my name. At least, after tomorrow it will be again."

"Viva's more you."

How would Blaze have any idea what's me and what isn't?

"It's okay for you. You didn't find out what I found out."

"No," he says. "Not exactly that."

"What, something even bigger?"

I mean, as if.

There couldn't be anything bigger than Julius. That's about the biggest thing anyone could ever need to forget.

"Alex told me how they recruited the trial participants. Rich kids from fancy mental hospitals whose parents agreed because they were basically willing to try anything."

He stops. He won't look at me. In the blue room, lights buzz and equipment beep. Every sound is made by machines instead of people or animals or Dot herself.

Between Blaze and me, though, there's a heavy, thick silence.

"Except with me, it was different."

Blaze takes a folded piece of paper from the pocket of his blue-printed sungarb and hands it to me.

Teen Found Guilty of Chilling Murder

Local student Luke Beaufort was today sentenced to a twenty-five-year minimum jail term for the vicious killing of a priest, Father Michael Repton.

"Father Mike" Repton was a long-serving staff member at

St. Joseph's School, where he both befriended and mentored disadvantaged boys. The unconventional priest was a passionate surfer who organized regular surfing trips and an annual beach camp for his charges.

The court heard Beaufort entered the school on a scholarship and quickly became one of Repton's protégés.

The prosecution maintained Beaufort went to Repton's residence out of school hours and killed him in a jealous rage when he discovered Repton had a younger boy visiting. Throughout the trial, the defense admitted Beaufort beat Repton several times with a shovel, fatally wounding him.

By his own account, the youth "snapped and went insane" when he discovered Repton sexually abusing the younger boy, who cannot be named.

Beaufort's defense rested on the claim that Repton had also forced Beaufort to perform oral sex on a number of occasions during 2010 and 2011, while the priest recorded the alleged acts.

However, the defense was unable to substantiate these allegations to the satisfaction of the Supreme Court, with Justice Gemmell directing that the jury note the impeccable character witnesses for Father Repton provided by St. Joseph's and the local church authorities.

Due to the severity of his crime, seventeen-year-old Beaufort is expected to serve his sentence in a maximum-security adult facility.

I fold the paper. I open it and refold it a few more times, which it doesn't remotely need.

I start to say, "Oh my Dot."

But I stop myself in time, and instead I just say, "Oh, Blaze. I'm so sorry."

He looks away. "Not your fault."

It isn't, but that doesn't stop my cheeks from turning pink, the way Blaze's always do. I guess I thought I had some exclusive claim to misery because of Julius. But the whole time there was Blaze, with his own terrible things going on.

It's then I remember yanking Blaze's sungarb by the lagoon, and going on and on about hooking up. And how he just stood there, all weird and still.

Did he already remember that man back then? Did he know what happened?

Because if he did, the way I was acting must have made the whole thing way, way worse.

"You've seen it? That . . . stuff happened?"

"Father Mike was the first thing to break through."

I don't think I can stand hearing anymore. I feel like I'm going to implode or something, just collapse in on myself, knowing how that man must have made Blaze feel.

Knowing how I must have made him feel.

Quietly, Blaze says, "He said I couldn't go on surfing trips if I didn't do what he said. He told me God would get mad. I was so young, I believed him."

I want to smother Blaze with sorries then, but I don't. I figure that would be more for my benefit than his. So the two of us sit there together. We just absorb it all.

It's Blaze who starts talking first. "Now you know. I killed someone."

You had your reasons. Anyone would, in your position. I can think of plenty of things to say, but none of them seem quite right.

Basically, I just don't want to think about it, let alone talk about it.

I want us both to forget.

But Blaze goes on. "They couldn't wait to hand over their youngest violent offender for the Grace trial."

He takes the paper and puts it back in his pocket. "Alex says the police love Lainie Shepherd. Imagine all the criminals on Grace." Blaze snaps his fingers. "A lot of problems would go away."

He starts talking about the helicopter. "Remember how it suddenly flew off? Lainie basically offered the police a subsidized supply of Grace if they stopped what they were doing — searching for Dennis."

Blaze doesn't have to say anything for me to know what he thinks of this. Why should one person have all that power? How does she know what's best? Who says she should be the ruler of everything?

Except I don't feel like that. I'm not completely outraged the way I'm pretty sure Blaze wants me to be.

All I know is, both of us are hurt. One thing can take that away, so why wouldn't we use it? We don't have to worry about the not-so-good parts of Grace anymore. Not after tomorrow.

"Stay," I say. "We'll get the new implants and make everything okay again. Let's be happy."

"If we leave," Blaze says, suddenly uncomfortable, exactly like he was by the pond on completion night, "we could be happy anyway."

"How could we be, with everything we know? Give me one possible way."

"Bad things happened to us. But that doesn't mean good things can't too." He grabs my hand. Then he drops it. He goes for it again, but he ends up pulling away.

"Between the two of us, I think we could . . . you know . . ."

"No, actually, I don't know."

Suddenly, I'm all precalm. *Mad.*

I go on, "Because to me it looks like life without Dot is just a whole lot of . . . I don't know . . . gray days, one after the other. And then at the end of it all, guess what? Hooray! We die."

Blaze stands, and a folded pile of blue material lands in my lap. "Alex got you these," he says. "If you're coming, put them on and we'll go. Right now, down this hall, across the parking lot to the side gate. Then we run."

I take the material from Blaze and shake it out. It's a full set of Shepherd clothes, small enough to fit me.

"There's this group, the Circle. Alex is a member — that's the only reason he works here. There's more of them too, here and outside. They want to stop Grace launching Phase 2 of the trial." He pauses. "They might even help us find Dennis."

I'm kind of stroking the unfamiliar fabric in my hand, thinking about Julius and Dennis and everyone else. But the fabric feels stiff compared to the soft, colorful silk I'm used to wearing. Too stiff to ever imagine putting it on.

"Millions of people are going to buy this drug, you know." Blaze corrects himself. "Millions of consumers."

"Who'll end up feeling a whole lot better about themselves than they ever did before."

Blaze shifts his weight. "I get it. You're not coming. You won't even try." He reaches out again, but before he touches me, he lets his arms fall back down by his sides.

Everything inside of me tightens. My chest feels too small for my heart.

Blaze turns, opens the door, and closes it behind him. He doesn't shut it all the way, I notice. Just leaves it resting closed.

Sit down, I tell myself. *Even better, lie down and close your eyes. Think about Dot and happiness and newfruit and swimming and fun. Think about how you've been chosen to do Dot's work.*

And I try, I really do. I even hum "We Belong 2 Dot" while I'm lying there. It's just there's a part of me that wants to take another look at Blaze. You know, one last time.

So I get up, go to the door, and push it open. It makes that wheezing sound. Outside there's the long, bright hall. The screens on the walls are still flashing. All the doors are closed. Is Dennis behind one of them? Are all the others?

I notice there's a rounded thing farther along down the hall. *Desk.*

There are two women behind it and a bank of smaller screens showing pictures of the building we're in. I figure they're supposed to be keeping watch. But what they're actually doing is showing each other the devices around their wrists.

"This is him with his soccer team. They didn't win a game all season. Do you know, I don't think he even noticed? He loves it that much."

"What a sweetheart. Do you go to the games?"

"Do I *go*? I'm the biggest soccer granny there is!"

The women break into laughter, which is when Blaze goes past the desk. He has his head turned away, just enough so it isn't easy to tell who he is, but not so much that it's obvious he's trying to not to be noticed.

All the women do is glance up at him, then they're right back to their conversation.

In all that bright, shiny whiteness, it isn't long before Blaze turns into just a tall, solid shape in the distance.

I keep watching until he reaches the double doors leading outside. I'm pretty sure I even hear the bleep as he swipes Alex's pass. Then the doors open, and Blaze disappears through them.

That leaves me with nothing to do except shut my own door. This time it clicks closed.

34

DURING THE NIGHT, someone delivers a brand-new Books of Dot unit and a folded sungarb for me to wear during the procedure. The sungarb's the bright, shimmering blue-green of a Shepherd butterfly's wings. All over it are teeny-tiny coral beads in a starburst pattern. It's the most beautiful thing I've ever seen, easily the dotliest sungarb ever created.

That must be why I end up bawling when I put it on. In relief, probably. Happiness.

The entire morning, there are people checking me over and others with papers to sign. I'm told Shepherd has been in touch with my mom to let her know what's going on.

No one tells me what she said, but I can guess. She didn't approve of it the first time around, so why would she the second?

She thought counseling could fix me. As if. Mom has no idea what it's like to live with what I did.

The next visitor is Alex. When he blips open my door and comes into the room, I see that he's holding a tiny clear cup with two capsules inside.

"Something to help you relax," he says as he offers me the cup.

But he yanks it away when I reach out for it. "Not that you need it. It's all blue skies and dotliness ahead of you now. No reason to be uptight."

Alex's pass is swinging around his neck, where it should be. I guess that means Blaze made it out.

"Have you heard from him?"

"You should forget about all that."

"Is he okay, though? Just tell me."

"We both are," Alex says. "So far. But they're investigating."

Alex digs in his pocket and pulls out a rectangular box. He taps out a cigarette and puts it in his mouth. Then he takes a smaller box, which slides open.

Matches.

Alex takes one out, strikes it, and a flame flares on the end. There's no window in the room, naturally, so he fiddles with a switch on the wall, until the duct in the roof starts humming louder than before.

Alex lights his cigarette, closes his eyes and inhales.

"These'll kill me before Lainie Shepherd can." He holds out the pack. "You want one?"

I shake my head. The last time I smoked a cigarette was the night Julius . . .

"C'mon. When else will you get the chance to do something bad?" Alex pushes the pack closer, and I end up taking one. He hands me the matches, and I light up, watching the duct suck the smoke up to the ceiling. I turn the matchbox over in my hand, squeezing it until the cardboard goes limp.

"You sure you want to do this?"

I nod.

"Because you don't look like it."

I guess he's talking about the way my eyes are all red and puffy, my skin pasty-pale. Kind of an inevitable side effect of lying awake all night thinking about Julius and Mom and Dennis, but mostly about that figure disappearing down the hall.

"You're smart enough to figure things out for yourself, you know. You don't need Lainie Shepherd telling you how to live."

"That happens to be exactly what I need."

"Dot isn't the only one who'll love you, you know. No matter what happened before the Grace trial."

I guess I scowl at him.

"I can name at least one real person who does. He just hasn't worked out how to say it."

I inhale again and blow out smoke.

Blaze. Did he say something? Were there things Blaze could tell Alex that he couldn't say to me, because of everything that happened to him?

"Let's just say I wasn't sure," I say. "Isn't it too late anyway?"

"Nothing's decided until the implant is under your skin. There are steps you could take. Not easy ones, but there are always steps." Alex grinds out his cigarette on my breakfast plate, full of uneaten, congealing eggs. "There are ways you can be useful too. You don't know this, but the Circle has —"

But I don't want to hear. I stub my own cigarette out as I hear the door opening. Just in time, Alex clamps the warming cover over the ash-covered plate and says, "Marion," as a nurse comes in.

He sounds cheery, almost as upbeat as Marion does when she says to me, "So, the big day!"

"I've administered the medication," Alex tells Marion, which he hasn't. The empty cup is on the wheeled table in front of us, but I'm pretty sure the capsules are in Alex's pocket. "Over to you now."

"Ready, honey?" Marion asks. Her stomach strains at her Shepherd uniform. The crook-patterned fabric buckles over her thighs. Under the name on her pass there's a round yellow sticker of a smiling face.

"I guess."

"Let's go change your life!"

* * *

I'm lying facedown with my eyes closed. Marion sweeps my hair to one side.

"Hold still." She takes a marker, and I feel its cool tip draw a little line on my skin. "The new implant will go right above the old one," she explains. "Closer to your brain. That's the technical reason, I'm sure."

I hear her tearing something, and right after that, there's a cold, wet swipe across my neck.

"The swab numbs the area. You can hop up now."

I lift my face, all red and wrinkled from where it's been pressing into the sheet. Marion brushes a few strands of hair out of my eyes for me.

"You seem nervous, honey."

"I'm fine."

"You probably don't recall the last time. It's painless, I promise. No worse than a little nick with a kitchen knife. And after that? Well, you'd know better than me. No feeling blue. No fat days. No getting lonely. No broken hearts." Marion sighs. "One perfect day after the next."

There's a stool on the floor by the bed. Marion helps me down it. At the bottom, she holds onto me like she thinks I'll collapse if she doesn't.

"I might even sign up myself, when it comes onto the market." She swipes the air with her hand. "What am I saying? My kids would have ten heart attacks each. They're dysfunctional when I'm not there. Oh well, nice to be needed, I suppose."

She steps toward the door. "I'd say they're ready for us out there."

* * *

Lainie Shepherd's curved office has been redecorated for the procedure. The table and golden chair are gone. In their place are planters overflowing with newfruit blossoms. The screens have been rolled away too, revealing windows made of little panes of colored glass. There's a design to them — abstract I guess you'd called it. Shepherds' crooks with newfruit twined around.

On the far wall there's a huge silky banner with Dot's cleverly designed face. Underneath the banner is a raised platform, and that's where Lainie Shepherd stands in her black clothes, her blue diamond crook swinging at her chest. Her smile is serene and warm and welcoming.

Next to her is a woman in that same blue crook-patterned sungarb, only she's wearing gloves, a face mask, and mesh covering her hair.

On a little stand between Lainie and her assistant, there's a tray with a cardboard box and a scalpel, which looks like a miniature version of the coconut knife.

Between all that and me stretch rows and rows of chairs. Every one of them is full and every person sitting there is dressed in blue. When the double doors click closed and I walk into the room with Marion holding onto my arm, all the heads turn.

The people smile and nod at me, as though right now is the most wonderful moment in creation and they're all so thrilled to be here.

I recognize the girl with the curly blond hair and fig-colored lips. Alex is there too. I actually spot him first, since he's looking at the floor. Out of everyone there, he's the only one without a smile plastered on.

"Here she is," says Lainie Shepherd. "Our chosen one!"

Between the chairs there's a curving aisle down the middle of the room, and that's where Marion guides me. Behind us, a cluster of people has stepped in front of the doors. In their hands, those black objects again, the ones that shot out the white clouds of gas.

Guns.

As I walk down the aisle, no one says anything. Not to each other and not to me. They just stare and stare at me until I get to the little platform, which is when Lainie Shepherd says, "Would you please kneel?"

So I do. The carpet feels soft underneath my bare knees. Then Lainie begins to talk. How fortunate I am, just like everyone else at the Shepherd Corporation.

How wonderful it is to be part of Phase 2 of the Grace project, destined to bring hope to so many children as they grow, to give ordinary people the love they crave, unconditionally. After a while, I notice my knees beginning to itch and then to ache.

So when Lainie says, "Viva, are you ready to accept Dot as your creator?" I just blurt out a yes in this get-on-with-it way.

It doesn't matter what Alex says. It's not like I could say no, even if I had changed my mind.

"Wonderful," says Lainie Shepherd. With a soft hand, she brushes my hair to either side of my neck. I feel the pink shells of her fingernails on my skin. There's this little *tink* sound as Lainie's assistant takes her knife from the tray. A click, a rustle, and a tear as the assistant opens the box and takes out the implant.

My implant, the strongest ever created. The implant that's going to override my doubting genes and make me feel loved forever.

"Just a small nick," the assistant murmurs, and I feel the blade against my skin. The cut doesn't even hurt because everything's numb, inside my body as well as out. Then the assistant's fingers close around my neck, holding everything steady to make sure the implant slides into the exact right place.

There's this suspended feeling, like me and everyone else in the room are holding our breath until it's in and I'm reborn.

So when the doors at the back of the room shake, everyone exhales at the same time. In the rush of air that follows, I lift my head. The doors are open. There's a whole other group of guards standing there. Naturally, they have guns too.

"Room for another?" one of the guards says.

From behind him comes another person. His Shepherd sungarb is damp and dirty. His long hair is gone, hacked off in uneven chunks. But it's obviously him.

It's Blaze.

"Found him trying to get back in. Changed his mind, he says. Didn't want to leave the other one behind."

Everyone spins to look at me. With my head raised, I feel drips run down the back of my neck. There's a lot of blood from one little nick.

"Touching," says Lainie Shepherd as the guards lead Blaze to the front of the room. "Really, it's quite beautiful."

She motions to him, and he kneels down next to me. Close, but — even after everything — still not quite touching.

"Luke," Lainie says. "Are you ready to welcome Dot back into your life?"

Blaze kind of shrugs. "If I have to."

He turns his head toward me so that for the first time since he came through the doors, we're looking right at each other.

"If that's what I have to do to be with her."

35

BLAZE AND I are side by side. My head is bent, but through my curtain of hair I can see his profile, the one familiar thing in all this strangeness.

Lainie Shepherd's assistant wipes away the sticky blood from my neck, then runs another cool swab over the skin. She leans over me. "You'll feel a slight pressure now. No pain. Nothing to worry about."

And then . . . well, it's hard to explain the next part exactly. This single word comes to me, and I don't mean someone like Dot tells it to me or anything like that.

It's more like the word blooms inside me. As in, it's me, finally telling myself what to do.

No.

Blaze was free, but he came back. To have the procedure just so we can be together. That's enough for me to be sure I can't let either one of us have it. Ever.

So the next thing I do, I sort of haul my head upward. I slam it into the underside of the assistant's jaw, crunching her mouth closed. She yelps, with surprise or pain, I don't know which.

When she reels backward, I get up on my feet. Beside me, Blaze is standing too, and he's yelling and yelling and the entire room just erupts.

Woven through all the shouting I hear Lainie Shepherd. "I suggest you stay right where you are."

Blaze and I start trying to move through the crowd.

"You signed a contract. You do realize you're obligated to have this procedure? The terms clearly state —"

"Go!" I tell Blaze. "Run!"

But there's nowhere *to* run. The aisle is heaving with people. The double doors are blocked. All around are security guards with those black gas guns, each one pointed directly at us.

The guns make a snapping, cracking kind of sound as they fire. A cap hits the silky banner on the wall behind my head, explodes, and releases its contents with a hiss.

Lainie Shepherd is moving through the crowd.

"Keep your mouths and noses well covered," she's saying, a blue mask already covering her own face. "Don't breathe anything in."

More cracks. Caps are everywhere now, ricocheting off the walls and the chairs and the roof. A planter is hit, sending water and newfruit blossoms arcing through the air.

The air smells like smoke and gas and panic.

The space between the guns and us is getting smaller. My head feels like it has swollen to twice its normal size. My neck is too reedy-thin to support it. My eyes are doing that burning thing, and I'm sort of swaying on my feet.

I swing around, grabbing for anything to support me. I end up banging into the stand where the equipment was. The top of my leg slams into it so that I suddenly feel the twisted shape of Alex's matchbox in my pocket.

Gas and fire.

Somehow, the two things are linked in my head. I don't remember why I think so, but I'm pretty sure that something big will happen if I light a match in here.

I try taking out a match, but my fingers feel too thick and stumpy to handle the tiny little mashed-up box. When I do manage to pick one up, it snaps in my trembling hands.

Another match.

The shaking in my hands is even more intense. But the match lights this time, and I flick it into the air. It spins there, and every sound is wiped out by this one gigantic *woomph*.

I haven't heard a sound like that since the night Julius died.

This time, it's deliberate.

That night, I realize now, and everything that happened was a terrible, awful, painful accident.

Flames mushroom up and out. Heat crackles after them, and vents on Lainie's roof release a stinking foam that's meant for putting out fire.

There's smoke, flashing lights, alarms, everything. So many people are running and shouting that it's pretty much impossible to work out who is who.

Blaze snatches up a chair. It hurtles over our heads and right into a window. Shards of Shepherd-blue glass fly out and clear, bright light rushes in through the jagged hole.

The silky banner with Dot's face is torn between the eyes where the cap hit it, rippling and billowing now in the sudden gust of air.

Blaze and I just run for the window, hands up to push our way through.

I'm afraid to jump through the hole and slash my skin, and maybe that's why I stop. Only for a second, but it's enough.

Someone grabs me and yells, "That's her!"

I'm just waiting for a knee in my back or an arm round my throat. But it never comes. Right beside me another voice yells. "Nah, she's an intern. The girl went that way."

The hand lets me go, and suddenly I'm jumping through the window with Blaze right behind me. And then we're running.

* * *

We are free.

Behind us, the Shepherd complex. It's daylight, and I see the whole building from the outside for the first time. It's long and low, every window shrouded in blue-frosted glass apart from the one we just smashed. One long hall with a curved section at one end.

I get it. It's a shepherd's crook.

Flames are already jumping from Lainie's office at the curving tip of the crook. They're working on swallowing the whole building, where Fern and Gil and everyone else are.

286

Except now there are guards and orderlies and whoever else spewing out of every entrance. There are sleeping bodies on stretchers, but I can also see people I recognize up on their feet.

Sage, still groggy and staggering, and Luna too, coughing up her insides from all the smoke.

"It's this way out," Blaze says, plunging forward.

In front of us, all I can see is this endless tarmac full of cars. I follow him, though. Blaze has been out there once before, so I figure he knows how to weave his way through the cars and find the fence he has been talking about.

And that's when I hear a voice shouting my name. I spin around, and someone's running toward us. It's Brook, barefoot, a Shepherd hospital robe flapping around his lean legs. Behind him, a bunch of security guards with guns. "Viva!" he shouts.

I stop. I'm trying to make sense of what I've just seen and heard.

Okay, so Brook is awake, just like some of the others. But how does he know my real name?

"What are you stopping for?" Blaze says. "We have to keep moving!"

Dust and grit swirl around my ankles. Ash rains down around us, turning the Shepherd parking lot into an even duller shade of gray. Shouting voices, compete with the angry sound of flames.

But all I hear is what Brook says next. "Dennis is in there." He jerks his head at the crook-shaped building. It's really blazing now. "You have to go back for him. He says he's only coming out if it's with you."

I don't ask how Dennis got there. I just grab hold of Brook and look at him closely. His eyes are this pale, clear blue without their normal big black circles in the middle. For some reason I think about that mark on his ankle, a circle.

A circle-shaped tattoo, not a dotmark after all.

"Where?" I say. "Which room?"

At the same time, Brook tells me that Dennis is in his room, I think of Alex talking about the Circle, trying to tell me more, but me not wanting to hear it.

Something sails through the air and lands at my feet.

Alex's pass. I snatch it up and put it around my neck. I spin on my heels and head toward the straight section of the building.

"Don't!" Blaze yells. "It's *Brook*. Don't trust him."

And he lunges out to stop me, but Brook elbows Blaze hard in the stomach. There's this *ooof* sound, and Blaze staggers backward. He goes on calling my name, yelling at me to stop, to think about what I'm doing, telling me that getting myself killed won't save Dennis if he really is inside.

I'm pretty sure Blaze is about to punch Brook, but I don't wait to find out. I just run and hope they'll figure something out before security grabs both of them.

As I go, I'm wondering a billion things at once. Like, how Brook must be Circle and was he always that way, the whole time we were doing the trial?

How did he fool everyone? Did he get Dennis out and keep him hidden somehow?

But as my feet slap the tarmac, I'm mainly thinking of Julius, and how everything's going to be different this time.

36

SMOKE HANGS THICK in the air. It wraps itself around me, blanketing my body, coating my mouth, whipping my eyes until they sting.

The noise is just as suffocating.

Alarms screeching. People screaming. Running feet. Gas guns firing. A helicopter above us raining down a chemical spray.

Shepherd might have reinvented paradise, but right now it feels pretty much like hell.

Inside, windows are exploding and a section of the roof has collapsed. Every entrance is crammed with people, trial participants dazed and wandering, medics with other participants flat out on stretchers.

Choose an entrance, I tell myself. It doesn't matter which. Every door is as dangerous as the next.

So I dive for the nearest door. Bursting out the other way is a stretcher, two men in Shepherd uniforms on either end.

I squeeze to one side.

"His arm," one man shouts, and I see the figure on the stretcher has a pale limb thrown over the edge.

Five long fingers are trailing the air. Fingers that have crawled over my skin. Fingers that only recently were hurling rocks at my head.

I don't stop to take another look at Gil. One of the men is busy replacing his arm on the stretcher. The other one looks right at me. I freeze.

Jordy.

"Hey, watch what you're doing, buddy," says Jordy to the other man.

"Me watch out?" the man snaps back. "That was your fault."

A slight nod from Jordy, and I duck my head and dodge through the door. Is Jordy Circle? How many others are there?

Heat shimmers, and smoke obscures everything. I try to think clearly, work out which way Brook's room is.

And then — do I imagine it? — I hear Dennis's voice.

Viva! Help!

"Coming!" I scream. It comes out like a seal bark, as coughs grab at my chest. "Where are you?"

I'm scared, quavers the little voice.

"It's okay," I tell Dennis. "Even big kids get scared sometimes."

I'm running in the direction of the voice, even though I don't know if it's real. It's the only thing I can think to do. I have to find him, even though I don't know which room is Brook's.

Now, before the entire building burns. Or falls.

"Hey." A hand clamps my shoulder. "How'd you get in here?"

I can feel the butt of a gas gun in the small of my back.

"It's this way," the guard says, and he propels me forward.

But it's weird. He's pushing me into the hall, not out.

"There's me, Alex, and a few dozen others," the security guard pants. "We're Shepherd, but we're Circle too. And Brook is . . ."

I'm sure this is all really interesting. And I'd like to hear what the guard has to say, I seriously would. It's just that my head is already full of Dennis's little voice calling to me, on top of my own reminding me what I have to do.

"I know," I snap. "Just get me to Dennis."

And the two of us run down the hall, the endless handle of the shepherd's crook.

"4–0–2," says the guard. "This one."

By now the air is pretty much solid with smoke. I can't see any numbers on any of the doors, but when the guard blips one open I have all the confirmation I need. I mean, it's hard to miss Dennis's wailing cry and the sound of his voice saying my name over and over again.

And then I guess Dennis recognizes my voice because suddenly this small, shivering shape catapults out from under the bed.

"It's you," says Dennis, happy and relieved and hysterical all at once. Dennis grabs on around my knees, so I unclasp him and hoist him into the air.

"I can carry him," the guard says.

But at the exact same time, Dennis and I both squeak, "No!"

It has been such a long time since I have felt this kind of weight in my arms. Now that I have it, there is no way I'm letting go. I don't care that flames are starting to lick their way along the roof of the building. It doesn't even matter that there's a whole pack of security guards outside looking for me.

All I know is I'm hanging onto Dennis, and the two of us are getting out of here. Right now.

Together.

37

"WAIT," SAYS LUKE. "You can't start yet."

I stop mid-lick, my tongue pressed to my ice-cream cone. "It's dripping all over me."

"So let it."

Luke is laughing. His hands are literally covered with sticky green splashes of melted ice cream, the same way mine are. "We have to be on the sand before we start eating."

"Why?"

"That's the rule."

"I thought we didn't have them anymore."

"We don't have Books. There are still rules."

"Okay, then. What are they?"

"Still working them out."

"In that case . . ." I swirl my tongue around my ice cream while Luke pretend-huffs, his free hand in mine.

To be honest, it's getting late and pretty cold, but we clatter our way down the wooden staircase to the beach anyway, our long shadows crinkling over every step. The stairs are hardly wide enough for one of us, let alone the two of us next to each other, hands firmly clasped together.

But we don't let go.

At the bottom of the stairs, we take our shoes off. Straightaway, Luke plunges his feet into the sand and wiggles his toes around.

"Exactly how I remember it," he says.

And then he sort of goes inside his head and I let him, because that's what he does when the same thing happens to me.

We're both recovering stuff, and we still have a ways to go. Some things we're not sure we'll ever completely remember.

Other things, like Father Mike for Luke and Julius's accident for me, are back completely and won't ever go away.

I think about Julius all the time now. Not just the accident, but Julius when he was alive. Sometimes I even talk to him, although not the way I talked to Dot. I mean, I definitely know Julius isn't up there in the clouds or anything.

He's gone, and that makes me more than sad every single day.

But the one way I can hold onto him is to remember him, so that's why I talk to him. To keep him alive inside my head at least.

I lean over and take a big bite out of Luke's cone, and that's when he comes back to right now. "It's okay to eat mine as well as yours now, is it?"

I shrug. "We're still working on the rules, aren't we?"

"Goes both ways, then," he says, taking a huge bite of my ice cream.

So I steal another bite of his. Even though I'm pretty sure ice cream is something people are supposed to eat in summer, now seems like a perfect time to me.

In front of us, gray-green waves are breaking, churning into messy foam before sloshing their way up the sand. Behind us are huge dunes held together with some tufty kind of grass. Then beyond that, almost hidden by the dunes, is the place we're staying.

When the Circle people asked us where we wanted to go, Luke immediately said the beach. In his head, he was reclaiming it from Father Mike or something, I guess.

Anyway, it turned out Brook — who's really called Guy — knew someone with cabins that are basically always empty in winter.

I guess no one really goes to the beach in the cold weather, except for a pair of escapees and some activists figuring out their next move against a humungous drug company.

"So what was that one about?" I ask Luke.

Without my having to say it, Luke knows I mean what he saw in his head.

"Not about Repton."

"What then?"

"Nothing from way back," Luke says, which is our term for everything that happened to us before Grace. "It was something from Dot's place."

"And that would be?"

"By the pond. I never told you who my someone was."

And then, of course, he stops talking. We might be free, but Luke and Blaze are pretty much the same guy and neither is the best at saying what he feels.

"You can't start something like that and then go quiet."

Luke blushes. "It's kind of . . ."

"You can look away, remember."

So he does. Luke stares the other way across the beach as he gives his little speech all over again, the one about the point of things being ice cream on the beach.

But even more important than that, Luke tells me, is doing those things with someone who matters to you. As in, your *someone*.

This time, he adds the last part. That for him, that someone is me.

So it's sort of obvious that I should put my hand on his neck and move his face toward mine again, so that the two of us can join our sticky, ice-creamy lips.

Which is exactly what happens.

Luke doesn't pull back or anything like that. Afterward, he rests his cheek on my shoulder and even puts his arm around me.

The two of us are *connected* and suddenly I get it. Luke's totally right. Seriously, it isn't some type of magical being in the sky who's going to make this whole living thing worthwhile.

It's actual, real-life people.

The hard part comes when those people die or disappear or leave you behind or hurt you. But as impossible as it sounds, even those things you can find a way to handle. You and your someones, together.

I'm about to start telling Luke all about it when I realize there's someone behind us.

I turn sharply.

Guy.

"It's risky, you two being out here," he says. "If someone from Shepherd saw you . . ." He stops. He doesn't need to say any more. If anyone knows what's risky, it's Guy. I mean, he and Alex faked his entire implant procedure. And then Guy spent a full year in a Shepherd facility acting like he believed in Dot, wearing special contact lenses to give him the authentic big-eyed look.

He had the job of watching how Grace really affected us, and keeping us safe if the drug turned anyone a little loopy. Which was why he stuck so close to Gil, and also why he noticed that the drug seemed to be wearing off me.

"We know," I say. My sticky hand finds Luke's. "We're coming."

I don't want Guy to think we're not grateful for his help. It's because of the Circle that the two of us are safe right now. And otherwise we could never have gotten Dennis back to his Mom and his brother Nathe.

"Anyway," Guy says, "there's something I want you guys to see. There's an ad for Grace out. It's all over my device."

He can barely keep from shuddering. Right now, Guy's life is pretty much about trying to tell the world what Grace can do to some people.

"Yeah?" Luke's really eager to see it, I can tell.

If it weren't for me, Luke would probably join Guy and Alex and everyone else. He'd hang around here and help out with their campaign. I guess Grace reminds him of Repton and all of that.

Mind control, he calls it.

I'm no huge fan of Grace, either. I mean, I can't tell you how sick I felt when I found out that Fern and Gil had put themselves on the waiting list to buy the first commercial batch of Grace.

How they'd already decided they couldn't deal with normal life and weren't even going to try. And how no one was going to stop Gil from buying Grace, even though they knew what it did to him.

It's just, I'm not convinced that stopping Shepherd is what I want to do with my life. At least, not at the moment. Right now, all I really want to do is be with Luke and, when it's safe, get on my device and call my mom and tell her I love her.

To say sorry for running away like I did.

The wind is blowing. If I still had my long hair the way the Books said I should, it would have been whipping my face right now. But my hair is all gone, cut off by Luke on our very first night of freedom. So now I can feel the wind on my neck, the old scar and the scab of the new cut. And anyone who chooses to look can see them too. I won't be hiding that Grace is part of me. I just won't be making it my whole entire life.

Luke's hand feels warm and heavy in mine. Guy is walking ahead of us, keeping his distance and giving us space.

"You okay?" Luke asks me.

"Yeah," I tell him. "Just thinking."

"Just having a Viva moment," Luke supplies.

"That would be it."

"I like Viva moments," Luke tells me. "I like Viva, too."

Inside I feel this quivery thrill. "Yeah?"

"Yep."

I forget about Grace. I forget about Guy and Fern and Gil and Lainie Shepherd. I forget about everything apart from me and Luke and this actual moment.

The only thing I'm aware of is this crazy desire to jump on Luke's back and put my arms around his neck and just cling onto him forever and ever.

Luke looks across at me with his dark, intense eyes, dreadlocks gone, just this gleaming brown cap of hair in their place. He does his mouth thing, twisting sideways and down.

"How do *you* feel about Viva?"

I tell him the absolute truth, because that's how I want it to be between us from now on.

"I'm only just getting to know her," I tell him. "But you know what? I actually think she's pretty okay."

Acknowledgments

Thank you to Switch Press for bringing *State of Grace* to a new audience and to Hardie Grant Egmont for supporting the book so enthusiastically from inception to publication. In particular, I am so grateful to Hilary R. for guiding me but also letting me find my way. And for never once asking why the manuscript was taking so long!

Thanks to Arma and Arpa for being there, minding the children, and believing I could do literally anything.

And to Rob, Caspar, and Romy . . . I love you.